All I Want
Is You

All I Want Is You

KAYLA PERRIN
and
DEBORAH FLETCHER MELLO

Kensington Publishing Corp.
http://www.kensingtonbooks.com

DAFINA BOOKS are published by

Kensington Publishing Corp.
119 West 40th Street
New York, NY 10018

All Kensington Titles, Imprints, and Distributed Lines are
available at special quantity discounts for bulk purchases for
sales promotions, premiums, fund-raising, and educational or
institutional use. Special book excerpts or customized print-
ings can also be created to fit specific needs. For details,
write or phone the office of the Kensington special sales manager: Kensington Publishing Corp., 119 West 40th Street,
New York, NY 10018, attn: Special Sales Department, Phone:
1-800-221-2647.

Dafina and the Dafina logo Reg. U.S. Pat. & TM Off.

ISBN-13: 978-0-7582-6867-9
ISBN-10: 0-7582-6867-X

First printing: October 2011

10 9 8 7 6 5 4 3 2 1

Printed in the United States of America

Contents

Holiday Seduction

Kayla Perrin

Chapter 1

"Boring in bed?" Isabel asked, her eyes as wide as saucers as she spoke in an exaggerated tone. "Those were his exact words?"

Mikki Harper lifted her mug of beer as she looked at her two best friends in New York City, Isabel Rodriguez and Debbie Mott, who were standing next to her at a crowded midtown bar. "An exact quote," she told Isabel with as much passion as if she had just pointed someone in the direction of the restroom. She had to keep her emotions in check, or she was going to fall apart. "Right after we finished eating our appetizers." Plastering a smile on her face that didn't match her mood, Mikki raised her glass high and said, "Cheers."

Mikki clinked her mug against Isabel's and Debbie's, then proceeded to down the entire contents in five seconds flat. That was a record for her. She didn't guzzle beer, and she didn't typically drink to excess. But tonight she was going to make an exception.

She was getting drunk.

It had been a long time since she'd gone to a bar with her girlfriends, drinking beer and shooting the breeze. One year, eleven months, and four days to be exact. Ever since she had started dating Alexander.

She'd been to restaurants with her friends, of course, and coffee shops. She'd gone with them on shopping trips. But Alex hadn't wanted her to go clubbing, warning her that men—including the bartenders—couldn't be trusted not to slip something into her drink and take advantage of her.

Mikki had figured him overprotective, or even a little insecure, but she had heeded his warning and had gone to bars and clubs only with him.

Tonight, however, she was saying screw it to Alex's advice. He was no longer in the picture. She didn't have to listen to him anymore.

Mikki audibly put the mug down onto the counter and pushed it toward the bartender, who looked friendly and harmless, not at all like a potential serial rapist. "Another," she told him.

"I can't believe he said that to you." Isabel's face had an expression of almost gleeful horror, the kind of look you get when you're sharing dirty gossip. "I mean, really."

Mikki couldn't believe it either. "It's ridiculous, right? We didn't have problems in the bedroom. In fact, I'd say we had a very active sex life. You know how I told you Alexander liked to have sex *all the time.* Sheesh, you'd think he was training to compete in the newest Olympic sport!"

Debbie snorted. Isabel, who had just taken a sip of her beer, began to laugh, then covered her mouth as beer spilled out. "Girl, you gotta warn a person when you're gonna start talking about Alexander and sex. Dang, I'm going to miss those stories about Alexander the Great."

"Though I guess he's more like Alexander-the-not-so-Great now," Debbie said.

Mikki was silent, remembering the amount of times she'd made love with Alexander. He'd had an insatiable sexual appetite—in the beginning. But in the last few months, his interest in sex had completely waned. He'd gone from one extreme to the other, something she had been embarrassed to share with her friends.

The bartender put another draft beer in front of her, and Mikki quickly lifted the mug to her lips for a sip. This one she would drink like a respectable woman—not like a woman trying to drown her sorrows in booze. She hadn't been out drinking in a while, but she knew that it was important to pace yourself.

"Here's the thing," Mikki began. "He pretty much stopped being Alexander the Great a few months ago."

Debbie narrowed her hazel eyes. She was biracial, with a thick mane of curly brown hair that she always wore in a ponytail. "What does that mean?"

"What it means is . . ." Mikki stopped, sighing. "Well, he sort of stopped wanting to have sex."

"Get *out*!" Isabel's eyes bulged at the news. She was Latino, from Nicaragua, and reacted in grand style to everything. "No wonder you haven't had any more stories about sex in public places. You know, one of the reasons I quit the law firm was because I couldn't handle going into the conference room without thinking about—"

"Enough!" Mikki said, raising a hand to silence her friend. She didn't want to remember how Alex had convinced her to get down and dirty on the law firm's conference room table after-hours. She had given in, and while the experience had been exciting, Mikki's back had hurt for days.

"You didn't really quit because of that," Mikki went on, more of a question.

"Naw, I'm just messing with you," Isabel said. "You know I had to leave because of Calvin. He thought my job description included sleeping with him."

Isabel had been the firm's receptionist, which was how she and Mikki had met. Isabel had already been friends with Debbie, whom she'd gone to college with, and once Isabel quit her job, she went to work at the high-end lingerie boutique where Debbie was a manager. As far as Mikki was concerned, that job was a much better fit for Isabel. At the boutique, she didn't have to tone down her sexuality and could dress like a vixen to her heart's content.

"You're not serious about Alexander," Debbie said. "He didn't suddenly lose his interest in sex. . . ."

"I figured he was busy with work," Mikki explained. "Or that he'd finally tired himself out. But in the last three to four months, I'm definitely the one who's wanted it more than him."

"I think icicles are forming in hell," Debbie said, shuddering. "I never thought the day would come."

"Shit, *I* just got a chill," Isabel added.

"You want to know what really sucks?" Mikki asked. "I did everything to turn him on over the past four months, and most of the time he came up with excuses as to why *he* was too tired. Now he's breaking up with me because *I'm* boring in bed?"

"That kind of relationship always burns out," Isabel

said, the sour expression on her face a sure sign she was speaking from experience.

"After nearly two years?" Mikki asked. "I thought . . . I thought we had something real."

What she'd really thought when Alexander had suggested they go to their favorite restaurant for dinner was that he was going to propose. Considering that Christmas was right around the corner, as was her sister's wedding. She was certain he'd had love and commitment on his mind.

What an idiot she had been.

"All I can say," Isabel began, "is, good thing you didn't move in with him. It's no fun being kicked out on the street. Trust me, I know."

Stupidly, Mikki had believed that that would be the next step. Perhaps a formal engagement first, then she would move into his Manhattan condo.

"I can't believe he broke up with me *now*." Mikki frowned, the emotion of the breakup getting to her. "When he knew how much I was looking forward to going to my sister's wedding with him. Now I have to head to Miami like a loser . . . with no date."

"Men." Debbie shook her head sadly. "You know he was sleeping with someone else, right?"

Mikki's heart slammed against her chest. "Pardon me?"

"You don't go from sex all the time to doing it once in a while . . . not for a guy like Alex. How do you think he got that nickname Alexander the Great? If he stopped sleeping with you, he must be sleeping with someone else."

"Did you hear something?" Mikki asked, the very idea of Alex cheating on her making her feel ill. She'd had her suspicions but never had been able to confirm anything. Before she'd gotten lured into an office romance, she had heard that Alex liked to play the field. But he had assured her that he'd sown all the wild oats he'd wanted to, and indeed, their relationship of nearly two years had been a testament to the fact that the thirty-seven-year-old was ready to settle down.

In response to Mikki's question, Debbie shook her head. "I didn't hear anything in particular, no. But if a man isn't sleeping with you, he's sleeping with someone else. Plain and simple."

To hell with drinking this beer slowly. Mikki put it to her lips and guzzled it.

But as she put the empty glass onto the counter, ready to order another one, she knew that no matter how many beers she drank, she would not be able to escape the painful memory of Alexander's words.

Face it, Mikki—you're boring in bed.

"Cheer up," Debbie said. "I never liked Alex anyway."

It didn't matter that Debbie hadn't liked him. Mikki had loved him. After a handful of failed relationships, she had finally found the man she believed she would marry—and he was a lawyer, no less.

"And look," Debbie went on, gesturing to the bar at large. "There are a lot of cute guys in here. *That's* the real reason Alex didn't want you partying with us—because he feared you'd find someone else who would treat you better."

"I so don't want to do this," Mikki said glumly. "I don't want to be a thirty-year-old single girl in New York again."

"You're back in the single girl's club, whether you want to be or not," Isabel said. She raised her beer mug. "Go with the flow, and you'll see it can be fun."

Easy for Isabel to say. With her olive complexion, thick head of hair that hung to her midback, naturally full lips, and expressive eyes, she was gorgeous—supermodel material. There was no shortage of guys wanting to date her. Men loved her hourglass figure—especially that well-packed booty. That booty had led to one of the New York Yankees approaching her in the lingerie shop, and a hot and heavy romance had ensued. For two months, he had wined and dined her and spoiled her with expensive jewelry—until Isabel broke it off after seeing his engagement announcement on page six of the *New York Post*.

"There are some hot guys right there," Debbie said, indicating the direction with a jerk of her head. "And the bonus—they don't look like lawyers."

Mikki nodded, but she didn't particularly feel like checking anyone out already. Alex had just broken up with her two days ago. Even if he was a jerk, her heart was crushed.

"You know, the best way to get over an old guy is to jump into bed with someone new," Debbie went on.

"Debbie, I swear, where do you get this stuff? Ann Landers for the young and brokenhearted?"

"You think I'm lying?" Debbie challenged. "Remember my friend Christina? Dating for five years, only to learn that her boyfriend wasn't proposing because he'd been sleeping with some other girl for half of their relationship?"

How could Mikki forget? Talk about the lowest of the low in terms of unscrupulous behavior. He'd strung Christina along and stalled every time she brought up marriage, when his real issue had been that he'd had some little tart on the side. And a stripper, to boot.

"Well, as much as Christina was in love with Joe, she was out with me one night, met some hot guy at a bar, and went home with him. Days later, she was totally over her ex. *Totally.*"

Mikki had forgotten that part of the story. Now she leaned forward, intrigued. "Really?"

Debbie nodded. "Yep."

Mikki looked around the bar in earnest now, to see if anyone struck her fancy. Perhaps her problem was that she'd always been a little old-fashioned. Not boring, as Alexander had so rudely said, but simply a present-day woman with old-fashioned sensibilities.

Unlike a lot of the women she knew, Mikki wasn't the type to jump into bed with a man on the first date.

But maybe Debbie was right. Maybe the best way to get over Alexander was to have a fling with someone else.

"Bartender," she said, gesturing to the man. "Another beer, please."

"You driving?" he asked.

"In New York City?" Mikki guffawed. "Not a chance."

As the bartender poured her another draft beer, Mikki looked around. For the first time that evening, she noticed that there were quite a few attractive men here tonight. As her gaze continued to wander, one in particular caught her eye.

He was staring directly at her. Or was he? Mikki glanced over her shoulder, almost certain he was checking out Isabel. But when she faced the man once more, he shook his head and smiled. Then he raised his mug in a toast.

Yes, he was definitely looking at *her.*

"See?" Debbie said. "You've got a hot one interested already."

"He's probably checking out Isabel," Mikki said, but she didn't believe her own words.

"Oh no, honey." Isabel shook her head. "He's looking at *you*."

Mikki turned again, and her stomach fluttered when the man in question stood from his table and started toward her.

"And talk about a hottie," Isabel added. "Mmmm-mmm-mmm."

And he was. At about six foot two, he had golden brown skin, a bald head, and full lips framed by a neatly trimmed goatee. Unlike the men in this bar who were dressed in suits at the end of the workday, this guy was wearing a pair of denim jeans and a black dress shirt that was open at the collar.

As he made his way through the crowd, unquestionably heading in Mikki's direction, Debbie whispered, "If you don't do him, I will."

Chapter 2

Mikki couldn't remember the last time a man this hot had approached her, and the realization that he had her locked in his gaze was making her heart pound. She wished she was wearing something sexier, or heck, that she'd put on a bold color of lipstick before she'd left the office. But she hadn't agreed to head to this bar in order to meet guys. In fact, that had been the furthest thing from her mind. She had come with her friends to drown her sorrows in alcohol.

The man wove his way through the throng of people, holding Mikki's eyes as he did. Normally, she would look away. But tonight, she did something out of character.

She stared right back.

The sexy stranger smiled widely as he reached her, revealing a perfect set of white teeth. "Hello."

"Hi, there," Mikki replied, a shuddery breath oozing out of her. She did a quick sweep of his body. Even though his shirt wasn't form-fitting, his strong arms and pecs were still evident beneath it.

On the hot meter, this guy was a ten out of ten.

Why was he interested in *her*? With her hair pulled back in a ponytail, her white shirt buttoned almost to the top, and her gray pleated skirt hanging below her knees, she could be the poster child for Plain Jane.

But as soon as the thought came to her, Mikki silently chastised herself for it.

No, she told herself. *You're not going to do that. You're not going to act as though you're not an attractive, desirable woman. Just because Alex dumped you doesn't mean you don't have it going on. You don't have to be all dolled up for a guy to notice your beauty.*

"What can I get you to drink?" the man asked.

Mikki glanced at the bar. Her draft beer was there. "I've got a beer, but thank you." She sipped it. "I haven't seen you here before." A lame line, perhaps, but it was true.

"No, you wouldn't have."

Mikki extended her hand. "I'm Mikki."

"Hi, Mikki." The man took her hand in his, holding it a beat too long as he shook it. "I'm Barry."

"Please tell me you're not a lawyer, Barry," she said, but she doubted it. A model, perhaps. But a lawyer? She'd never seen a lawyer quite as fine as him before.

"Actually, I'm in advertising," Barry said.

"I'll bet you are," Mikki replied, her tongue feeling loose.

"What does that mean?"

He had the cutest smile, and she loved the way his eyes lit up as he looked at her. "It means," she said in a husky voice, "that I'm sure you've graced the pages of many magazines. A guy as cute as you . . ."

His chuckle was endearing and floated over her like a warm breeze. "Not a model. Definitely not."

Mikki drank more of her beer, feeling like a new woman. She was *flirting*. Two days after she had been dumped by the supposed love of her life. And it felt good.

"So, how come I haven't seen you here before?" Mikki asked.

"Probably because I'm from Chicago."

"Aah, that would explain it."

"I'm in town on business."

Even better. If Mikki took Debbie's advice and went to bed with him, she wouldn't have to worry about a possible relationship. He could be a true palate cleanser.

But she'd need a bit more liquid courage if she was going to leave the bar with him. She lifted her mug of beer and polished off half of its contents.

"You really like your beer," Barry said.

Mikki laughed. To her own ears, she sounded drunk. But she didn't care. She was having fun. "I guess I do. But I was thinking of having a shooter. Irish cream. Want to do one with me?"

Barry held her gaze for a long moment, and Mikki had the sudden thought that there was something familiar about him. Something about his eyes that made her wonder if she had met him before. But if she had, she wouldn't have forgotten. She would know.

Barry flagged down the bartender, and this time the woman behind the bar hurried over. She smiled coyly as she asked Barry what he wanted.

A minute later, she put two shooters onto the counter. Barry lifted them both and passed one to Mikki.

"To new beginnings and second chances," he said, and clinked his shooter glass against hers.

"Cheers." Mikki tipped her head back and drank the Irish cream in one swallow. It warmed a path down her throat.

As her head came up, her mind registered what Barry had said. "Hold on. Did you say 'second chances'?"

His eyes twinkled, as if he knew some secret that she did not. "Yep."

A beat passed. He couldn't be referring to her breakup with Alexander, could he?

"What did you mean by that?" Mikki asked. She wrapped a hand around her mug and brought it to her mouth. Not the most tasty of beverages after Irish cream, but, hey, she was well on her way to feeling no pain.

"You don't remember me, do you?"

Mikki had just sipped her beer, and now she nearly choked on it. That wasn't what she expected this man to say. "Excuse me?"

"You don't remember me."

Now she narrowed her eyes. Had he approached her thinking she was someone else? "If you're going to tell me we slept together after a night in a bar, then you've got the wrong woman."

Barry chuckled. "You're Mikki Harper, right?"

Now Mikki's mouth fell open. This man knew her name. How? She whirled around, noticing that her friends were gone.

And then it hit her. Either Debbie or Isabel had put this guy up to approaching her. One or both of them had told him her name. She was betting Debbie was behind it, in an attempt to get her into bed with some random guy as a way to mend her broken heart.

"I get it," Mikki said. "My friend Debbie. Right?"

"Pardon?"

"My friend put you up to this," Mikki said, nodding as she spoke. "Told you to come over and talk to me. Heck, she probably paid you."

"High school," Barry said.

"High school?" Mikki repeated, not understanding.

"Mrs. Miller's English class. Eleventh grade. Surely you can't forget that."

Mikki's eyes narrowed again, and again she thought that something about his face looked familiar. Familiar, and yet . . . different.

"Barry Sanders," he said, a question in his voice.

Barry, Barry, you're a fairy. The old chant from high school sounded in Mikki's mind.

"Not Barry the Fairy?" she asked, too tipsy to consider censoring her words.

Barry's eyes crinkled. "I don't like to go by that name anymore. I didn't mind 'Boring Barry' so much, but the fairy one . . . hated it."

"Oh my God!" Mikki exclaimed. "*Barry*? It's really you?"

"Yep."

"You look so . . . different."

"Thank God."

"I can't believe it!" The last time Mikki had seen him, he had looked . . . well . . . nothing like this. Then, he'd had a full mouth of braces—which explained the perfect teeth now. He had probably been just as tall, having been one of the few guys in high school to experience an early growth spurt, but he'd been a good forty pounds lighter. Maybe more. Poor Barry the Fairy had been tall and lanky, all arms and legs. And surrounded by jocks who'd worked out tirelessly to hone their teenage bodies, he had been teased something fierce at their South Florida high school.

But the way he looked now, no one would dare tease him.

Talk about a metamorphosis.

Mikki couldn't help telling him so. "Barry, I can hardly believe it's you. I mean, seriously. You look amazing."

"So do you. But then, you always did."

Mikki touched her ponytail, self-conscious. "You're being too kind, but thank you. I'm looking a little frumpy today."

"'You' and 'frumpy'—two words that don't go together. You always looked great, even when you were balking at conventional fashion."

Mikki grinned. She remembered how she had made the conscious decision to defy all the fashion trends that the girls in high school had followed. "Ah, high school. Dark days I'd rather forget."

"You? You had it easy compared to me."

"Perhaps."

"What was the worst name anyone ever called you? Bitchy Mikki?"

Mikki groaned. "And that nickname was totally unfair. I wasn't bitchy. Just shy and misunderstood."

"Still, a far better moniker than Barry the Fairy."

"I'm not so sure about that."

When Barry's eyes widened with incredulity, they both shared a chuckle. As her laughter died, Mikki said, "So you're in New York for business?"

"Yep. I'm overseeing a big campaign for a sporting goods company."

Mikki sipped more beer. "Well, I meant what I said. You could easily be the model for any campaign."

And then she stared at him with narrowed eyes, wondering if the beer had caused her to imagine things. Because surely this couldn't be Barry the Fairy in front of her.

"What?" he asked.

"I'm sorry. I know I keep looking at you. It's just . . ."

"A big change, I know. But, hey, high school was thirteen years ago."

Very true. A lot could change in thirteen years. Clearly.

"So, what about you?" Barry asked. "Are you living in New York? Or just visiting the Big Apple?"

"I'm living here. Five years now. I'm working for a law firm."

"A lawyer?"

"No. Not a lawyer. I'm a legal secretary."

"Nice."

At the mention of her job, Mikki couldn't help thinking about Alexander, and she did *not* want to think about her schmuck of an ex. She lifted her mug and finished off her beer.

Her head swam a little as she put the empty mug onto the bar. But as she looked at the fine specimen of a man in front of her, she grinned like a fool. She was feeling a lot happier. Because she was here with Barry, who was definitely no longer a fairy.

"So, Barry, are you single?" She hoped he hadn't simply come over to her to say "hi" to an old friend.

Not now that her body was tingling in reaction to his masculine hotness.

"As a matter of fact—"

Barry didn't even finish his statement before Mikki moved forward and placed her hand on his chest. "Good. Then dance with me."

Taking his hand in hers, Mikki led the way to the dance floor. An upbeat Usher song was playing, and she began to shake her hips, moving in front of Barry seductively.

She couldn't stop feeling amazed at just how gorgeous he was. How could he be the same Barry who'd once been her friend in high school?

Mikki didn't question it. She simply went with the flow, as Isabel had said she should. And the flow right now was causing her to snake her arms around Barry's waist and get close to him.

He grinned down at her, and Mikki felt a bolt of heat.

No, he was more than a ten out of ten. At least a twelve.

He smelled incredible. And the way his hard body felt against hers . . .

Mikki's body was thrumming. Lust was undeniably coursing through her veins.

She wanted to kiss him. She *needed* to kiss him.

Moving her hands to his broad shoulders, she eased up onto her toes. And when she pressed her lips against his, Alexander was the last thing on her mind.

Chapter 3

Mikki's eyelids fluttered open, but when bright sunlight nearly blinded her, she promptly squeezed them shut. That was the first sign that something was odd, because she always closed her blinds at night. She must have been too drunk to do so when she got home from the bar.

Rolling over onto her side, she stretched her arm out. And that's when she got the second inkling that something was wrong. Because her arm brushed against something warm and smooth.

Warm and smooth . . . Mikki's eyes flew open as alarm spread through her body. She saw the form in her bed, the golden-brown skin of a man's back. She saw the white sheets strewn around his waist and the strong calf that had slipped from beneath the bedspread.

Something was wrong. Seriously wrong, indeed.

Because this *wasn't* her bedroom. She currently had beige sheets on her bed, not white.

Not to mention the room at large. She looked around in horror, not recognizing it at all.

Where *was* she?

Oh God. Had she been kidnapped? Kidnapped and forced to satisfy some strange man? As wild as the idea was, what else could explain the fact that she was in some other person's bed?

Her head pounded and her stomach roiled, and in a flash, the previous night came back to her. At the bar with her friends. Drinking too many beers. Meeting up with Barry the Fairy.

Now Mikki bolted upright. Barry the Fairy. Oh God, she'd slept with him.

Her eyes scanned the room more intently now. The small space. The delicately wallpapered walls. The television in the large cabinet console.

She was in a hotel room.

His hotel room.

He had mentioned something about the Waldorf Astoria, hadn't he?

Oh shit! What have I done?

Mikki didn't realize that she was holding the sheets up to her chest, and now she dared to look down at herself. Though she couldn't feel a stitch of clothing on her body, she pulled the blanket back to be sure.

She cringed as her worst fear was confirmed. She was naked.

Completely.

Looking around the room again, she now saw her clothes. Her shirt was by the hotel door. Her skirt was about a foot away from the shirt, closer to the bed.

Then came her bra, followed by her frumpy granny panties, which were on the floor next to the bed.

Nooooo.

One more glance at Barry made it all too real. His clothes were also thrown about the room, which meant he was also naked. But if he was wearing briefs, she would feel a world of relief.

Gingerly lifting the sheet covering his behind, Mikki gasped when she saw his naked butt.

Oh, good God in heaven. What exactly had happened between them last night?

Dumb question. Mikki knew what had happened.

Well, what *must* have happened. Because the last thing she could remember was being in the bar, on the dance floor with Barry.

Everything after that was a blank.

Mortified, Mikki slipped out from under the covers and off the bed. She picked up her panties, then her bra and the rest of her clothing. Creeping across the floor so she didn't make any noise, she made her way into the bathroom.

No more alcohol for her. Clearly, being under the influence messed with her brains. Because she was *not* this person. She wasn't a woman who slept with a guy the first night she'd met him.

Granted, she'd known Barry for two years in high school, but still. She hadn't seen him in thirteen years.

This was unacceptable.

And she couldn't even remember it!

Maybe she'd been drunk and Barry had taken her to his hotel room. Maybe he'd undressed her and put her in his bed so she could get some rest. Maybe there was a perfectly good reason why he had taken off every stitch of her clothing that had nothing to do with doing the dirty.

Yeah, right. And maybe Isabel had decided to join a convent.

Her nipples were throbbing, sensitive. It was clear Barry had played with them—a lot.

Groaning, Mikki glanced at herself in the mirror. Damn, she *looked* guilty. "You slept with him," she said accusingly to her reflection. "My God, you're a slut."

She had to get out of here. She couldn't face Barry in the light of day. If *she* thought she was a slut, what would *he* think of her? Sure, he had been party to whatever had happened in his bed, but still. Men were forgiven for behaving promiscuously. Congratulated, even. Women were not.

Mikki quickly got dressed. Then she opened the bathroom door and peered in the direction of the bed. Barry was still on his stomach, his one leg still jutting from beneath the sheet. She was certain he hadn't moved, which meant he was still asleep.

Hopefully soundly.

Mikki found her pumps and slipped into them. Her leather jacket was also on the floor beside the door, and she shrugged into it.

She was about to open the door and make a hasty exit when she remembered her purse. A quick scan of the area and she couldn't see it. There was no way she'd left it at the bar . . . had she?

Silently cursing, Mikki moved through the room, fearing every second that Barry would wake up. Not seeing her purse anywhere, something came to her.

It was likely under a piece of Barry's clothing.

His shirt was thrown into a heap on the armchair, and Mikki lifted it with one finger.

Bingo. The purse was there.

She slipped the leather strap over her shoulder, then went back to the door. One more glance at Barry, who thankfully still appeared to be asleep, and Mikki knew it was time to make her move. She opened the hotel door as quietly as possible, then crept out of the room.

In the quiet of the hallway, the door closing sounded like a bomb going off. Her heart beginning to pound, she rushed down the corridor. She came upon the bank of elevators but didn't stop. If Barry had heard the door closing, he might be getting his clothes on to come after her.

Instead, Mikki raced to the far end of the hallway, toward the stairwell. When she saw the exit door, she finally looked to her right to figure out what floor she was on.

Fifteen!

No matter. She went into the stairway nonetheless and began her descent. Two flights down, she stopped, took off her pumps, then continued going.

"I'm a slut. I'm a slut." Mikki repeated that mantra over and over again, shamefully.

How could she have slept with Barry?

She'd been drinking, yes. And she remembered how good he had looked, even before she'd known he was Barry from her past. And she remembered pressing her body against his on the dance floor . . .

But what had happened next? Why couldn't she remember?

She paused in the stairwell, a memory coming back to her. There had been a kiss. Yes, she remembered his mouth coming down onto hers as they'd danced. Or had she initiated the kiss?

Make that plural. They'd kissed more than once, and damn, it had felt good. Scorching hot. Barry's skillful kisses had made her giddy and light-headed.

Granted, it could have been the beer that had made her light-headed. The beer that had made her do something so completely out of character.

Suddenly, Alex's paranoid warning about men— even the bartenders—putting drugs into a woman's drink didn't seem so paranoid. Was that what had happened? Had something been added to the beer that had made her lose control?

And just how out of control had she been? Her body was throbbing in a variety of places, and her inner thighs felt strained, making it clear that whatever they'd done in Barry's bed had been . . . a workout.

But no matter how much she racked her brain for a memory of what had happened in the hotel room, she couldn't conjure it.

"If you're going to be a slut," Mikki said, panting slightly as she reached the main floor, "you at least want to remember the experience."

She took a moment to catch her breath before slipping back into her shoes. She tightened her jacket around her, then opened the door leading to the lobby.

As she began to stride with her head held high, she once again felt the strain on her inner thighs. It had been a long time since her body had felt muscle tension after making love. Just how wild had she and Barry gotten?

Well, she would never find out. Because Barry lived in Chicago. That was one thing she remembered that he'd said the previous night. The chances of them running into each other again were slim to none.

Whatever she'd needed to do, she'd gotten it out of her system. Debbie had told her that having sex with someone else would help her get over Alex. But the sad reality was, sex with Barry hadn't made her forget that Alex had broken her heart.

Perhaps because she couldn't remember the experience. But she certainly wasn't about to look Barry up and ask him for a play-by-play of what they'd done.

And she definitely hoped that Barry didn't try to find her. Though if he did, good luck. New York was a big city, with a gazillion law firms. She hadn't given him any specific details as to where she worked.

Had she?

She certainly hoped not. And if Barry reached out to her on Facebook, she would deny his friendship request.

Because no matter how much she might have enjoyed her night with him, Barry wasn't her type. Not a man who had once been known as Barry the Fairy.

Mikki strode across the beautiful lobby, not making eye contact with anyone for fear that they would see in her eyes the truth of what she'd done last night.

Sex with a stranger. He may as well be, given that they hadn't seen each other in thirteen years.

As Mikki exited the hotel, she felt a little bad for

leaving Barry without so much as a note or a good-bye. It wasn't that she didn't like him. Indeed, they'd been friends in high school. From what Mikki remembered, she'd been one of his very few friends. Where Barry was concerned, people hadn't looked past the exterior. And the fact that he'd come to their high school two months into their junior year made him easy prey for those who'd already formed their clique of comrades.

But Mikki had liked Barry. Unlike most of the insensitive jocks at her school, he was easy to talk to, something they'd done often. And while most of the other kids had seen Barry as a geek, Mikki hadn't. A little awkward perhaps, but a nice guy at heart.

She wondered what had ever happened to Tiffany, the object of Barry's desire back then.

No, she told herself. *Don't wonder about Barry; don't wonder about Tiffany. Just get to Brooklyn and make sure you have everything packed.*

Because she had to head to Florida on a flight this afternoon. Her younger sister by a year and a half, Chantal, was getting married.

Chantal, the one who had always been popular throughout high school. The one who had been a cheerleader and valedictorian. The one for whom love came easy.

Chantal was about to get married, while the man Mikki had thought would propose to her had dumped her instead.

It was embarrassing to head to Florida without Alex, having to answer all the questions Mikki knew would come. Especially after telling Chantal that she thought he would propose over the holidays. And worse than the questions would be the pity. The pats on the back and the assurances that, hey, one day she'd find her Mr. Right.

Mikki was sick of it. She was sick of being single with no hope of marriage on the horizon.

And sadly, not even a night of hot sex could make her forget that fact.

Chapter 4

"Just touched down," Mikki said into her phone while the plane taxied to the gate. "I think my mother is picking me up, and tonight will be a quiet dinner with family. But tomorrow, I have to head for a fitting at the bridal shop. And I still have to do my Christmas shopping," she added with a little sigh. "Who plans a wedding for three days before Christmas?"

"In a way, I can't blame your sister," Debbie responded. "Ken put off the wedding twice before, didn't he?"

"Conflicts with golf," Mikki said, stating the reason Ken had given. Yes, as well as being handsome and from a wealthy background and pretty much perfect in every way, her future brother-in-law was a professional golfer.

"Forget Ken," Debbie said, her voice growing with excitement. "Tell me what happened!"

"What do you mean?" Mikki asked. But she was playing dumb. She knew exactly what her friend was getting at.

"Um, you leave the bar with one of the hottest guys I've seen in a long time and you pretend you don't know what I'm talking about?"

Mikki leaned closer to the airplane window. "This isn't the best time to talk. I'm still on the plane."

"Aah, I get it. The details are too dirty to talk about in public. Nice! But you'd better call me the moment you have a minute. I want to hear every one of those naughty details." Debbie laughed.

"Sure. I'll call you back in a bit, okay?"

Mikki hung up, knowing that when she called Debbie back, her friend would be disappointed. Because there was nothing to tell her.

Well, that wasn't exactly true. She could tell her how she'd woken up naked in Barry's hotel room, but she couldn't give the details her friend wanted to know.

Naked in his bed. Mikki had been thinking of nothing but that for practically the entire day. Meeting up with Barry again after all these years. How *good* he'd looked. How incredible he had smelled.

Even amid her alarm at waking up in his bed, there had been a part of her that had felt a secret thrill when she'd lifted the sheet and taken a peek at his naked butt.

As butts went, it was pretty darn perfect.

The memory made her body flush, and as the passengers began to move toward the plane's exit, Mikki mentally chastised herself. She should be ashamed of herself, not feeling any measure of heat over an illicit night she couldn't even remember.

She wondered what Barry was thinking now, if he had missed her once he woke up. If he was upset that she had taken off without a word.

Or if he even remembered having slept with her. If he, like she, had been too drunk, he might have awakened and not even remembered that a woman had been in his bed.

No matter. It was over and done with. Mikki was going to move on and put the disturbing truth behind her.

As she made her way to the baggage claim area, any thought of calling Debbie back anytime soon was quickly erased. Because her sister and Ken stood there waving at her, matching smiles on their faces and matching clothes on their bodies. Ken was in khaki shorts and a polo shirt, while her sister was wearing a polo shirt and a khaki skirt. They looked like an African American Barbie and Ken.

Mikki had first met Ken in New York just over a year ago when he and her sister had shown up to visit the Big Apple. She had gone out with them, feeling like a third wheel the entire time because Alexander had told her he was too busy to hang out. So Mikki had gone to restaurants with them and shown them the sights, all the time listening to just how wonderful Ken was and how amazing her sister's life was going to be now that she'd found her Mr. Right.

Mikki had wanted to throw up.

It wasn't that she didn't love her sister and wish her the best. It was just that everything happened so easily for Chantal. She had met Ken pretty much right after her high school sweetheart had moved to China for business. Out at a restaurant, the gorgeous son of a business magnate had approached Chantal, and the rest was history. He'd helped nurse her broken heart, and the two had fallen in love.

Mikki, on the other hand, had gone through all of high school without dating anyone. She had gone to college where she'd dated some, but not much. She went to New York for a change of scenery, feeling that she would never find the love of her life in Miami. She'd worked for two years at a law firm in Brooklyn, before a better opportunity came up at a bigger firm in Manhattan. She'd been hired, and that was where she'd met Alexander.

Slowly, her relationship with Alex had built. First as friends, because she had rejected his numerous advances, not wanting to be a notch on Alexander the Great's bedpost. When, after a year, he was still pursuing her, Mikki agreed to a real date with him, having believed that the slow and steady start to their relationship would give them a lasting foundation.

And after dating for nearly two years, Mikki had thought he might finally propose. Alex, on the other hand, thought it was time to move on.

Mikki's stomach fluttered as she knew that explanations would soon have to be forthcoming. Alex was supposed to have traveled to Miami with her. Chantal and Ken would have questions as to his whereabouts.

She didn't want to think about him, much less talk about him.

"Hey," Chantal said sweetly, moving toward her with her arms spread wide. She wrapped her in a hug. "How are you?"

"I'm great," Mikki responded. She felt a little guilty for any negative thoughts she'd had about her sister, including the ill timing of a wedding during the holidays. But she always felt like this when she first saw her, because they had yet to knock horns.

Ken hugged her next. "Hey, Mikki."

"Ready for the big day?" Mikki asked him.

"Definitely."

Chantal draped an arm around Ken's waist. "And *no* cancellations due to golf. Thank God."

Ken gave Chantal a kiss on the temple. "I know Chantal was angry with me for having to postpone the wedding a second time. But in three days, I'm going to make everything up to her."

Mikki inhaled a painful breath. Chantal and Ken, the picture of the perfect couple, while her relationship with Alex had gone down the toilet.

As if Chantal read her thoughts, her expression of bliss soon morphed into one of confusion. "Hey, where's Alexander?"

Of course, it had been too much to hope that Chantal and Ken wouldn't have realized he was missing.

"Um, he's not here."

"Obviously." Chantal smiled. "Where is he?"

There was no point delaying the inevitable. Alex wasn't coming, and pretending that he was going to show up at any moment would be stupid. As much as Mikki wished he would surprise her and do exactly that, she wasn't about to bet her life on it.

So she said, "He's not coming."

The serious tone of her voice clued Chantal into what was happening. "No," Chantal said, shaking her head. "No."

"We broke up." Mikki aimed for cool and nonchalant, but her voice cracked a little.

Chantal wrapped her in another warm hug, longer this time. "Oh my goodness. I'm so sorry."

Mikki drew in a deep breath, because if she didn't, she was going to start crying right here at Miami International Airport.

"What happened?" Chantal asked as they pulled apart.

Mikki waved off the question. "Later," she said.

"Sure. Tell me all about it this evening at the dinner."

"At the dinner? What dinner? The rehearsal dinner isn't tonight."

"No, but tonight Ken's parents are hosting a dinner at the club."

"The club?"

"Oh, sorry. The Deering Bay Yacht and Country Club." There was a hint of smugness to her sister's voice, one that hadn't existed before she'd started dating Ken. Chantal loved that she was marrying into a family with money, one that had memberships at exclusive clubs and whatnot.

"Tonight?" Mikki asked. "Because it's been a long day, and I was hoping—"

"Don't even think of trying to get out of it," Chantal interjected. "Because, yes, you have to be there. It's a dinner where we'll meet all of Ken's family. And you can tell me what happened with Alexander over a glass of wine."

The mention of alcohol made a vision of Barry's naked butt flash into Mikki's mind, followed by an odd stirring in her gut.

"I think I'll lay off the wine tonight," Mikki said. When Chantal gave her a questioning look, she added,

"There'll be plenty to drink at the wedding. I'll abstain until then."

Situated on the southern tip of Coral Gables and along the shores of Biscayne Bay, the Deering Bay Yacht and Country Club was a stunning property. The grounds were lush, with a bay-front golf course, serene waterways, and even mangrove forests. And in terms of amenities, the club had all a person could want. Tennis courts, a fitness and yoga center, and a junior Olympic-size pool. Topping it off were the private marinas that club members with boats could utilize.

The Crystal Room was decorated to elegant perfection. A pianist in the corner was playing a steady stream of Christmas songs. Outside, the palm trees were decorated with strings of white lights, adding to the festive holiday atmosphere. Servers wearing white gloves were making the rounds with hors d'oeuvres and wine. The room was filled with happy people, eating, drinking, and congratulating the engaged couple.

And everyone in the room was extremely well dressed, especially the women. They wore sleek dresses, designer boots, and strings of classy pearls. They looked like models.

Mikki, on the other hand, looked . . . well, not sleek and stylish. She was wearing a black skirt, a red top, and a black blazer—as if she was dressed for a day at the office instead of a party.

Nothing she could do about it now, so Mikki put it out of her mind and dutifully made the rounds, meeting Ken's parents, cousins, and other extended family.

There were certainly a lot of them. Chantal said that just over fifty were due to be here. According to Chantal, the bonus of having a wedding so close to Christmas was that it allowed family to get together to celebrate the holidays.

Mikki's parents looked as happy as the bride and groom, her mother's dream that one of her daughters would marry up finally coming true.

Turning to her right, Mikki noticed that Ken's uncle Wally was heading in her direction—again. He was holding two cocktail glasses, and Mikki was certain that one was for her. She rolled her eyes and quickly whirled around. She didn't want to spend another fifteen minutes entertaining the fifty-year-old flirt.

Mikki veered toward the wall of windows, her intent to head to the door at the room's far end so that she could escape to the restroom. But halfway across the room, she stopped dead in her tracks.

Her heart jumped into her throat. No. It couldn't be. Her eyes *had* to be playing tricks on her.

She closed her eyes. Reopened them.

Gulped.

No. It wasn't possible. Surely that couldn't be Barry-No-Longer-the-Fairy standing near the exit door, talking to Ken and her sister.

Mikki had conjured him. He was a figment of her imagination, here simply to haunt her because she'd gone to bed with him.

But as she continued to stare at that magnificent body and that bald head, she became certain that it *was* him. Somehow, some way, he was here in this room.

She hadn't seen Barry in thirteen years, and now

here he was, appearing in her life twice in two days, and in two different states.

Unbelievable.

Suddenly, he turned. Seeing her, his face lit up in a smile.

Mikki wondered for a moment if it was possible that Barry was following her. She had put on her Facebook page and on Twitter that she was heading to Florida for her sister's wedding. And now here was Barry.

"Ah, Mikki."

At the sound of Uncle Wally's voice, Mikki turned. He extended a cocktail glass to her.

"Um," she began, "will you hold that for me? I've got to use the facilities."

And then, squaring her shoulders, she moved forward, toward the exit as planned. Unfortunately, to get to the restroom, she had to pass the man who had occupied her thoughts all day.

"Hey," Ken said exuberantly, snaking a hand around her wrist as she tried to sneak by. "Barry was just telling me that you're friends."

"Um." Mikki fidgeted from one foot to the next. "Yeah. We went to the same high school."

"Long time," Barry said, and Mikki thought she detected a hint of amusement in his tone.

His voice sounded deep and sexy, and Mikki had a sensation of a tongue trilling her earlobe. Much to her horror, her nipples hardened.

Not daring to look at Barry, she said, "*Very* long time."

"Thirteen years or so, right?"

He was taunting her, clearly. "About that," Mikki said in a clipped voice. Then, "You're the last person I expected to see here." She paused briefly. "Why *are* you here?"

Ken slapped Barry's back. "Barry's a second cousin. Small world."

"This'll work out well, then," Chantal said. "Since you already know each other."

"Excuse me?" Mikki asked.

"Barry is Ken's best man," Chantal explained. "You're my maid of honor. So you'll be paired up. Which works well, given your history."

"Ah, right." Mikki's head began to pound. This couldn't be happening.

"If you'll excuse me," Mikki began, aware that she sounded a little breathless. "I'm heading to the bathroom."

Quickly, she scooted past Barry, her pulse racing so fast she wondered if she would end up having heart failure. She hurried into the bathroom and locked herself in a stall. Two minutes later, she was still in there, leaning against the wooden door, taking deep breaths as she assessed the situation.

So much for a one-night stand not coming back to haunt you. Goodness, could Mikki have worse luck?

After another minute passed, Mikki asked herself what she was doing. She couldn't hide out in the bathroom all night. So what if she'd slept with Barry and then sneaked out of his hotel room like a thief in the night? Life went on.

That thought in mind, Mikki exited the stall—which she hadn't used—and then made her way to the restroom exit.

She opened the door and stepped outside.

And ran smack into Barry.

Her heart pounded so hard, she thought it might explode. She stared up at Barry, at the humorous smile on his face, and swallowed.

"So, we meet again," he said.

Chapter 5

Mikki's chest rose and fell with each heavy breath as she stared at Barry. She said nothing.

"Tell me," Barry went on. "Was I ever going to hear from you again?"

"Sure," Mikki lied.

"That's why you slipped out of my bed and didn't even leave me your phone number on the night table."

His eyes danced as he spoke. He was enjoying this. Enjoying humiliating her.

"What do you want me to say, Barry? I woke up in a strange room, discovered that I was naked in some-one's bed—"

"*My* bed."

She swallowed again. There was a lump in her throat that wouldn't dissipate. "Your bed," she whis-pered, her chest tightening when she saw the victori-ous smile on Barry's face. "And why was I naked, by the way?"

Barry chuckled, the warm sound causing Mikki's

stomach to flutter. And then another image flashed into her mind.

Barry's full lips wrapped around her nipple.

Mikki jerked her gaze from his, disturbed by the thought that had come into her mind. She couldn't actually be aroused, could she?

No. Of course not. She was simply uncomfortable at seeing him again, when she never expected that she would.

"Why were you naked?" Barry asked. "Don't tell me you don't remember . . ."

"I don't," Mikki stressed. "All I know is that I woke up and discovered I was naked and that you were naked beside me." She paused. "What did you do to me?"

"What did I do to *you*?" One of Barry's eyebrows shot up, humor playing on his face. "I think the more appropriate question to ask is what did *you* do to me?"

Mikki's breath caught in her throat.

After a moment, Barry's expression changed from playful to serious. "You really don't remember?"

Mikki shook her head.

"Damn," Barry said. "Damn."

Mikki suddenly realized how her words might have been construed. "I'm not saying you took advantage of me. I'm just saying . . . I don't remember . . . what went on."

"Too bad," Barry said, his eyes holding hers, his voice deep and husky as he spoke into her ear. "Because you had a good time."

* * *

Barry watched Mikki all but trip over herself as she scurried back into the dining room, and he couldn't help grinning.

What were the chances? He'd woken up this morning, found Mikki gone, and had been hugely disappointed. Because last night had been one of the best nights of his life.

Never had he experienced such an explosive sexual encounter before. Mikki had made no secret of the fact that she had wanted him, starting on the dance floor. The moment she'd kissed him, his body had erupted in heat, and the way she had grinded her perfect figure against his as the music played, Barry had become hard almost instantly.

He'd had to hide his throbbing erection as he'd left the bar with Mikki, and the way she'd kissed and groped him in the back of the taxi . . . well, it was a wonder they'd made it to his hotel room before she'd started to take her clothes off.

She had been wild with lust, but Barry wasn't stupid. He knew she had consumed a large amount of alcohol. He'd suggested she drink water, lie down, and take a breather. But he was a man, one who had dreamed of Mikki wanting him sexually in high school, and when she hadn't been able to take her hands off of him, he had been powerless to resist her.

He was surprised to hear her say she didn't remember what had happened, because last night, he had jokingly asked her if she knew her name, how many fingers he was holding up, that sort of thing. She had been aware of everything. And even after she'd gotten naked and had then helped him out of his clothes, Barry had restrained from making love to her right away. He'd taken her to the bed and lain with her and talked for a good half hour.

Actually, *she* had talked—all about the ex who had just dumped her. But she'd also said how glad she was to have run into Barry and continually told him how hot he was.

Only after being certain that she had her wits about her—and after Mikki had asked, *Didn't you want to do this back in high school?*—Barry had caved to Mikki's seduction.

And then they'd made love, and the sex had been phenomenal.

Barry hadn't considered himself the type to believe in fate, but the fact that Mikki was here, in Florida, and that Ken was marrying her sister . . . if that wasn't fate, what was?

It was also something else—pretty damn perfect. Because after the night he'd had with Mikki, he knew that one taste of her would never be enough.

Because you had a good time . . .

Mikki thought about the words all night long. Strangely, she couldn't forget them. In fact, she found herself flushed when she remembered the deep timber of Barry's voice as he'd whispered in her ear.

Aroused.

And when she fell asleep, she dreamed of him. Of deep kisses as his hands tweaked her nipples. Of enthusiastic, steamy, toe-tingling sex. She had dreamed of his lips and tongue tantalizing all the hot zones on her body. The dream had been scorching, definitely

X-rated, and Mikki woke with a sensation of lust coursing through her body.

Because you had a good time . . .

Just how good of a time had she had? That's what Mikki wanted to know. She wished she could remember what had happened.

Her dream had been so vivid, Mikki could almost feel Barry's lips and hands on her body as she thought of it now. Almost as if the dream had actually been real. She couldn't help wondering if on some level the dream had been a memory of what had happened the night she'd ended up in bed with Barry.

All she could say with certainty was that the dream had been so hot, it left her craving sex.

And this wasn't like her. Not at all. She hadn't even been attracted to Barry in high school. Why should the thought of him turn her on at all now?

Because he's a totally different guy than the one in high school, came the whisper of a reply in her mind.

Who was she kidding? She may not be able to wrap her mind around the physical changes, but Barry's hotness factor had gone up about one thousand percent.

Was that what was causing Mikki to think of Barry and sex in the same sentence? Because Barry was now undeniably smoking hot?

Perhaps. But as Mikki lay in her bed, she thought of another reason, one that was more likely. Alex had broken her heart, and her self-esteem had suffered. Barry's attention was helping to repair her bruised ego.

Surely any guy who paid any attention to her would cause the same reaction.

Because you had a good time . . .

Maybe there was yet another reason. The mystery

behind exactly *what* had happened in Barry's bed. Maybe the wondering about what they had done had the effect of a sexual stimulant.

Because Mikki was definitely not used to waking up and thinking about sex. Not with anyone.

Doing her best to push all thoughts of Barry and sex out of her mind, she got up, took a shower that was more cold than warm, and then sent text messages to both Isabel and Debbie to let them know she was at home and that she had survived the first night.

But by the time she'd finished her breakfast and she still couldn't put Barry out of her mind, she knew she needed to talk to someone about the latest, unnerving development. She called Debbie, since she'd already spoken to her about waking up in Barry's bed. But Debbie's number went to voice mail. So Mikki did the next best thing. She called Isabel.

"Girl!" Isabel exclaimed when she answered her phone. "I've been waiting to hear from you. What happened that night?"

"Did you talk to Debbie?" Mikki asked.

"She didn't answer her phone, since she was traveling to California, but she sent a text to say I needed to talk to you. I called last night, by the way, and you didn't pick up. So, what happened?"

Mikki said frankly, "I don't remember what happened."

"What?"

"I don't remember. I have no memory of that night."

"You blacked out?"

"I . . . I don't think I blacked out. I just . . . I just can't remember. Everything's a blank from after I left the bar until the morning."

"No way, chica," Isabel said. "But I guess I shouldn't be surprised. You were drinking a lot."

"Why did you let me leave with him?" Mikki asked, feeling the need to blame someone. Debbie and Isabel had seen how drunk she was and really should have intervened on her behalf. If only her friends had stopped her from leaving with Barry, she wouldn't have done something so out of character.

Because you had a good time . . . Mikki felt a tingle of desire in her belly.

"Don't you remember the conversation in the bathroom?" Isabel countered.

"No."

"You were all excited, told us how turned on you were just by dancing with Barry and that you were going to take Debbie's advice and get laid."

Mikki cringed. "I said that?"

"Oh, yeah. Like I said, you were real excited. We tried to suggest that maybe you should slow down on the alcohol and even offered to get you home in a cab. But you told us absolutely not. You said you were looking forward to spending the night with Barry because he looked good enough to eat."

"Okay, I get the picture." Mikki couldn't quite stand hearing this account of how she had behaved. Because it was completely unlike her. What had the bartender put in her beer? Surely he had put something in there to knock the sense out of her. Because Mikki didn't behave like this, drunk or not.

"You don't remember *anything*?"

Isabel was one of her best friends. She could tell her everything. "All I remember is waking up in bed and there was a naked guy beside me. I was . . . unsettled, to say the least."

"Damn," Isabel said. "I was hoping to hear the details."

"Isabel!" Mikki rolled her eyes. "So you're not so much concerned that I don't remember the details, only that you're not going to be able to live vicariously through me!"

"Sorry," Isabel said sheepishly.

"Here's the thing," Mikki went on, sighing softly. "And it's really thrown me for a loop. Guess who I just saw last night at a dinner for my sister's fiancé's family?"

Isabel paused briefly; then she said, "Get out."

"He's *here,*" Mikki said, hearing the note of alarm in her voice. "Thirteen years I haven't seen him, and then suddenly I'm seeing him twice in twenty-four hours."

"He didn't tell you he was going to Miami?"

"I have a feeling we didn't talk much that night."

"But afterward. In the morning."

Mikki hesitated a moment, knowing that this was going to sound lame. But she said, "I snuck out of the hotel room."

"What?" Isabel shrieked.

"I panicked. I woke up, realized that I was next to some naked guy, and I panicked. It wasn't like me to go to bed with a guy on the first night. I got out of there as fast as I could. And before you ask, no, I didn't leave my phone number. I never thought I would see him again. And then I come to Miami and here he is?"

Isabel muttered something in Spanish that Mikki didn't understand.

"What does that mean?" Mikki asked.

"It's fate."

"Pardon me?"

"It's fate," Isabel repeated. "You tried to escape him, but there he is in Florida. The two of you are destined to be together."

"Is that some sort of cultural superstition?" Mikki asked. She was slightly annoyed.

"You mark my words. And I have to tell you, I've never seen you so excited about the idea of getting laid. *Never.* I just thought you should know."

Mikki's face flushed. Again, there was a sense of arousal. Did her subconscious mind remember what had happened while she couldn't recall it on a conscious level?

"I have to go," Mikki said. "I've got to head to the bridal boutique to try on my dress, make sure it fits. So I'll talk to you later, okay?"

"You better tell me how things go with Barry!"

"Of course." Though there would be nothing to tell. "Talk to you later."

Mikki hung up the phone, frowning. Debbie hadn't told her that she had acted like some wanton slut in the bathroom.

But perhaps she shouldn't be surprised at what Isabel had relayed to her. The fact that she had woken up naked, and seen her clothes thrown around the room should have been a huge indication that she'd been all too eager to do the nasty.

Well, the wedding was in a couple of days. After that, Mikki wouldn't have to see Barry again.

Chapter 6

Mikki and her sister went to the bridal boutique in Coral Gables so Mikki could finally try on her dress. She was still surprised that her sister had asked her to be the maid of honor at the wedding. They weren't as close as sisters could be, but neither were they enemies. But given the fact that Mikki was living in New York and not around to help her sister with any of the wedding planning, she figured Chantal would have asked one of her friends to stand up with her on her special day.

But Mikki was happy—and touched—to be the maid of honor. She only hoped that her sister had respected her wishes in terms of the dress.

When they got to the boutique, Chantal all but ran out of the car, excited. She was about to become Mrs. Ken Pearce, and it was clear the wedding day couldn't come a moment too soon.

Mikki followed her into the store. They'd had many discussions over what the dress should look like and had mostly knocked horns over the color. Chantal had insisted on fuchsia, but Mikki looked ghastly in fuchsia and had pleaded with Chantal to choose another color. Mikki wanted something more understated, like a pale yellow or baby blue.

Time to see what Chantal had decided on.

The store was small and quaint, and decorated to a woman's sensibilities. The various mannequins wore an array of bridal gowns and other kinds of dresses, in a mix of classic and more elaborate styles.

"Everything here is one of a kind," Chantal explained. "The designer is exceptional."

"The gowns are amazing," Mikki said, feeling hopeful. Surely she had worried needlessly about how her dress would look.

Mikki perused the floor as her sister went to the cashier and asked for someone named Emily. Less than a minute later, a tall redhead with a bright smile joined Chantal, and the two made their way over to Mikki.

"Emily, this is my sister, Mikki. Mikki, this is the designer's assistant, Emily."

Mikki shook her hand, saying, "Nice to meet you."

"Are you excited about your sister's wedding?"

"Oh yes. Definitely."

"Well, your dress is over here," Emily said, gesturing toward the back area of the store. "Come this way."

Mikki followed Emily to the dressing room area, where a gown was hung on a changing room door. Mikki's stomach knotted.

Fuchsia. Bright fuchsia.

"I told you I didn't want fuchsia," Mikki said.

"And gold. I think it looks great." Chantal smiled. "Just try it on."

Sure, there was gold threading amid the fuchsia bodice, but it was hardly the dominant color. To make matters worse, the dress had an enormously wide skirt made of layers of organza and netting. It looked like a tutu.

Granted, it wasn't as short as a tutu. Still, it was the kind of dress guaranteed to pack at least twenty pounds onto her hips.

Mikki glanced at Emily, whose face was still lit up in a perpetual smile. "Isn't it gorgeous?"

"It's . . . different." Mikki closed her eyes and breathed in deeply, reminding herself that this was about her sister's special day. So she walked toward the changing room and lifted the dress, then went inside and tried it on.

And just as she expected, the dress hardly looked flattering on her. The bodice, made of satin, was form-fitting and felt a bit snug over her breasts. She could barely get the side zipper up. Perhaps she would have to wear it without a bra. Holding up the bodice were straps about an inch wide that were positioned to rest at the far edge of her shoulders.

Mikki could deal with the bodice of the dress. It was the layers of organza and netting flowing everywhere that were a bit too much.

And as if there wasn't enough organza already, there was an organza sash that came from the right shoulder. This was in gold, to match the threading on the bodice.

Mikki frowned at her reflection. Honestly, how could her sister think that this looked good?

Mikki exited the changing room feeling as though

she were walking toward her executioner. Chantal, on the other hand, beamed.

"Oh my God, it looks amazing!" Chantal exclaimed.

"I don't look good in fuchsia," was Mikki's reply.

Emily, still grinning, said, "I think it looks darling on you."

"I told you," Mikki went on, "any color but this one. Not to mention it looks like I'm about to star in a Disney princess movie. This dress will be pretty hard to move around in."

Chantal's face crumbled, and then the tears came. "Why can't you just like it? Why can't you just let me have things the way I want them for *my* day?"

Mikki groaned as her sister ran off toward the front of the store. "Chantal!" she called. But her sister didn't stop.

Emily walked toward her and began to fuss over the organza sash and skirt. "Your sister was going for a princess theme. Since she said she's marrying her prince. She wanted something different, complete with tiaras for all of the bridesmaids." Making her way to a dressing table, Emily lifted a small tiara with fuchsia-colored jewels. "Every bridesmaid is wearing a similar dress in different colors, like peach and royal blue and burgundy." She placed the tiara on Mikki's head. "For what it's worth, I think the dress looks wonderful on you."

Hearing Emily explain her sister's reasoning, Mikki couldn't help feeling like a bit of a bitch. Chantal had always loved princesses and fairy tales, so the idea of princess-themed dresses made sense. Ultimately, it was her sister's dreams and desires that mattered right now.

Mikki drew in a deep breath and let it out in a rush. "One day. It's my sister's wedding. I can deal with this."

Emily guided Mikki to the full-length mirror so that she could check herself out. Looking at her reflection now, outside of the small dressing room where she had filled up the entire mirror, the dress didn't look all that bad. Her hips didn't look as giant as she had originally thought. And her waist, courtesy of the bodice, looked quite thin.

Chantal appeared, dabbing at her eyes and sniffling.

"I'm sorry," Mikki said without preamble. "You're right—it's your wedding. The day is all about you. What you like, what you want. Planning a wedding is stressful enough. It's not up to me to make things harder on you." Mikki paused. "And looking at the dress now, I'm sorry about my knee-jerk reaction. Because it *is* pretty. Very princessy. It's just that it wasn't what I expected. But it's not about what I expect or want; it's about you." Mikki smiled as she took her sister's hands in hers. "So let's get on with the task of planning the rest of your phenomenal wedding."

Chantal's eyes misted, but a smile spread on her face. She wrapped Mikki in a hug. "Thank you, sis."

"Does the dress feel okay?" Emily asked. "Because the fitting looks right."

"It's a little snug over the bosom," Mikki said. "But nothing major."

"It needs to be a little snug," Emily explained, "to avoid any wardrobe malfunctions."

"Of course. Otherwise, it's fine."

"Excellent," Emily said.

Mikki went back into the changing room and took

off the dress; then she and Chantal left the boutique and went to the florist, where Chantal made sure that the orders for the flowers were coming along with no hitches.

They were on their way back to the car when Chantal said, "Any word from Alex?"

"No," was Mikki's quick reply.

Chantal's Hyundai Elantra beeped as she pressed the remote key to unlock the car door. "Have you tried to call him?"

"No. Definitely not."

"Why not?" Chantal asked once they were inside the vehicle. "You were together for two years. Surely your problems can't be insurmountable."

"Problems? I wish we had problems, some specific reason I could pinpoint for our breakup."

But instead of giving her a concrete reason why they weren't getting along, something Mikki could work with, Alex had given her the "boring in bed" excuse, which had pretty much left her not knowing how to respond.

"I don't understand," Chantal said.

"If you want the truth," Mikki began, "Alex just dumped me. He didn't say that he needed space or anything like that, only that he thought it was time for us to go our separate ways." Which was pretty much true, except for the part about her being boring sexually.

"So you fight," Chantal went on. "You fight for the man you love."

Mikki was silent for a long moment. Then she faced her sister and said, "I hear what you're saying, and normally I would believe in fighting for the relationship."

"Then do it."

"Did you know I thought he was going to propose?" When Chantal met her gaze, Mikki went on. "Alex invited me out to our favorite restaurant. Made a big deal about that particular date. I thought . . . I thought he was going to propose. But he ended things instead." Mikki paused, inhaling deeply. "When Alex broke up with me, days before we were supposed to come down here for your wedding, and for no good reason . . . well, I just got the sense that we're irrevocably over."

"After two years?"

After two years, Alex should have known if I was good enough in the bedroom for him or not, Mikki thought. But she said, "Yeah."

Mikki had been hurt by the breakup, no doubt, but she didn't feel the urge to call Alex and ask him to work things out. Maybe it was the callous way in which he'd dumped her that had stripped her heart too bare to believe there was hope for a future with him.

Or maybe it was . . .

No, it's not. It's not because of Barry.

"Does it have anything to do with Barry?" Chantal asked as they came to a traffic stop, as if she had read Mikki's mind.

Mikki's eyes widened. "What? Why would you say that?"

"I'm just teasing you," Chantal said. "Though I kinda always thought you and Barry would end up together back in high school."

"W-what?" Mikki sputtered.

"I did."

"Where is this coming from?"

"Barry told Ken that he ran into you in New York. Two days ago."

"He did?" Mikki chuckled a bit nervously. What else had Barry said?

"Yeah. Something about you two reconnecting."

Mikki couldn't figure out if this was a fishing expedition, or if Chantal knew more than she was letting on. "It was a total coincidence," Mikki explained. "It was the day before I left for Florida, I ran into him at a bar. I had no clue who he was, but he remembered me. We hung out for a while. No big deal."

"I didn't say it was a big deal," Chantal said. "Just that you guys ran into each other." Pause. "I guess . . . I just figured you would have mentioned that."

"There was nothing to mention. And definitely no time. This is the first time we're really talking."

"Though, come to think of it, at the dinner you made it seem like that was the first time you were running into Barry in thirteen years."

Mikki forced a laugh, hoping it came off sounding casual. "I saw him in a bar; then I got on a plane to Florida the next day. I was shocked when I saw him here. That's all."

"Mmm-hmm," Chantal said.

"Funny coincidence about him being related to Ken," Mikki went on. "Small world."

"Yeah, small world," Chantal agreed.

But the curious look in her eyes, as well as the questioning tone in her voice, made Mikki wonder if she had just rambled so much that her sister couldn't help but figure out that she had gone to bed with the man.

Chapter 7

When Chantal dropped Mikki off at the house, Mikki all but ran out of the car. She was certain that her sister had figured out that something had happened between her and Barry. How could she not have, with all of Mikki's blubbering about the man?

But maybe Chantal hadn't figured anything out. Maybe Mikki was simply being extra-sensitive. Though what was that whole part about Chantal thinking she and Barry would have gotten together in high school?

As if! They'd been friends, nothing else.

Mikki didn't want to think about Barry and whether her sister would soon put the pieces together of their raunchy night. She needed a distraction.

She would go to her old stomping grounds where she'd done plenty of thinking as a teen. The mall.

And she would kill two birds with one stone. Because she wanted to clear her head *and* get some new clothes for the next wedding dinner. She didn't want to be the only one in the room dressed for the office.

No, tonight she was going to wear newer, sexier clothes.

Seeing Barry last night had been more than alarming. It had been embarrassing.

It was one thing to have behaved shamelessly with him. It was another thing to have realized that she'd been wearing her comfy undergarments at the time— undies that her friends had labeled *granny panties*. But it was the ultimate embarrassment to have been wearing granny panties and then having to see the man again.

If the occasion arose a second time, she wanted to have something decent underneath her clothes—

Mikki stopped the thought abruptly. What was she thinking? Was she actually considering going to bed with Barry *again*?

Where on earth had that thought come from?

It was hypothetical, of course. *Whoever* she went to bed with next would benefit from her sexier choice of underwear.

And what if Alex called her up and wanted to reconcile? She would prove to him that she wasn't boring in the bedroom, starting by having a wardrobe that wasn't boring.

Although Alex had never cared what she wore and had been more interested in getting her naked as quickly as possible. He didn't need any enticements in terms of lingerie and sexy clothing. Alex had been turned on all the time.

But perhaps there was nothing wrong with changing her style. She hadn't caved to societal pressures before in terms of clothing, mostly because she hadn't been part of the popular crowd in high school. She had seen how superficial people got regarding the right shoes, the right purse, and all that nonsense. Mikki had always dressed for her own comfort.

So on some level, she thought it was ridiculous to start caring about dressing to impress when she hadn't thus far in her life. Clearly, Alexander had really done a number on her self-esteem, making her determined to show people—at least outwardly—that she was a sexy woman.

No more frumpy panties for her. She only hoped that whatever had happened with Barry, he had been taking off her clothes so quickly that he hadn't noticed her pathetic undies.

Mikki borrowed her mother's car and went to Miami International Mall, which was fairly close to her Coral Gables home. It had been her favorite mall to shop at while she'd lived in South Florida. Her sister was off tending to last-minute wedding plans, which gave Mikki the opportunity to head to the mall on her own.

It was stupid, going lingerie shopping in Florida when she could have had all kinds of discounts at the shop in New York where Isabel and Debbie worked.

But at that time, she hadn't run into Barry again . . .

I'm not doing this because of Barry, she told herself, but that felt like a lie. All Mikki knew was that every time she thought of Barry, she felt a tingle of arousal.

Her first stop was Frederick's of Hollywood to check out their selection of lingerie. But she blushed when she saw some of the racy panties. Which was weird, because she saw all kinds of racy lingerie at her friends' boutique in New York.

But then, she hadn't been thinking of items to buy for herself. Items that would drive a man wild.

Alex had needed no lingerie to get in the mood, which was perhaps why Mikki hadn't bothered with any of it. But she couldn't go from conservative to risqué. So she left Frederick's of Hollywood, because this store was definitely not for her.

She went to Victoria's Secret, where she found more classic lingerie. This was more her style. Delicately embroidered push-up bras and lacy panties. Items that were pretty and sexy at the same time.

Mikki went into a changing room and undressed. As she slipped off her bra, she stared at her naked breasts.

And then came the image that had flashed into her mind yesterday, of Barry's lips wrapped around her nipple. She was lying down, arching her back. Moaning. And as Barry gently suckled one breast, he tweaked her other nipple.

Mikki drew in a shaky breath and closed her eyes. She went with the thought, allowed herself to enjoy the image.

Then her eyes popped open. A memory?

Her body felt flushed, and in the privacy of the dressing room, she closed her eyes again. This time, the image that came to her was of Barry's face between her thighs.

Wetness pooled between her legs, and Mikki jerked her eyes open. What was she doing?

Fantasizing about Barry in a Victoria's Secret dressing room? That was crazy, wasn't it?

Trying to push the man out of her thoughts, Mikki

set about trying on the various bras and liked the way her breasts looked in them. They gave her great cleavage, made her look bountiful.

She exited the changing room, prepared to buy most of what she'd tried on. En route to the cash register, she passed a table filled with thongs, and she paused to check them out. Some were lacy, some frilly—but all were the kind of panty she had never worn. Isabel swore by them, said that thongs were the best because you had no panty lines.

But there was something else Isabel had said. She claimed that wearing sexy lingerie made a woman feel sexier.

Mikki was prepared to discover just how sexy.

As she brought her mound of items to the cash register, a part of her once again wondered if she was doing this for Barry. As a way to eradicate the embarrassment she felt over the fact that he had seen her in the cotton undergarments she wore for comfort as opposed to style.

But how was buying sexy lingerie going to erase her embarrassment . . . unless she was actually considering sleeping with him again?

Gritting her teeth, Mikki realized that she had more than once considered the idea of going to bed with Barry again. More than once today alone. Not to mention the erotic images of him and her together that were definitely turning her on.

What Barry had said must be getting to her, those words he had whispered hotly into her ear.

Because you had a good time . . .

Those words, she was sure, had led to her erotic

dream. To the steamy images filling her mind now. More and more she was wondering if she was beginning to remember their night together.

"Find everything okay?" the clerk at the register asked her.

"Yes," Mikki said. She didn't meet the woman's eyes directly, still rocked by the erotic thoughts in the changing room. Rocked by the way her body, even now, was thrumming with sexual desire.

Leaving Victoria's Secret, Mikki hit more stores and bought short skirts, low-cut tops, and a few pairs of sexy boots and shoes. The items in her bags were not the kind she would typically wear, but she was ready to embrace her sexy side.

Several bags of purchases in her hand, Mikki went back through Sears and to the doors that would lead to her parked car.

But when she stepped out of the door and outside, her heart sank into her stomach.

Because there was Barry, walking toward her.

Chapter 8

Mikki gulped. The object of her lust was standing not ten feet away from her. How was it conceivable that he was once again at the exact same spot on the planet that she was?

Now she really had to wonder if Barry was possibly following her. He just *happened* to be at this mall at the same time she was, and at the same part?

His lips curled in a wide grin, making it clear he had seen her.

"Mikki," Barry said cheerfully as he reached her. She had stopped walking, seeming to forget how to.

"Okay, be honest," Mikki began. "You *are* following me, aren't you?"

Barry chuckled. "Maybe it's fate that we keep running into each other."

Mikki's eyes widened, the fact that Barry was stating the same thing Isabel had making her feel unsettled.

"Do I scare you?" Barry asked suddenly.

Mikki guffawed. "Scare me? Of course not."

"The way your eyes just widened—"

"So?"

"And then there's the fact that you seem unable to look at me . . ."

"I can look at you." She met his gaze but didn't hold it.

"Only briefly," Barry told her. "You look at me for a few seconds, and then you turn away."

Mikki laughed. "Sounds to me like someone has ego issues."

"Ouch."

Mikki swallowed. She didn't mean what she'd said. It was just that a part of her wanted to run in the other direction when she saw him.

Either that or throw herself at him.

"If you were serious about not following me, then I assume you've come to this mall to shop. I'll let you get to it."

"Victoria's Secret," Barry said, a hint of amusement in his voice. "Looks like you did some serious shopping. Not going to show me what you bought?"

"That's a little bit forward, don't you think?"

"Is it?" Barry challenged. "I've already seen you naked, after all."

Mikki's eyes bulged once more. Barry did *not* just say that. Had he become a different person simply because he no longer looked like the geeky teen he had once been? Was that why he was being so bold with her?

And why did Mikki want nothing more than for him to kiss her?

But the last thing she wanted to do was acknowledge what he'd said, much less make it appear that his words were getting to her. Because he was enjoying this. Enjoying the knowledge that he had turned her into some wild woman in the bedroom.

"And you used to like showing me your radical purchases back in the day. All those outfits that went against the grain. Remember?"

A smile touched her lips. She did. "Well, that was a long time ago. A lot has changed."

"Oh yes, it has. Most definitely."

Was that his way of referring to the fact that they'd slept together? If so, Mikki had led him right into that one.

But she wasn't going to go there, so she said, "I've got to go. Lots to do before the wedding. Happy shopping."

Mikki hustled off in the direction of her car, which was a short distance away, not daring to look over her shoulder. She hated that she would have to see Barry later, or ever again, given how much fun he was having at her expense.

She wasn't entirely sure that he wasn't stalking her. Irrational, maybe. But not impossible.

Even as she had the thought, she knew it was ridiculous. Barry was related to Ken. He had a perfectly logical reason for being in Florida, just as she did. It's just that she was flustered. She'd broken up with Alex, she'd slept with Barry, and now she would have to deal with him until her sister's wedding was over. Could life get any worse for her?

Mikki got to her car and searched for the keys in her purse but couldn't find them anywhere. "Come on," she muttered. They *had* to be in her bag. "Where did I put you?"

As her fingers failed to close around anything metal, Mikki peered into the car. And she saw the mistake she'd made. Both the keys and her cell phone were on the passenger seat.

"Dammit," she cursed. This could *not* be happening. Not now.

She stood there for at least a minute, wondering what to do. Then she glanced over her shoulder and saw that Barry was still standing where she had left him. Looking at her, he was clearly wondering what was going on.

Mikki didn't want to go back over to him. Perhaps it was the ease with which he spoke to her about what she'd purchased. Perhaps it was the fact that embarrassment ran through her veins every time she looked at him, given that she'd slept with him and couldn't remember it. And like a bad habit, she couldn't seem to escape him.

But she wanted to keep her distance. As much as physically possible.

Still, she was in a bind right now. Once again she glanced at Barry.

He was still standing in front of Sears, staring in her direction. Of course.

Oh, what the hell. If she needed his help, she needed his help. She didn't have to make a federal case out of it.

Drawing in a deep breath, she made her way back across the parking lot to the front of the mall where Barry stood.

"Car trouble?" he asked. "Or did you come back to spend more time with me?" He softened the question with a smile.

"I locked my keys in the car," Mikki told him frankly.

"Fate," Barry muttered.

Mikki narrowed her eyes at him. Now wasn't the time for jokes. "Do you have a phone? I also left that in the car."

"Sure." Barry produced a BlackBerry. "Who are you going to call?"

"Triple A," Mikki told him. "My mother gave me the membership card when I took the car. And here I thought she was being extra cautious."

"Word to the wise—the last time I called Triple A, it took two hours for the tow truck to arrive. And there's that dinner for the bridal party tonight. Food for thought."

Mikki frowned. Then something came to her. She was borrowing her parents' car. Certainly they had another key at home.

"Actually, I'll just call my mother. She probably has an extra key for the car. Of course, she said she'd be baking all day, and my sister would have to go pick up the key since my parents only have one car . . ." Mikki groaned. Her sister likely wouldn't have the time to spare right now. "Damn, I just figured I would come out here, grab a few things, and then head back home. So much for that plan."

"You know," Barry began, "I can take you home. It's no big deal."

Fate. That was the word that popped into Mikki's

mind. Because it certainly seemed as though the gods were conspiring to keep them together.

"If there's an extra key at the house, we can get it, I can drive you back here, you get the car—problem solved. No need to have your mother or father track down your sister when I'm right here."

Barry was right. And there was no need to call AAA. In fact, no time to call them. She had to get home and get dressed for the dinner, as well as do her hair and makeup. Tonight, she was going to unveil her new image. It would be Mikki's way of showing to the world—and Alex perhaps, even though he wasn't there—that she was not boring sexually.

"I guess that makes sense," she told him. "But don't you have your own shopping to do?"

"When I get you back here, I'll do my shopping."

Mikki followed Barry to his vehicle, a black Ford Explorer that he was renting for his trip. It was large and roomy. Opening the passenger door for her first, he let her get seated, and then he took her purchases and put them in the backseat.

As Mikki got comfortable in the front seat, she remembered the last time she had been in a car with Barry. It had been the night of the Spring Formal, and she'd been devastated because she'd found her date, Chad Who-Cared-Anymore, in a corner of the darkened gym with Keisha, a cheerleader who was known to put out for all the guys. Barry had gone to the dance hoping that Tiffany would grace him with at least a smile and perhaps some time on the dance floor, but it hadn't happened. And once Mikki had learned that Chad was hoping to get lucky with someone who *would* put out, she had turned to Barry for comfort. As he'd driven her home, Barry had put her in a better mood by telling her all the ways he would torture Chad if he could get away with it.

As Barry got into the car, she looked at him. Really looked at him. Since running into him again, she hadn't done that—looked at him like he was the friend she'd once been close to.

Maybe it was hard to face him because they'd crossed that friendship line.

"What ever happened to Tiffany?" she asked.

"Tiffany?" He sounded surprised.

"You remember. You had a wicked crush on her in high school."

"Ah, right. Well, as you know, that went nowhere."

"I always thought she was stupid not to date you. You were such a sweetie, much nicer than that jerk she was involved with."

"Only one girl I ever loved in high school." Barry shrugged. "But she didn't love me back."

Barry held her gaze, and Mikki felt a stirring in her gut. She glanced away.

"I'm assuming your parents still live at the same house?" Barry said.

"You remember where?" Mikki asked.

"Of course. How could I forget?"

"Thirteen years is a long time."

"Not so long that you forget the important things."

Silence fell between them as they drove, Mikki thinking about a past she would be happy to forget. She didn't have the worst high school experience ever, but it had been far from the best. She hadn't had a ton of friends, and she hadn't run in the popular circles.

Maybe that's why she and Barry had connected, because he had definitely not been in a popular crowd.

"Why do you look so unhappy?" Barry suddenly asked.

"I'm not unhappy."

"If you're not," Barry began, "you're doing a pretty good impression."

Was she? Even as the question sounded in her mind, she realized that she was leaning against the car door, as though trying to put as much physical space between her and Barry as possible.

"It's just . . . it's being home," she told him. "Remembering the past. Remembering that feeling in high school that things never quite worked out for me."

Barry narrowed his eyes. "What are you talking about? You're in New York, working for a law firm. That doesn't sound like things not working out for you."

"How about the fact that I was supposed to come down here with my boyfriend? But he broke up with me last week, just in time for Christmas—and just in time for me to go to my sister's wedding like a spinster in the making."

"Alex-the-Not-So-Great," Barry said.

Mikki whipped her head in his direction. "You know him?"

"You told me all about him."

"I . . . I did?"

Barry nodded. "Uh-huh. In the taxi. And in my hotel room, before . . . well, before. And afterward . . ."

Mikki stared at Barry. "Afterward what?"

"Afterward, you kept telling me how much better I was in bed than Alex."

Mikki's face flushed hotly. Had Barry really just said that? Had she?

"Just keeping it real," Barry explained as she looked at him. "In fact, you went on about how you only dated him because you thought he was the kind of guy you *should* be dating, and you were a little pissed that he turned the tables on you and broke up with you for such shallow reasons."

"Oh my God." What exactly had Mikki said?

"And for the record, you are not boring in bed. Absolutely not."

Mikki couldn't look at him. How could she look at him? She didn't remember what she had said, what she had done.

"No need to be embarrassed," Barry told her. "You were sharing your problems with me . . . just like old times."

"Except for the sleeping-with-you part," Mikki quipped. There, she'd said it.

"Yeah, there was that." Barry breathed in deeply. "But you want the truth?"

Mikki looked at him, her pulse racing as she wondered if he was going to tell her that he had been messing with her all along. That they *hadn't* really slept together.

But he said, "I thought you were going to sleep it off in my hotel room. Because, yeah, you were pretty tipsy. But you . . . you weren't having it. I told you no, let's wait, but you were . . . Let's just say you were pretty eager to make love."

Mikki promptly looked away, her stomach twisting intensely. She gazed out the window at the massive oak trees that lined many of the roads in Coral Gables. Their large, sprawling branches hung well over the streets, looking majestic during the day as they provided much-needed shade from the Florida sun. But at night, those same trees created an eerie feeling. She had always loved those oaks, but the sight of them gave her no pleasure now.

Perhaps it was a fitting punishment that she had run into Barry here. That would teach her better than to jump into bed with someone she had no plans of having a relationship with.

But she was beyond ready to stop talking about their one night of passion, even though she was definitely aroused. So she said, "You're a cousin of Ken's. What are the chances?"

"Second cousin," Barry explained. "It's a big family. We weren't that close growing up, though, but we reconnected when he came to Illinois for some golf tournament and we hung out."

"And is he a decent guy?" Mikki found herself asking. "Is he going to do right by my sister?"

"Why would you ask that?"

"I don't know . . ." Mikki had simply been making conversation, but maybe there was something more to her question. She said, "When I met Ken in New York, he seemed like a pretty nice guy . . . but I just got a sense about him. I don't know. Maybe that he's the kind of guy who knows how to charm a woman."

"Wow," Barry said. "You got all that from one meeting with him? I'm impressed."

"So what does that mean?" Mikki asked. "He's a player?"

"Ken's had his share of women, no doubt about it. But I think his player days are behind him."

"You *think*?"

"As far as I know, Ken's a changed man. He was always spoiled, but even the most entitled kids have to grow up at some point."

"I guess you're right," Mikki said, but hadn't she thought the same thing about Alex?

The difference, of course, was that Ken had proposed to Chantal. Alex had dumped *her*.

And they were getting married in two days. That spoke volumes about his commitment to her.

Ken wasn't Alex.

"Ah, here we are," Mikki said as Barry pulled onto the street where her parents lived. By the time he reached her house, Mikki was already unlocking the door.

She exited the vehicle the moment it came to a stop. "Thanks again."

Barry put his hand on her arm. "Wait."

Mikki turned to look at him. "Yes?"

"Why do you make it sound like you're heading into the house and not coming out? I've got to take you back to the mall."

"Right." What was wrong with her?

But then Mikki realized that her sister's car was there. Which meant Chantal could drive her to the mall. "Actually, my sister is home. So either she or my mother can take me to the mall."

"Are you sure? Because I don't mind."

Mikki opened the back door and collected her bags of purchases. "Yeah, I'm sure. But thanks for the ride home. I'll see you later."

And then Mikki closed both doors and hurried to the house.

Chapter 9

Mikki had felt like a different woman as she'd gotten dressed for tonight's dinner, but stepping into the wine cellar at the club for the bridal party dinner, she saw the difference in everyone's expressions.

Eyes swept over her body from head to toe. Eyebrows rose with interest. The people who had seen her yesterday dressed like a librarian had to be wondering if she was the same person.

The black skirt she was wearing hugged her hips like a second skin and stopped a good couple of inches above the knee. She was wearing black leather boots with a spiked heel higher than she normally wore, but as she'd checked out her image in the mirror, she had acknowledged that the high heel definitely made her legs look sexier.

The bright red scoop-neck blouse with the plunging neckline completed the outfit. No blazer tonight.

Mikki scanned the room, which was a more intimate setting than the much larger Crystal Room. From what she could tell, all the groomsmen and bridesmaids were here.

Everyone except Barry.

No one was seated at the large L-shaped table. Rather, people were mingling around the room.

Ken, who had been standing at the far end of the room with one of his buddies, a glass of wine in his hand, looked at her with widened eyes. He promptly excused himself from his friend and approached her.

"Wow." His gaze swept over her from head to toe. "You look amazing."

Even her sister seemed surprised by her appearance. Coming to join her and Ken, Chantal said, "Look at you. Look at that bosom!"

Mikki leaned forward and whispered to her sister, "The magic of a push-up bra."

"I almost want to ask, who are you?" Ken went on, chuckling.

"I just thought it was time to spice up my image a bit," Mikki said. She wasn't about to say that her ex-boyfriend had destroyed her confidence and had sent her to extreme measures.

"Well, you've certainly done that," Chantal said. "If Alex could see you now . . ."

"Barry tells me he ran into you in New York," Ken said.

"Yeah." Mikki forced a grin. "Total fluke."

"And speaking of my best man . . ."

Mikki whirled around and looked in the direction of the entrance. And there stood Barry.

All the air in the room seemed to be suddenly sucked out. Mikki's heart began to pound so hard that it was the only thing she could hear as she checked Barry out.

My God, he looks good.

Tonight he was wearing black slacks, black cowboy boots, and a white dress shirt that was unbuttoned at the collar. A tantalizing amount of that golden brown skin of his chest was revealed, and it was easy to see his sculpted biceps and pecs.

It struck Mikki again that Barry had done a total one-eighty. He was a completely different person than the one he had been in high school.

Then, he had been a boy.

Now he was all man.

Talk about making an entrance. Barry stepped into the room, and once again Mikki registered the sounds around her. Happy chatter, the music.

Her heavy breathing.

Barry was walking right toward her, as if she were the only one in the room, and Mikki felt a rush of heat. His eyes held her captive, and she wasn't sure she even breathed.

As he reached her, his lips curled in a sexy smile, and Mikki suddenly found herself thinking about kissing him. It was the one thing she remembered, his slow, hot kisses and the way her body had come alive.

It was alive right now. Oh yes, it certainly was.

"Sorry I'm late," he said, and greeted Ken with one of those hugs that was more about bumping chests while gripping hands. And then he turned to Mikki.

"Damn, look at you," he said, his eyes sizing her up. The way he checked her out made the small fortune Mikki had spent on clothing today entirely worth it.

Snaking his arm around her waist, Barry drew her close and whispered, "You look incredible."

Barry's voice washed over her like warm chocolate, smooth and delectable. She savored the feeling . . . until she saw her sister looking at her oddly.

Mikki promptly stepped away from Barry, saying, "Thanks. Just something I picked up today."

"Worth every penny."

Why was it that Mikki wanted to take Barry's hand and leave with him, go somewhere they could get naked?

Thankfully, she didn't have to think about the question much longer because she heard the clinking of a fork against a glass.

"Excuse me," Chantal said. "Can I have your attention, please?"

The chatter died, and the bridesmaids and groomsmen all turned to look at Chantal, who was now standing at the far end of the L-shaped table with Ken. "First of all, thanks for coming tonight. I know many of you probably want to be out doing last-minute Christmas shopping, so I appreciate you sparing time for me and Ken. But I wanted everyone to get together in a more intimate setting than last night so you could all get acquainted. We know some of you got to meet last night, and some of you may have known each other before, but in case you didn't, this is the time to break the ice and say hi."

"Hi."

The deep whisper in her ear caused her belly to tickle. Casting him a sidelong glance, Mikki said, "Hi."

"Are you wearing anything else you bought at the mall today?" Barry asked.

Mikki's heart fluttered. "Excuse me?"

"You heard me."

"I heard you, but I can't believe you would ask me something like that." Who was she kidding? The question had turned her on.

Barry smiled, the kind that gave her butterflies. "Sorry if I can't get that night we spent out of my mind. I keep thinking about it. Over and over . . ."

This was madness. Why did the deep timbre of his voice send a chill of excitement racing down her spine?

"And now, everyone," Chantal went on. "I've been informed that dinner is ready, so let's get seated so we can eat."

Somehow, Mikki survived being seated across the table from Barry, who looked at her during the entire meal as if *she* were the main course.

It had been disconcerting, to say the least. Mikki wasn't used to this bolder, sexier version of Barry.

Most of the time, she had tried to avoid eye contact with him but was all too aware that he had continually checked her out.

The guests duly acquainted, Ken and Chantal had gone over the logistics of the wedding day—who was walking down the aisle when, to what music, and that sort of thing.

Everyone had gotten along very well, and there was lots of laughter and lots of wine. Mikki had tried to avoid drinking, given how out of control she'd been that night at the bar, but once the desserts came around, she knew she needed something. She'd been far too on edge for the dinner; perhaps a drink would help her unwind.

She had Irish cream with her cheesecake, and it definitely helped loosen her nerves. But if she was going to get through the last part of the evening, she needed one more.

Many people were standing now, stretching their feet, some still mingling, some saying their goodbyes. Mikki got to her feet as well and all but ran toward the server as she saw him approaching with her second drink.

"Thank you," she told the man, and promptly took a sip. The Irish cream went down warm and smooth.

Suddenly, the glass was being removed from her hand. Whipping her head around, Mikki looked at Barry in surprise.

"No," he told her. "Not tonight."

"I'm not driving."

"Maybe not, but I don't want you inebriated. I want you to remember everything this time."

This time? Two words, but they said so much.

He intended to take her to bed again.

Mikki felt a rush of heat. She should feel offended at his brazenness, and yet, the very idea of going to bed with him turned her on to no end.

Damn it, she wanted the drink. If for no other reason than to be able to blame it on alcohol, as Jamie Foxx sang in his song. Because the truth was, Barry was looking downright scrumptious. Those broad shoulders, that tantalizing glimpse of skin below his neck . . .

Yes, Barry was looking delicious. And she was seeing him without the haze of liquor.

She wanted him—and that was hard to wrap her head around.

Yet Mikki found herself shaking her head and saying, "You want me to remember everything *this time*?"

"When I take you home."

Mikki's heart was beating a mile a minute. "Barry—"

"Your sister asked if I'd take you home. Didn't she tell you?"

"W-what?" Mikki was confused. Was Chantal suddenly trying to act as matchmaker?

"Oh, good," Chantal said, appearing at Mikki's side out of nowhere. "Have you told her?"

"Just did," Barry responded.

"Chantal," Mikki began. "I'm not sure I understand what's going on here. . . ."

"Ken and I need to go somewhere, and I didn't want Mom to have to come back and pick you up, so I asked Barry to take you home."

"Oh. *Ohhh*." How had Mikki so totally misconstrued what Barry had meant?

Sex on the brain, clearly. Damn it, she needed her Irish cream.

"I didn't think you'd mind. Since you already know each other. No big deal, right?"

It *was* a big deal. Because Barry wasn't simply some old friend.

She'd slept with the man. And now she was being forced to spend all kinds of time with him when she didn't want to. She had barely been able to sit across the table from him without serious discomfort.

"What's the matter?" Chantal asked.

Mikki couldn't very well tell her sister the truth—

that she'd shamelessly bedded Barry and therefore felt unsettled around him. So she said, "Nothing. Nothing's wrong."

Chantal grinned. "Good. Now, if you'll excuse me . . ."

Barry's eyes crinkled as he said, "Looks like you're stuck with me." He placed her drink on the table. "Ready to leave?"

"Almost." Quickly lifting the tumbler of liquor, Mikki downed the Irish cream. "There." One more drink wouldn't make her lose her mind like she had the night at the bar. "Now I'm ready."

Barry slipped his arm around Mikki's waist as he led her out of the room and to the car. Mikki didn't say a word and neither did Barry. But she was aware that as she got into the SUV beside him, her pulse was racing.

Why did it always race around him?

It had to be shame. Shame that she had slept with him and didn't remember. He held some secret over her head simply because her brain couldn't recall what had happened.

As Barry started the car, Mikki asked, "Are you staying with your parents?"

"No. They've moved. They're in Ocala now. Quieter. Not as much hustle and bustle as South Florida."

"Ah," Mikki said. "Are they coming for the wedding? I didn't see them at the dinner last night."

"Sure," Barry said. Then, pausing, he stared at her. "Is this what you want to talk about? Because I'm thinking there are other . . . more interesting things we can discuss."

Nerves tickled Mikki's stomach. "Like?"

"Like whether you want me to take you home. Or to my hotel room."

"You're going to keep doing this, aren't you? You're going to keep making suggestive comments because we went to bed together and I don't remember it."

"More like because I want to take you to my bed again."

Heat enveloped Mikki. Good Lord, what was it about Barry that was stoking her desire so intensely?

"I hate that you remember what happened and I don't."

"I can rectify that."

"What, you're going to give me a play-by-play of what happened?" Her voice sounded deep and flirty. Good grief.

"I was thinking I could show you."

Mikki stared at Barry, saw that he was sinking his teeth into his bottom lip. She couldn't help thinking that he wanted to sink his teeth into *her*.

"You're being very . . . forward."

"Am I?" Barry asked, his eyebrow rising. "Because I'm willing to bet my last dollar that the heat I felt every time I looked at you tonight was mutual. I've been waiting for this moment when I could finally get you alone."

"Barry—"

"Tell me I'm wrong," he said. "Tell me I'm wrong, and I'll drop the subject."

Mikki said nothing. She may look sexier in her outfit, but old habits died hard. She simply wasn't used to aggressively going after what she wanted.

Well, at least not while she was sober.

Barry suddenly jerked the car to the right, pulling into the parking lot of a strip mall. "Better yet," he said once he put the car into park and faced her, "tell me you don't feel anything when I do this."

Then, moving forward, he gently cupped her face, planted his lips on hers, and kissed her until she was panting with need.

Barry broke the kiss, his own breathing ragged. "I want nothing more than to take you back to my hotel room. And this time, we'll share a night you won't soon forget."

Chapter 10

Something became very clear to Mikki as she looked into Barry's eyes, their heavy breaths mingling. She wanted him. She had wanted him again from the moment he'd walked into the Crystal Room her first night in Florida.

Maybe she simply needed a second dose of him to really put Alex out of her mind. Or maybe she simply wanted to experience—as a sober woman—just how hot they were together.

And there was nothing wrong with that. She was a grown woman, nearly thirty-one years old. She could embrace her desire for a man without making excuses for it.

Because her desire was all too real. Like a living, breathing force within her.

Mikki was in Florida, so was Barry. Isabel had spoken of fate, but Mikki preferred to think of it as good timing. Clearly she was lusting after him, and he after her. Soon enough, she'd be heading back to New York and he back to Chicago. What was wrong with having a hot-and-heavy fling during their time here in Miami?

Nothing.

Mikki pressed her fingers into Barry's shoulders. "Yes."

"Yes?"

"Take me to your hotel room. Take me now."

Barry's mouth came down on hers again, and Mikki purred into his mouth. God help her, had anything ever felt this good?

Mikki was the one to break the kiss this time, and Barry quickly restarted the car and swerved back onto the road. He drove faster than the speed limit, but they made it to the hotel without being pulled over by a cop.

Barry was staying at a Courtyard Marriott hotel in Coral Gables, so it was nice and close to Mikki's home, the church, and the golf club where the prewedding dinners were being held.

What mattered to Mikki was that Barry had gotten there quickly, because she was ready to get naked.

Now.

Barry held her hand as he whisked her through the hotel lobby. Held her hand as they rode the elevator to the fourth floor.

Mikki's eyes swept over Barry's back as he fished his electronic key out of his wallet. She noticed everything. His wide shoulders and muscular arms. The way his muscles strained against the fabric of his shirt as he moved. And that tight behind.

He was hot. No doubt about it. And she was about to do him.

She also noticed his hands. They were large, his fingers long. Her eyes were glued to them as he inserted the key card into the door and opened it.

Mikki's heart began to beat rapidly as she stepped into the room behind Barry. She was nervous and excited at the same time.

Letting her pass him, Barry closed the door and then bolted it—as if to stress that he wanted to make sure they had no interruptions.

Immediately, he closed the distance between them and drew her into his arms. Mikki gasped a little, but the gasp soon turned to a moan when Barry brought his mouth down onto hers.

And just like that, heat enveloped her. She eased onto the tips of her toes and wrapped her arms around Barry's neck. His mouth worked over hers skillfully, drawing out pleasure through her entire body. And when his tongue slipped between her parted lips and swept into her mouth, she moaned and pressed her body against his.

Mikki hardly recognized the woman she was right now, so consumed with fiery need. It had never been like this with Alex, no matter how many times they had gone to bed. Alex's kiss did not inspire in her this kind of crazy fever. And that was what she was feeling for Barry right now. Her entire body was on fire, simply from the touch of his lips.

It wasn't enough. She lowered her hands from his neck down his back, savoring every touch of his muscles. He had an amazing body. One that was electrifying her both to be touched by him and to touch.

But Mikki wanted to touch him without clothes.

She needed to feel him, skin on skin. Opening her mouth wider to deepen the kiss, she reached for the buttons of his shirt and fumbled to undo them. Her fingers were working hastily, her urgent need for him growing with each second.

Barry groaned into her mouth, the sound a potent aphrodisiac, turning her on even more. His hands went from her shoulders down to the small of her back, and then over her behind. He pulled her against him, and Mikki felt the very real evidence of his desire for her. He was hard. And the idea of making love to him was more exciting than anything she had ever felt before.

Unable to unfasten the last button because of her haste, Mikki pulled on it and heard the thread pop as the button snapped. Barry growled, as though her obvious lust was making him even more horny.

With his shirt open, and his skin bared, Mikki tore her lips from his and brought them to the base of his collarbone. She planted kisses there, and then lower. All the while her fingers explored his skin, the muscles of his chest. She sank her teeth into his flesh as her fingers went over his flat nipples.

In an instant, something changed in Barry. With a deep growl, he scooped her into his arms and walked to the bed. He all but threw her onto the mattress, that action exemplifying his need.

He wanted her with the same fervor that Mikki wanted him.

And then he lowered himself onto her, his lips finding hers, his hands finding her breasts. He fondled her through the material of her blouse, then moved his fingers to the exposed skin of her cleavage.

"Mmmm," Mikki moaned.

"Don't worry," Barry whispered hotly into her ear. "I know how much you love for me to play with your nipples."

"You . . . you do?" But of course he did. They had done this before.

"You made that very clear the first time."

Desire was thrumming through her veins, and Mikki wanted to get laid now, but she was suddenly curious for the details of exactly how she had behaved. "Just how clear did I make it?"

Barry lifted his head from her neck and looked into her eyes. "You want that play-by-play now?"

Talk about an erotic suggestion. A hot play-by-play of what they'd done in New York . . .

"Yes," Mikki told him, breathing heavily.

Barry grinned. "Okay. But you need to be on your feet for that."

"I do?"

"Mmm-hmm."

Mikki got up. "Like this?"

"Move to the door."

Mikki did as he told her. Barry walked with her. At the door, he pulled her against him, and a gasp of air escaped her lungs.

"The moment we came through the door, you pressed your body against mine. Like this. And then you started to kiss my neck."

"I did?"

"The door wasn't even closed. I had to use my foot to do that job."

"Oh."

"I said something to the effect of, 'Hey, no need to rush. Let me get you some water first.'"

"And I said?"

"You said you didn't want any water. That you only wanted me."

Mikki closed her eyes, embarrassed. She felt the brush of Barry's knuckles against her skin.

"No," he said, "don't feel any shame. I liked your aggressiveness. Very much."

"I'm not normally aggressive."

"I'm surprised to hear that. Because you were . . . well, determined on the dance floor."

"I kissed you," Mikki said. "I . . . That much I remember."

"What about in the taxi?"

Mikki shook her head. "In the taxi?"

Barry grazed his lips against the underside of her ear. "You were all over me. We gave the driver quite the show."

"Oh my God. That's so unlike me."

"Then I'm glad you were a different person with me. Because I liked it. A lot."

Mikki drew in a deep breath. "What happened next? Once we were in the room?"

"After you kissed my collarbone, you did this." Barry brought his lips onto hers and kissed her deeply, all tongue, and Mikki's knees nearly buckled. He pulled back without warning, and Mikki moaned in protest.

"No, Barry. Don't stop."

"I have to stop . . . to show you what you did next."

"What?"

"You started to take off your clothes. Your top first."

"Like this?" Mikki pulled her blouse over her head and tossed it onto the floor.

"Yes, like that. And then your bra." He paused. "Wow. Your breasts . . . they look incredible in that bra. You bought that today?"

"Uh-huh." Mikki kept her eyes on Barry's as she reached behind her back and unsnapped her bra. Feeling a surge of feminine power, she slipped her fingers beneath the shoulder straps and fiddled with them, but didn't pull her bra off. She watched Barry's eyes, which volleyed between her face and her hands, and saw his anticipation.

"You pretty much threw your bra off—then pressed that beautiful body against mine again. There was no . . . no teasing."

"You mean like this?" Mikki let the bra fall from her body and onto the floor.

She saw his Adam's apple rise and fall. "Yeah. Kind of like that. Damn."

Barry's heated gaze on her breasts caused sensations of pleasure to spread through Mikki's body. She felt as though a sexual part of her had come alive in a way that had never existed within her.

"And what next?" Mikki asked, already reaching for the button on her skirt. "This?"

Barry's lips parted, and Mikki heard his audible intake of breath as she shimmied the skirt down her hips. She was nearly naked in front of him, and instead of feeling even a little bashful, she was emboldened. Emboldened by the powerful realization that Barry wanted her.

"Barry, what next?"

"Screw it," Barry said. "We'll create a new playbook."

He advanced and pulled her into his arms. Mikki's heart beat furiously, and as he edged his mouth toward hers, she closed her eyes. His warm breath fanned her face, and God, how erotic that felt.

"The first time, it was all fire and passion." Barry kissed the corner of her mouth. "This time"—he kissed the other corner of her mouth—"we're going to take it more slowly."

Mikki melted as he softly suckled her bottom lip. After what seemed like hours of torture, he finally covered her lips completely.

And then his tongue delved into her mouth, and his hands ventured from her hair down the expanse of her throat to her breasts. She moaned, his fingers setting her body on fire.

"Tell me, Mikki. Did you wear any of these clothes for me? Because you knew that this outfit, this bra, and God, this underwear, would turn me on?"

"I . . . I did," she admitted. "Do you like it?"

"Like it?" Barry stepped back as his eyes swept over her entire body. "You look incredible."

Slowly, Mikki did a three-hundred-sixty-degree turn, allowing Barry to see that she was wearing a thong.

"Damn, you are so beautiful."

Reaching for her, Barry stroked his thumbs back and forth over her nipples until they puckered and pouted beneath his hands. While his fingers worked their magic, he trailed seductive kisses from her mouth to her ear.

"Yes, baby. I'm going to be the one to seduce you this time."

Mikki shuddered as delicious heat flooded her core.

"That's it, Mikki. I want to feel you surrender in my arms. I'm going to tease you and please you all night long."

"Oh my God . . ."

Barry brought his lips down onto hers, swallowing her moan of pleasure. He was lost. Lost in this incredible woman.

He wanted her. Wanted her with a need that was foreign to him in its intensity. He had felt the same kind of raw need only once before.

In New York, when he'd run into Mikki in the bar.

He broke the kiss and said, "In New York, you told me how much you loved it when I played with your nipples."

"I did?"

Nothing sounded sexier than her breathless little gasps. He wanted to make her whimper and moan all night long.

Lowering his head to her breast, he took her nipple in his mouth. He grazed it with his teeth, then circled it with his tongue before drawing it completely into his mouth and suckling it.

Mikki cried out and clutched her hands to his head, holding it there as though she never wanted him to stop suckling her. He loved the way she responded to him. Every time he touched her, stroked her, her body reacted.

He hadn't stopped thinking about their night in New York, reliving every hot moment. He knew he could spend forever making love to her and not get bored.

Pulling his mouth from her breast, he lowered himself onto his haunches in front of her and ran his palms down her abdomen and over her stomach. As he kissed her belly and felt her shudder, a groan rumbled in his chest.

His right hand went lower, over the delicate lace of

her red thong. He stroked her intimately, and she purred in response.

In a flash, Barry rose to his feet and swept Mikki into his arms. He carried her to the bed and laid her down gently this time. Once she was on her back, he guided her thighs apart and kissed his way to her center.

"Oh, Barry . . ." Mikki moaned, and once again, her body quivered.

"Do you know how hot you look? Lying like this on the bed, almost naked except for these sexy boots?" Barry reached for the sides of her thong and maneuvered them off of her thighs. And as he drank in the sight of her nakedness, his erection throbbed. He had never seen a woman more beautiful.

He had to taste her, something he hadn't done the first night. Then, the sex had been frantic and wild, and all about the act of making love.

But tonight, Barry was going to make sure they savored the experience.

As he stared at the treasure before him, her pubic hair shaved into a trim square above her most private spot, he eased his chest down between her thighs. He trailed a finger over her nub. "This is one thing we didn't get to do the first time."

"What?" Mikki asked.

"I didn't get to taste this sweet pussy."

Mikki drew in a sharp breath, his words an aphrodisiac. She watched him, waiting, desperately wanting this intimate pleasure.

He brought his mouth down onto her, flicking the tip of his tongue over her clitoris. Heat erupted in her lower region and spiraled through her body.

"Yes, baby," Barry moaned, pressing a hand against

her belly as he teased her with his tongue. Mikki arched her back, the sensations of pleasure overwhelming her body.

"Oh, God, oh God, oh God . . ."

Barry groaned and increased the pressure, adding his teeth in gentle bites in addition to the hot swirls of his tongue. Mikki rocked her head back and forth, the pleasure so intense she could hardly stand it.

And then he was devouring her, his lips and tongue all over her nub. Mikki gripped the bedspread and moaned long and loud, feeling her orgasm start to build. Barry didn't relent in his erotic attack, and soon, Mikki's body exploded, tentacles of pleasure gripping her in the sweetest of climaxes.

"Barry . . . Oh my God."

She grabbed at his shoulders, and he eased his body upward, bringing his lips to hers. He ravaged her mouth like a man who'd been starved of affection all his life.

She wanted him inside her. Gripping his buttocks, she pulled him against her as he kissed her senseless.

"I want you naked," she rasped. "I need you to make love to me."

Barry broke his lips from hers and quickly rose. Mikki lay quivering on the bed, the aftermath of her orgasm leaving her weak. She watched as Barry stripped out of his clothes, the sight of his glorious naked form making her breath catch in her throat.

He was beautiful. Six-pack abs; strong, muscular biceps; well-sculpted pecs; and, good Lord, what an erection! He was an African American Adonis.

Mikki extended her hand, reaching for him, and said, "Do me."

Barry took her hand and linked fingers with hers. Then he settled his body on hers, his lips finding her mouth.

He kissed her deeply, his tongue twisting with hers as his free hand worked between their bodies. Not breaking the kiss, he guided their bodies together and filled her completely with one hard thrust.

Mikki cried out. She thought she had experienced all the wondrous sensations she could, culminating in a powerful orgasm, but the feel of him inside her brought pleasure even more intense.

Barry withdrew and plunged into her again, groaning as he did. Soon, they found a rhythm. Arching against him, she pushed her breasts out, and Barry lowered his head to greedily take one of her nipples into his mouth. Each suckle drove her nearer to the edge of the abyss.

He drove into her hard and deep, the sensations far beyond the physical. Something about being with Barry like this just felt right.

Fate . . .

Was it?

When Barry reached for her other breast and tugged at the nipple, Mikki fell over the edge. Crying out, she rode the wave of passion, this orgasm even better than the first one. She gripped Barry's back, digging her fingers into his slick skin and pushing up her hips so his strokes could reach even deeper.

And then, grunting, Barry drove into her with a blinding thrust as he succumbed to his own release.

Nothing had ever felt this amazing. Nothing.

Spent, their ragged breaths filled the hotel room. Mikki kept her arms wrapped around Barry's back, holding him close. The way she felt right now, she never wanted to let him go.

She sighed with pleasure as his lips brushed across her cheek. Then his mouth met hers and they kissed until neither had any breath left.

"How do you feel?" Barry asked.

"Amazing," she told him.

Barry grinned, that charming, sexy grin that made Mikki's insides melt.

"Good," he whispered into her ear. "'Cause, baby, that's just the beginning."

Chapter 11

Mikki woke up with a smile on her face. Her night with Barry had been nothing short of phenomenal.

Mikki hadn't known that it was possible to have so many orgasms in one night. Her friends had talked to her about great sex, and she'd always thought she was having it. But her night with Barry had proven that everything she had experienced before now was simply a pale imitation.

"Looks like someone's in a good mood."

At the sound of Barry's voice, Mikki opened her eyes, found that he was staring at her. "Hey, you."

"You didn't take off this time."

She grinned at him. "Kind of tough when you had the only car."

"You could have taken a taxi."

Mikki stretched, then turned her body toward Barry, draping her leg over his. "Trust me, I didn't want to take off."

"Did I live up to my promise? That I'd give you a night you wouldn't forget?"

"No chance of me ever forgetting last night," Mikki told him. "That had to be one of the most erotic experiences of my life," she added, then giggled.

"One of?" Barry asked, an eyebrow shooting up.

"Okay, *the* most erotic experience of my life. Barry, that was hot!"

Perhaps she should have played coy, not told him exactly what he wanted to hear right off the bat. But she couldn't help herself. Having sex with Barry had been nothing short of amazing.

No wonder she had gotten flustered and aroused at the mention of having gone to bed with him, even though she couldn't remember it. Somewhere in her subconscious, her body knew what she had experienced.

And she'd wanted to experience it again.

"So, what are you up to today?" Barry asked.

Mikki looked at the time. It was shortly after ten in the morning, and she was surprised she was even awake. She and Barry had spent the better part of the night making love. And even when they'd fallen asleep after two, they'd woken up around four to make love again. It was as though they'd both been starved sexually and had found something so completely amazing that they couldn't stop doing it for most of the night.

"Well, it's the day before the wedding," Mikki said. "We had the rehearsal last night, but there'll be lots to do. My sister's going to need me. I'd better get home."

Last night, she hadn't given any thought to the fact that if she spent the night with Barry, she would have to head home in the morning and deal with a curious family. And it was too late to do anything about it now.

She would have to face them, come up with some

explanation as to where she'd been. She couldn't exactly tell them that she'd been busy undergoing a sexual metamorphosis.

Barry took her hand in his and kissed it softly. Then he pulled the blanket from her breasts, brought his head down, and took her nipple in his mouth. Pleasure flooded her instantly, and moaning, she arched her back.

She could so easily sleep with him again. Right now. She could spend the entire day in bed with him and not feel guilty.

Except that she knew she couldn't. Not before the wedding.

"Barry, I wish I could stay, but I'd better get ready. Can you give me a ride home?"

"No worries, baby. I can wait until tomorrow night."

Mikki was glad when she got to her parents' house and saw that the car wasn't there. She could only hope that one or both of her parents were out running errands.

Chantal's car, however, *was* there.

Mikki tried to enter the house as quietly as possible, hoping that wherever her sister was, she wouldn't hear her. She glanced in the living room and kitchen and didn't see her sister there. Pausing to listen, she heard no sound.

Perhaps Chantal was still sleeping.

Hurrying down the hallway that led to the bedrooms, Mikki slipped into her room, then sighed with relief. She was home free.

But not more than ten seconds later, the door to her

room flew open, and Chantal breezed in, asking, "And where were you last night?"

"Sheesh, Chantal. You scared me."

"The way you scared me, Mom, and Dad last night?" Chantal countered.

Mikki frowned. She hadn't considered that her family would be worried about her whereabouts, just that they'd simply be curious. "Damn, I'm sorry. Did you think something bad happened to me?"

A sly smile formed on Chantal's face. "I had a pretty good idea that you were okay." She paused. "So, where were you?"

"I was . . . with a friend." That wasn't a lie. Barry was a friend.

"I didn't think you were wandering the streets on your own last night," Chantal said, tongue in cheek. "Fess up, sis."

"I was with a friend from high school," Mikki went on. Again, not a lie.

"The last I knew, Barry was dropping you home. Next thing, you don't show up. All night long."

Mikki's face flushed. She wondered if her sister could see on her face the exquisite experience that she had gone through.

"Well, it got late, so I just figured I would stay and sleep there."

Now Chantal was grinning slyly. "So who's this high school friend? Barry?"

"What?" Mikki asked.

"You can try to play dumb with me, but I wasn't born yesterday. I saw the way Barry was looking at you last night. The way you were looking at him."

Mikki's face grew hot, the memory of Barry's naked

body tangled with hers filling her mind. He had stamina, that was for sure. He had skill. Alex may have slept with many, many women, but Barry had mastered the art of making love.

"Okay," Chantal said, a knowing grin on her face. "It seems you want to keep your secret to yourself. That's fine. Every girl has to have her secrets, I guess."

Mikki said nothing, just smiled.

The thing was, what was she supposed to say? That she had gone to bed with Barry as a way to nurse her broken heart and now was having the time of her life?

She wasn't ready to get into the convoluted story.

Chantal left her bedroom, and Mikki plopped down on her bed and sighed with contentment.

Suddenly, she realized that she hadn't exchanged numbers with Barry. Again. They'd been anxious to get naked, and this morning, as he'd driven her home, they'd held hands, talked, and flirted.

Of course, if Mikki wanted to talk to him, she could call the hotel.

But as she lay on the bed, she considered that not seeing Barry until tomorrow, and not talking to him until then, would build up the anticipation. Because Mikki's sister wasn't going to be the only Harper sister enjoying one helluva wedding night.

As the thought came to her, Mikki wondered exactly what was happening between her and Barry. All she knew now was that she definitely wanted to see him again. She wanted more explosive sex; that was for sure.

But was this simply a fling? A hot and heavy one that would erase Alex from her mind once and for all?

"Alex," Mikki said with disdain, then snorted. She

had pretty much all but forgotten him. At least, she certainly wasn't pining over him.

And she definitely had Barry to thank for that.

Last-minute wedding plans took much of the day—getting the church decorated, getting their nails and toes done, and hitting South Beach for a bachelorette outing. Mikki didn't make the night too late, given that they had to be up early, but she'd made sure that her sister had enough drinks to let loose. She had worn a veil as they'd gone from one South Beach bar to the next, getting a lot of attention from tourists and partyers. Chantal had also gotten kisses from a group of guys from Scotland, who said it was tradition over there for the bride to kiss a variety of men during her hen party pub crawl.

Chantal had had a great evening, so Mikki was surprised when they got home around midnight and Chantal suddenly became an emotional mess. Clearly she had the prewedding jitters, all of a sudden fearful that something would go wrong tomorrow.

"We've got the dresses," Mikki told her. "All the floral arrangements are perfect. And the church looked gorgeous when we left it."

"I know," Chantal said, sniffling.

Mikki rubbed her sister's back. "Please stop worrying for no reason. Nothing will go wrong. You're going to have the perfect day."

Mikki's cell phone rang, and she left her sister sitting on the sofa to go get her purse. She dug out her phone, and when she saw Debbie's number flashing on her screen, she clicked the TALK button right away. "Hey, Debbie."

"Girl, I've been trying to reach you all evening," Debbie said without preamble.

"I was out. I didn't hear my phone."

"Well, I hope you're sitting down."

"Why?"

"Because of what I found out. Alex *was* seeing someone else. *Is* seeing someone else. He was cheating on you, Mikki—and that's why he dumped you."

Mikki's heart thumped hard against her chest at her friend's shocking announcement. She walked out of the living room and headed in the direction of her bedroom. "What?"

"Yep. I made some calls, and that friend of a friend who knows Alex? Well, she told me everything. He's been dating someone else for a while now."

Mikki was too stunned to speak as she slipped into her room and closed the door.

"I hear she's real beautiful. Looks like a model."

"She's a model?"

"I didn't say she was one, just that she looks like one. Apparently she's an assistant district attorney."

Mikki swallowed painfully. She had a pretty good idea who the woman was. And it was someone she had met.

The tall, leggy, dark-skinned beauty was stunning, and Mikki had heard that she and Alexander had been romantically linked in the past. Alex had denied that, however.

"Supposedly she's smart as a whip as well as gorgeous," Debbie went on.

"I know who she is," Mikki said. "At least, I'm

pretty sure. Son of a—" She exhaled harshly. "Debbie, I can't talk right now. My sister's having a meltdown, and I . . . I can't deal with this news right now."

"I'm sorry," Debbie said. "You wanted to know, right? You're not upset that I told you?"

"No, absolutely I'm not upset you told me. Of course you should have told me. You're one of my best friends. I would expect nothing less. It helps me to know the real reason behind the breakup." Mikki paused. "Even if I don't like it, it helps to know."

"Call me after the wedding, okay?" Debbie said.

"Yeah, definitely. Merry Christmas."

"Merry Christmas," Debbie returned.

Then Mikki ended the call and slumped down onto her bed. For a long while she sat there, gripping her phone and breathing heavily.

Alex had been cheating on her. And with Sandra Shelton.

If he's not sleeping with you, he's sleeping with someone else. That was what Debbie had told her, and her friend had been right. Mikki didn't need hard-core proof in order to believe the news. In her heart, she knew it was true.

She pressed the heels of her palms against her closed eyes. What was wrong with her? Why did she date the wrong man time after time?

Because if Alex had been the right man, shouldn't she have felt that Debbie's news wasn't true, that there was no way Alex would have cheated on her?

Yet Mikki didn't doubt the verity of it, not at all.

On a subconscious level, had she known all along that her relationship with Alexander was doomed to fail?

She found herself thinking of Barry's words earlier, when he'd told her that she had confessed to him that she had only dated Alexander because she thought he was the type of man she should date.

She couldn't deny that on some level it was true, that she'd been excited at the thought of dating a lawyer. Especially when her sister was dating the heir to a huge family business.

But she had cared for Alex. She hadn't dated him solely for his position. Their relationship had been real.

At least it had been for her.

Despite whatever she had told Barry in New York, it felt like there was a huge hole in her gut right now. A hole she had felt often as a teen.

More than once, she'd been disappointed by guys. Over and over again, she had cared for ones who would ultimately betray her. Maybe Mikki would never get it right.

It was the eve of her sister's wedding, and she should have been happy, but Mikki was instead feeling the familiar pain and insecurity she had known so well as a teen.

The fear that she would never find the right man.

But on the heels of that depressing thought came another one: *What if you've already found him?*

Chapter 12

Mikki was in a slump. It was her sister's wedding day, and she should be excited and happy, and yet she was miserable.

The news that Alex had been cheating on her had crushed her. She had stewed over the bombshell all night, unable to get the betrayal off her mind.

Even now, at the hair salon getting all dolled up with the rest of the bridal party, Mikki wondered if she should go into the bathroom and call Alexander. More than once in the night, she'd contemplated sending him a text.

Watching her sister smile at her reflection in the mirror as the stylist softly curled the front of her hair, Mikki's anger grew. Alex was supposed to have been here with her. The asshole was supposed to have proposed to her. And the snake had been screwing someone else.

Mikki took her phone from her purse and began to type:

You cheating scumbag.

But she didn't send it. Instead she erased it. No, she wouldn't give Alexander-the-Pig the satisfaction of caring.

She wished she didn't care at all. And it wasn't like she hadn't had the most amazing sex since him. It was just that . . . it was hard to totally erase a two-year relationship from your mind overnight.

Their hair and makeup done, the girls went back to Mikki's parents' house and got dressed. By the time the limo showed up, Chantal was already getting teary-eyed, and Mikki kept reminding her that she didn't want to ruin her makeup.

Chantal looked absolutely stunning. As brides went, she was the most gorgeous one Mikki had ever seen.

Seeing her sister so radiant, Mikki realized that this was what she wanted for herself. And that's why the news of Alex's betrayal on this day was especially hard. Because she'd believed that she would marry him, and now she had no clue if marriage would ever be in her future.

"You look radiant," Mikki said to Chantal before they walked out of the house to go down to the limo. "Absolutely stunning."

And she did. The whole princess-type dress on her and on the bridesmaids did make one think of a fairy tale. Her sister's bodice was form-fitting and made of satin, with crystal embroidered into it. The skirt—netting and organza like the bridesmaids' dresses—was exceptionally wide and also decorated with clear crystals. It was a magnificent dress, and Mikki only hoped it would fit into the limo.

"Thank you," Chantal said, and her eyes misted again.

"None of that," Mikki told her. "Though thank God you're wearing waterproof makeup."

When they got to the church and Mikki saw Barry, all thoughts of Alex fled her mind. He was wearing a tailored black tuxedo with tails—all the groomsmen were—but he was undoubtedly the most handsome of the lot. Good God, he looked like he had stepped off the pages of *GQ* magazine.

How could he be this damn attractive? Like a caterpillar morphing into a butterfly, his transformation had been magnificent and still a little hard to believe.

But the one thing that hadn't changed about him—and it was the most important thing—was that Barry was still a nice guy. His good looks could have turned him into a cocky asshole, and then he would have held no appeal to Mikki at all. Thankfully, he was still down-to-earth and decent.

His lips curled into a smile as their gazes locked from across the room in the basement of the church. And then Mikki felt the pull of desire and would have bet her last dollar that he was thinking about the amazing night they had shared.

But she tried to push the image from her mind, because her task now was to make sure all the men were accounted for, including the groom.

She gave Barry a little wave, then gathered her skirt and headed back up the stairs.

As soon as she entered the bridal room, Chantal hurried toward her. "Is he here?"

"He's here," Mikki told her. "Like I told you, no need to worry about a thing."

"So we're ready to do this?" Chantal asked.

"Ready if you are."

Chantal gripped both of Mikki's hands. "I'm scared."

"That's normal. Every bride has the jitters. But you're going to be fine."

Chantal grinned, some of the anxiety on her face ebbing away.

"If you're ready to get this party started, I'll go set everything in motion."

Chantal nodded. "Let's do this."

As ceremonies went, this one was beautiful. The bride and groom exchanged personalized vows, the kind that had many of the women—and some of the men—weeping.

Mikki noticed that as Ken and Chantal were standing at the head of the church exchanging vows, Barry had constantly had his eye on her. As though he was trying to tell her that he was exchanging vows with her.

The weather had held up for photos at the Miami Beach Botanical Gardens, and thus far the reception at The Delano, a chic South Beach hotel, was going off without a hitch. The five-star cuisine had been splendid, the décor of the reception hall the utmost in luxury, and everyone was in a happy mood.

Mikki's eyes misted as she watched her sister and Ken share their first dance as husband and wife.

The obligatory first dances over—father and daughter, mother and son—the DJ started playing more upbeat tunes, and everyone piled onto the dance floor.

Mikki took this opportunity to head to the restroom. With this kind of a dress, a woman couldn't go too often. But if she didn't relieve her bladder now, she'd be in trouble.

Mikki was on her way out of the bathroom when she saw Ken standing nearby. Seeing him, she grinned.

"Hey, brother-in-law." She walked toward him. "Congratulations again."

"Thanks."

"It was an amazing day. Everything went off without a hitch."

"Come here," Ken said, and opened his arms wide. He wrapped her in a hug.

It started off as innocent but changed when he held her a little bit too long and moved his hand over her bottom.

Mikki jerked back, looking up at him from narrowed eyes. Was he drunk?

"Ken, I think you ought to head back into the reception. Chantal's going to be wondering where you are," she added with a smile.

"You look incredible," he said. "Have I told you that lately?"

"Ken?" Mikki asked, her voice holding a note of uncertainty. "Are you okay?" Clearly he'd had too much to drink.

"Oh, I'm definitely okay." His eyes roamed over her from head to toe. And then he made his intentions perfectly clear. He pulled her against him, put both hands on her butt, and squeezed. "Damn, what I wouldn't give to have a taste of this."

"Ken—"

"Come on, let's go into the bathroom."

Mikki wriggled herself out of Ken's arms. She

stared at her brother-in-law in horror. He had just exchanged vows with her sister. Vows where he said he would love and honor her until death. How could he have just groped Mikki in a clearly sexual way and then suggested they go into the bathroom together?

It was a joke. It had to be.

"Come on," Ken urged. "No one has to know."

Mikki wanted to slap him. "Ken, I'm going to ignore what you said, because I'm sure you're going to regret having said it." She paused. "And lay off the alcohol, because it's obvious you've had too much."

Then Mikki spun around and went back into the reception hall.

For the next hour, Mikki contemplated what to do. As she partied on the dance floor, she periodically checked out her sister and Ken. Mikki noticed that Ken looked at her every so often, something that unnerved her. But other than that, they seemed like the perfect couple.

Mikki hadn't even been able to enjoy dancing with Barry, because her mind had been on the problem at hand. In fact, her opinion of the opposite sex was at an all-time low right now.

Maybe it was the news about Alexander, how he had been cheating on her, but Ken's sexual pass at her—and on her sister's wedding day—didn't sit well with her.

It confirmed her original misgivings about Ken. Even Barry had said that he *thought* Ken's player days were behind him.

But what if they weren't?

Alex had cheated on Mikki, and she would have wanted someone to tell her if they had known what he was up to. Didn't her sister deserve to know that her husband of only a few hours had already propositioned someone else?

Her decision made, Mikki went to get her sister, who was now dancing with some of the other bridesmaids to a funky song. She took her by the arm, saying, "Chantal, we have to talk."

Chantal, who was tipsy, smiled and hugged her sister. "You were so right, Mikki. I didn't need to worry at all. This has been the best day."

Her sister's happiness made what Mikki was about to do only harder. But Chantal deserved to know.

Mikki took her by the arm and led her out of the ballroom and into the bathroom. Thankfully, no one was in there. Placing her hands on her sister's shoulders, Mikki looked her squarely in the eye and said, "You have to listen to me. What I'm about to say concerns Ken."

The seriousness of her tone seemed to resonate, because Chantal's eyes widened in alarm. "What's wrong?"

"This is super hard for me to tell you. And I've debated it for the past hour. And I don't know . . . it could be just because he was drunk."

"What?"

Mikki drew in a deep breath, then said, "He came on to me."

There. She'd said it. There was no other way to do it. You had to just say it, the way people had to just rip off a Band-Aid so it wouldn't hurt as much. At least Mikki hoped it would hurt less this way.

For a long moment, Chantal said nothing. Then, a look of disbelief flashing in her eyes, she said, "What?"

"I thought he was just messing around," Mikki began. "Then he suggested we go into the bathroom together—"

Mikki didn't get the words out before Chantal snapped, "How could you? How could you say that?"

"Chantal—"

"No!" Chantal was shaking her head. "This is my wedding day."

"You think I don't know that?"

Mikki stared at her sister, saw the fury in her eyes. And she suddenly felt unsure about her decision.

Should she have said nothing? But if Ken was the type of man to proposition his own sister-in-law on his wedding day, with his new wife in the next room, didn't that show that he was a slimeball?

That's why Mikki had never totally taken to him. She had sensed that there was something untrustworthy about him, even though she hadn't exactly known what.

Now she knew.

"Chantal, I would never want to hurt you. Especially not on your wedding day. I guess I'm just saying . . . I'm saying you should talk to him. I don't know. I just thought . . . I thought you would want to know."

"Stop it!" Chantal exclaimed. "Stop telling lies. I'm sorry Alex dumped you, but—"

"You think this is about Alex?" Mikki asked, aghast.

"I think that Alex dumped you, and you're miserable,"

Chantal said. "And if you're miserable, I have to be miserable, too, right?"

This couldn't be happening. "You think I'm telling you this to hurt you? You think I'm making this up?"

"You've always been jealous of me. Always. I had more friends than you, more boyfriends. That ate you up, didn't it?"

"That's not what this is about!"

"I wouldn't put it past you to make up something like this today of all days—my wedding day."

"I'm telling you the truth. Ken came on to me. And it wasn't innocent. He knew what he was doing. For God's sake, he invited me into the bathroom to have sex, saying no one would know."

"If he said anything even remotely like that, it's because he's drunk and was goofing around."

Mikki tried another tactic. "Listen, Chantal. I just found out last night that Alex was cheating on me, and I wish someone had—"

"Ah, so that explains it." Relief streaked across Chantal's face.

"Explains what?"

"This isn't about me. This is about you. And let's face it, you never liked the fact that I was getting married before you were. I'm sure you're exaggerating what Ken said or did. He's not like that anymore."

The words stopped Mikki cold. *He's not like that anymore.* So he *had* been a player.

Had he cheated on Chantal before?

"Did you hear what you just said?" Mikki asked.

Chantal pointed her finger at her. "This is my wedding, and I won't have you ruining it. I'm sorry

Alex dumped you, but deal with it. Better yet, call him up. Work it out."

"Chantal—"

"I'm not listening to any more of your lies."

Mikki stared at her sister, as if seeing her for the first time. And suddenly, the sister she thought had such a perfect life didn't seem quite so perfect anymore. In fact, she wondered if her sister actually believed her own words. It was almost as if Chantal was protesting too much, and Mikki got the sense that Chantal didn't *want* to hear the truth.

Would she truly turn a blind eye if Ken was cheating on her? Even while married? Would Chantal ignore infidelity so that she could present to the world this perfect image she wanted to maintain?

"Please don't make the mistake Mom made." Their father had had a long-term affair, one that had crushed their mother, yet she had forgiven him. As far as Mikki was concerned, she shouldn't have, but her mother had argued that she was doing what was best for the family. But her parents' relationship had never been the same, and Mikki couldn't ever remember seeing her mother and father truly being loving with each other. Mikki didn't want that kind of marriage for her sister.

"So now you're turning a harmless comment into an *affair*?" Chantal asked, her chest puffing out with anger.

"Chantal, I love you. That's the only reason I said anything. I . . . I thought you would want to know."

"Well, you would. Only you would tell me something like this on my wedding day and expect me to say thank you."

"Chantal—"

"Go to hell."

Chantal marched off, and Mikki watched her go, feeling helpless.

Chapter 13

Mikki left the bathroom a few minutes after her sister did and went back to the elegantly decorated ballroom. Chantal and Ken were on the dance floor, and Chantal was looking into her husband's eyes while stroking his face.

It was an act, Mikki suddenly realized. She was playing the part of someone who didn't have a care in the world.

Funny how Mikki had never seen through the façade before. She was betting that Chantal had her own doubts about Ken, but maybe being married to the son of a megasuccessful business magnate was more important to Chantal than being married to someone who would be faithful to her.

"Hey."

At the sound of the deep voice, Mikki turned around. Saw Barry standing behind her. "Barry, hi."

"Where did you disappear to?" he asked.

"Ah, the ladies' room." Mikki forced a smile.

"Will you dance with me?"

"Of course."

Mikki let Barry take her hand and lead her onto the dance floor. He held her close, and she swayed her body with his to a love song by Mariah Carey, but she felt like crap. Her sister was pissed at her, and her brother-in-law had groped her.

Could life get any more peachy?

Barry urged her closer, and Mikki was aware that she was stiff. She was trying not to react to the touch of the hands that felt better on her body than anyone else's had.

But as the song continued, and Barry splayed his hands over the small of her back, Mikki closed her eyes and leaned against him. She rested her head on his shoulder, breathing in the scent of his cologne. It was intoxicating.

He was strong, and he was gorgeous. And in his arms, Mikki believed that there were still some decent guys left in the world.

Suddenly, Mikki was emitting a sob. The emotion of the day and all that had transpired finally got to her.

Barry eased back and looked at her. "Hey," he said gently. "What's wrong?"

"Nothing."

Barry wiped at the tear that had fallen down her face. "You're crying."

"Because I'm happy."

"Those aren't happy tears," Barry said. "Talk to me."

More tears fell, and Mikki brushed them away.

Then Barry was taking her hand and leading her out of the ballroom. He led her through the main entryway of The Delano, with its regal columns, wide lobby, bar, and chic seating areas.

"Tell me what's going on," he said.

Mikki shook her head, unable to find her voice.

"Tell me," Barry urged.

"I . . . It doesn't matter."

"Of course it matters," Barry countered. "And since it's got you upset, it matters all the more."

Instead of speaking, Mikki leaned against his very strong chest. He wrapped his arms around her, and she sagged against him. It felt good to be in his arms. It felt good to have him as a safe place to fall. He felt like an anchor in a stormy sea.

"Mikki . . ."

"My sister's new husband propositioned me about an hour and a half ago."

Barry eased back to look down at her. Confusion streaked across his face. "What?"

"That was my thought exactly. Here I was, coming out of the bathroom and I see Ken. I congratulated him again about getting married, and he asked if I would sneak into the bathroom with him. After groping my ass," Mikki added so that Barry would be certain that she hadn't misunderstood his intentions.

"Son of a bitch."

"He was telling me how good I looked, and what he wouldn't do for a piece of me. I . . . I couldn't believe it."

Barry said nothing, but Mikki could see that he was seething.

"I told my sister," Mikki went on. "I felt I had to. Ken kept looking at me while they were dancing . . . and she just looked so happy. . . . But Chantal thinks I'm making this up, that I wanted to ruin her day because I'm jealous. And because I'm miserable over being dumped by Alex."

Mikki began to cry again, soft little sobs that stabbed at Barry's heart. He didn't want to see her hurt. Not by Alex. Not by Ken. Not by anyone.

He never had.

He held her against his chest, her body quivering as she cried. Rubbing a hand up and down her back, he said, "For what it's worth, you did the right thing."

Mikki looked up at him, and he saw appreciation in her eyes. "I had to tell her," she said. "Maybe Ken was just being stupid, but if she talks to him about it now, maybe that will help him know better than to behave like an asshole in the future. Right?"

"Of course." Barry couldn't imagine marrying the woman he loved and hitting on anyone else, much less his own sister-in-law. He was thinking that *asshole* was too nice a term to describe Ken.

"I think I'll have a talk with him too," Barry said.

"I don't know," Mikki said, frowning. "If you talk to him, maybe Chantal will be more upset."

"Like I mentioned before, Ken was always spoiled growing up. We weren't that close, because . . . well, you know what I was like growing up. I would never run in Ken's circles, cousin or not. But if he thinks he's going to marry your sister and continue being a player, then it's time I have a talk with him, man to man."

"Not today, please. Chantal's already angry with me. Let her have the rest of her wedding day. Maybe that's what I should have done, told her tomorrow."

"Hey," Barry said softly, placing a finger beneath her chin. He could see in her eyes that she was beating herself up. "Any time you told your sister would have been a bad time. I'm sorry Ken put you in that position. I thought he loved your sister. Maybe he does but thinks fidelity is only required of other people, not him. Or maybe it was simply bad judgment. Whatever the case, I'm going to talk to him, make sure he knows that if he ever hurts her, he'll have to answer to me."

"I only wanted to protect her."

"And I'm sorry your sister didn't realize that." Barry stroked her soft cheek. She looked so beautiful. Her dark skin, her bright eyes, and damn, those succulent lips. Barry should be kissing her right now, not having to comfort this beautiful woman because Ken had acted like a bastard.

As he stroked her face and looked into her eyes, more tears fell. Barry brushed them away with the pads of his thumbs, suddenly certain that something else was wrong. "What else is going on, Mikki? What is it that you're not telling me?"

She eased out of his embrace and hugged her torso. "I guess I'm just starting to realize that love is an illusion. Here my sister has just gotten married, and her husband is already hitting on me. Then, last night, I found out that my ex was cheating on me. I can't believe that I was dumb enough to believe he was going to propose to me over the holidays, when the pig was actually having an affair. I feel like true love doesn't exist right about now."

"Is that how you really feel?" Barry asked, holding her gaze.

Mikki averted her eyes, and Barry moved forward, framing her face. He wanted to kiss her, right here in this hotel lobby, erase from her mind any doubt whatsoever. Because while there were loser men in the world whose sole goal was to get into as many panties as possible, there were also men who knew how to cherish and respect a woman.

"I don't know how to feel," Mikki said.

"Not every guy is an asshole, Mikki. Tell me you know that."

Barry gently stroked her face with his fingers, and damn if it didn't send a delicious thrill through her entire body. Mikki knew what he was asking her. To tell him that she knew *he* wasn't an asshole.

"I know that," she told him.

"Good."

He continued to stroke her face, his fingertips sending tingles of pleasure through her. She was supposed to be angry with men right now, not getting turned on by one.

But the truth was, Barry was no ordinary man. He had proven that in the bedroom and out of it. He had a gentleness about him, as well as strength. He was one of the good guys. Something she'd known back in high school.

"Want to get out of here?" he asked, his tone deep and sexy.

Just the suggestion of them leaving had Mikki's body awakening in a sexual way.

"We can talk. We don't have to—"

"But I want to."

Barry grinned. "I didn't get to finish my statement."

"You didn't have to."

And then Mikki encircled Barry's waist, tipped up onto her toes, and kissed him.

Mikki didn't bother saying her good-byes to anyone, just slipped out of the hotel with Barry so they could get a taxi to the Marriott.

A short while later, they were hurrying into his room. Once Mikki and Barry crossed the threshold and he closed the door, he swept her into his arms and planted his mouth on hers.

Unlike the last time, their kiss wasn't frenzied, speaking of an urgent need to make love. Instead, it was deep and gentle, the kind of kiss that conveyed tenderness and caring as well as heat.

Mikki slipped her arms up Barry's chest and across the expanse of his shoulders. She moaned against his lips, the feel of him turning her on.

Bringing both of her hands to the back of his neck, she opened her mouth wider, loving it when Barry's tongue swept into her mouth, twisting with her. Goodness, his lips felt amazing. Warm and sweet. He tasted of the red wine they had been consuming, and it was more potent on his lips than it had been from her glass.

He kissed her as his body urged hers to walk backward to his bed, and only then pulled his lips from hers. Mikki sat on the bed and looked up at him. And she couldn't help feeling lucky. Lucky to be connecting on such an amazing sexual level with a man like Barry.

Those broad shoulders beneath the tailored black blazer, the bow tie around his neck that she so badly wanted to undo . . . Every time she looked at him, she was aroused.

Barry sat on the bed beside her, his lips finding hers once more. With one hand, he gently stroked the length of her neck, and when Mikki sighed with pleasure, he lowered his hand to the bodice of her dress. He cupped her breast, and again she moaned, and Barry deepened the kiss. He tried without success to move the dress from her breasts. His hands went back up to her neck and to the straps, which he dragged down her shoulders.

But when he once again tried to get the bodice to budge, Barry broke the kiss and asked, "Is this dress made of iron or what?"

Mikki chuckled against his neck. "It's a form-fitting bodice. You have to undo the zipper under my arm."

And with that, Barry rolled her over. Rolled her over and then planted a kiss between her shoulder blades, one that sent a tingle of pleasure right down her spine. Then he took both of her arms and stretched them above her head. Finding the zipper, he began to undo it, and Mikki felt the material loosening against her skin. She was wearing a strapless bra, and Barry unsnapped that from the back. Mikki expected him to turn her back over, but instead, he used the tips of his fingers to tease the skin on her back. They went up, down, around, making her heady with desire.

Once again, his lips found her back. He kissed a path from the base of her spine up to her neck. Mikki couldn't remember anything feeling as good.

Then, placing a hand beneath her shoulder, Barry urged her over. His eyes met hers as he reached for the material at the front of her dress and now pushed it out of the way. His eyes held hers as her breasts were exposed. There was a look of heat and lust in his eyes, but also something else. Something that made the breath catch in Mikki's throat.

Because mixed in with the heat she expected, there was also a look of tenderness and appreciation.

Covering both breasts with his palms, Barry lowered his mouth to hers.

This time as he kissed her, Mikki felt a balloon of heat swallow them both. It was as though they were becoming one.

This was much more than simply sexual. At least, more than any sexual experience Mikki had had before. What was happening with her and Barry was ripe with meaning, although Mikki knew not what it meant—only that what she was about to do with Barry was going to be something beyond simply having sex.

His tongue delved into her mouth, tangled with hers, and soon she was panting. He began to tweak both of her nipples at the same time, and oh, the sensation. Her entire body was exploding with pressure points of pleasure. Her vagina was thrumming, and her nipples were as hard as rocks.

Barry moved his mouth from hers and brought it down onto one solid peak, sighing with satisfaction as he took her nipple into his mouth. Mikki gasped, tightened her hands into fists. He began to suckle her, slowly at first, and then more fervently, as if he couldn't get enough of her.

"You're beautiful," Barry whispered, and the words filled Mikki with warmth. He stroked her neck. "So beautiful."

Mikki reached for Barry's face, and he turned his mouth into her palm. "Make love to me," she told him.

"If you can get this dress off of me," she added, and then began to laugh.

"There *is* a lot of dress," Barry said, moving his hands to the heaps of organza and netting. He lifted and pushed, lifted and pushed, trying to get to her legs underneath. Finally, he succeeded, and Mikki felt his warm hands caress her thighs.

Then his head disappeared beneath the plentiful skirt, and Mikki giggled again—until she felt his lips kiss her through her panty.

"You're wearing another thong." He pushed the material aside and stroked her with his fingers. "Damn."

Mikki moaned. And then she frowned. "This won't do. I want to see your face, Barry."

He extricated himself from her skirt and looked at her. "You want to see my face?"

"When you . . . when you go down on me."

A grin tugged on his lips. "Then let's get you out of this dress."

Barry reached for her hand, helped her to her feet, and then worked the dress down her hips so that she was able to step out of it. Then he pulled her against him, her back to his front. One hand cupped her center while the other covered one of her breasts.

Mikki gasped in pleasure. Barry kissed her cheek, and she angled her head backward as his lips sought hers. The tips of their tongues playing over each other's, Barry's hand slipped into her panty. He stroked her clitoris and fondled all of her vagina until she was breathing heavily and already feeling like she could come.

"You feel amazing," Barry rasped. "I can't get enough of you."

In a flash, he whirled her around. And then he was

guiding her back down onto the bed and burying his face between her thighs.

The feeling was exquisite. His tongue tantalized. His teeth grazed her sensitive nub, leaving her breathless. But when his lips covered her as he suckled her so damn sweetly, Mikki came, and came hard.

"Barry, oh my God . . . I . . ."

Her voice trailed off, the words she'd been about to say startling her.

Because she'd been about to whisper, *I love you.*

Chapter 14

The next morning, Mikki woke up wrapped in Barry's arms. She felt warm and safe. Content.

"Are you awake?" Barry whispered into her ear.

Mikki rolled over and planted a kiss on Barry's cheek. "Yeah, I'm awake." She'd been awake for at least ten minutes, her mind replaying every wonderful moment of the previous night. "I'm awake and ready for round two."

"Is that so?"

"Uh-huh." Mikki kissed his lips this time, nice and slow as if to wake him into an erect state.

"You're insatiable, you know that?"

"You've brought out a part of me I didn't even know existed," Mikki admitted sheepishly. "And I'm liking it. A lot."

Mikki took Barry's penis into her hand and began to stroke him until he was erect. "Yes," she purred. "This is exactly how I want you."

"You touch me, and I'm powerless to resist you."

"Music to my ears." She kissed his cheek, then nibbled on his earlobe.

And when Barry groaned, Mikki climbed on top of him. She grinned down at him as she positioned her body over his and guided his penis into her.

"Oh yeah," Mikki rasped, Barry filling her so completely.

Barry covered both of her breasts with his palms, tweaking her nipples at the same time. She stared down at him, at the expression of raw desire on his face, and felt a surge of power.

She began to move against him, slowly at first, but increasingly getting faster. Barry urged his hips upward, matching her movements, pushing his cock deep inside of her.

Soon, their rhythm was fast, frantic, Mikki grinding her body against Barry's, the most delicious sensations washing over her.

"I'm almost there, Barry," Mikki said. "Come with me."

Barry's hands went to her hips, and he held her as he thrust into her. Then Mikki brought her face down to his, kissing him as fire consumed them both.

Barry wrapped his arms around her, and they moved like that, their lips entwined as they continued to make love. Mikki's breathing became more ragged, and Barry's did too.

And when Mikki's orgasm began, she felt Barry's begin too. It was as if hers had triggered his. They kissed deeply, moaning into each other's mouth as orgasms claimed them both at the same time.

* * *

Hours later, after two more rounds of making love, Mikki said to Barry, "I'd better go. My family's going to be wondering where I am."

Barry snaked his arm around her, holding her tightly against him. "I don't want you to go."

"I know. But I'll come back later. Because I'm enjoying every bit of whatever it is that we're doing."

At her statement, Barry held her eyes. "What *are* we doing?"

Mikki stroked his nose. "We're having an incredible time together."

"Obviously," Barry said. "But what comes next?"

Mikki looked at him. "What do you mean?"

"I'm talking about us. Our relationship."

"Our relationship?" Mikki echoed.

"I'm single, you're single, and there is no doubt that we've got amazing chemistry."

Mikki's heart began to pound in her chest. Suddenly, she felt anxious. Barry's question was making things more real. Up until this point, she had been enjoying spending time with him. Enjoying their hot and heavy affair.

But wasn't that all this was—an affair? Wouldn't it be disastrous to try and make a relationship out of a sexual fling?

"I don't know," she said honestly.

"I was hoping we could continue to see each other." Barry gave her a hopeful look.

"Honestly, Barry, I haven't thought past the here and now. Which has been incredible."

"Exactly. So why should it end now?"

"Are you asking me to commit?"

"What if I am?"

"I . . . I don't know. What we shared has been fantastic. But commitment? I'm not sure I'm ready for that."

Barry looked disappointed but said nothing.

"I mean, just because we've connected in bed doesn't mean—"

"Maybe it does. Maybe this can be the start of something else."

Mikki was silent for a moment, unsure what to say. And when her cell phone rang, she was secretly glad. Because she didn't want to have a talk about the future. Not when she was still confused.

"Excuse me," Mikki said, and rolled off the bed. Naked, she scurried to her purse and quickly retrieved her phone.

Alex's number was flashing on her screen.

Her stomach tightened. But she didn't answer it.

"Who is it?" Barry asked.

"Um . . ." Well, this was awkward. She was in bed with someone else, and her ex-boyfriend was calling.

Barry sat up. "Mikki?"

"It's . . . it's Alex," she told him.

Barry said nothing, and thankfully the phone stopped ringing.

But a moment later, her cell phone trilled, indicating that she had a text message.

Mikki pressed the button to open the message, and she read the words: Babe, call me. We need to talk.

"Alex again," Barry said, not a question.

"Yeah," Mikki said softly. She put her phone back into her purse and went back to the bed.

"Let me guess. He realizes he made a mistake by dumping you and wants another chance."

"I don't know. He said he wants to talk."

"You gonna call him back?"

"I don't know what I'm going to do," Mikki said, and then blew out a huff of air.

"Wow," Barry said, his disappointment unmistakable.

Mikki closed her eyes. This wasn't easy. She felt something for Barry; she couldn't deny it. But what was she feeling exactly? Yes, last night the thought that she loved him had come into her mind, but did she really? Or had she simply created artificial feelings for him based on the fact that she was trying to get over Alex?

She had to admit that her stomach knotted at the mention of Alex, at the fact that he had called her. But did that mean she still had feelings for him?

Yesterday, when her sister and Ken had been taking pictures, Mikki had told her mother about Alex's betrayal because she'd asked if she had spoken to him. Her mother had told Mikki that she should forgive him, that she should try to work things out if possible. That everything she knew about Alex said he was a good man, had a great career, and some things were more important than fidelity. Her mother had closed her argument by saying that infidelity didn't have to be a deal breaker.

Given the fact that her mother had forgiven her father, Mikki wasn't surprised that that had been her stance. But at the time, Mikki hadn't even considered the suggestion, in part because she was angry with

Alex, and also because she believed he would never call her after what he'd done.

Now, the impossible had happened. Alex had called. He wanted to talk.

Clearly, Alex was having second thoughts. And on the heels of Mikki's conversation with Barry, one where he was making it clear that he wanted more out of their relationship . . . well, she was suddenly more confused than ever.

"I'm not saying I want to talk to him or that I want to work things out with him," Mikki began. "I guess . . . what happened between us happened so fast. One minute Alex dumped me and I was hurting, and then the next minute you came along . . . and it's been fun . . ."

"Fun?"

"Yes, fun," Mikki responded, a little irritated. "Look, Barry. I like you. I always have. We were always friends. And now we ended up in bed together, and I don't know what that means. And heck, you're in Chicago. I'm in New York. How would we make it work?"

"We'd find a way."

"I need time."

"I leave tomorrow."

Mikki's eyes flew to his. "You do? When?"

"My flight's at three." He paused briefly. "I head back to Chicago."

"But what about Christmas? Your family's all here. I thought—"

"Not everyone," Barry explained. "I told you my sister just had a baby a few weeks ago, so she didn't want to fly—which is why she didn't come to the wedding. She's in Chicago too, and my parents are heading there. It's the one time of the year they enjoy seeing the snow. Plus, with their second grandson to meet, there's no way they'd be staying in Florida."

Barry's eyes searched hers, and Mikki knew he was trying to determine how this news was affecting her.

She hadn't expected their time together to end so soon, but she couldn't give him what he wanted. Not yet. Not until she knew what she wanted.

Rising from the bed, Mikki went to the chair where her clothes were and slipped into her thong. She hated that she had to wear her maid-of-honor dress out of the hotel, but she didn't have a choice.

"So you're just leaving," Barry said.

"We'll stay in touch," Mikki told him, hoping that didn't sound lame.

Barry chuckled softly, but the sound held no mirth. "Right."

"Barry . . . I don't know what you expect me to say. Every guy I've dated has been the wrong one. Every guy has hurt me. I thought Alex was going to propose, but instead he dumps me and I find out that he was cheating on me. I don't know that I can trust what I'm feeling."

Barry was silent as she put her clothes on, though she could read the disappointment in his eyes.

"I was in a relationship with someone for nearly two years," Mikki went on. "My mother, my sister, they both think I'm stupid to not try and work it out. Maybe they're right. Maybe I owe it to Alex to at least hear him out."

"Unbelievable."

"I didn't say I *want* to work it out." Mikki put her

bra on. "All I know is that I don't want to lead you on. And I don't want to make a mistake. Everything's great now, but . . ." Her voice trailed off.

Barry didn't say a word as Mikki continued to get dressed, and while she didn't look at him, she felt his eyes on her.

It wasn't reasonable for him to expect her to sail off into the sunset with him. Her affair with him had begun as a way to mend her broken heart. That was why she'd been all over him at the bar in New York—not because she was planning on having a future with him.

"I'll catch a taxi," Mikki said, since Barry hadn't gotten out of bed.

"If you really want to leave, I'll take you home."

"No. It's okay. I'll get home on my own."

Crossing the room, Mikki gathered her shoes. And that's when Barry got off the bed. Naked, he walked toward her.

Mikki's heart ached as she looked at him. Leaving him like this didn't feel good.

Barry stopped in front of her but didn't touch her. "Remember when we talked about high school, about the one girl I loved who broke my heart?"

Mikki nodded. "Yeah. Tiffany."

"You assumed I was talking about Tiffany, but I wasn't. I was talking about you."

Mikki stared at Barry, not understanding. "But you . . . you were always into Tiffany."

"That's what I told you, because I was scared to tell you how I really felt. And you were in love with Chad. I didn't think telling you the truth would make a difference. But mostly, I was scared that if I told you how I felt about you, you would run. Kind of like you're doing now."

And with those parting words, Barry headed into the bathroom, leaving Mikki speechless.

Chapter 15

Mikki hadn't known how to respond to Barry's proclamation, and when she'd heard the shower start, she had quickly left his hotel room.

She went back home and straight to her bedroom, relieved to find that her parents weren't home, even though she wondered where they could be.

She felt . . . She didn't know what she was feeling, except a definite sense of unease. As much as she'd like to have all of the answers, she simply didn't.

Why didn't Barry understand that?

Mikki undressed and got into the shower, Barry's surprise announcement playing in her mind the entire time. He'd been in love with her in high school.

How had she not known?

Or had she on some level always known? Was that why she had trusted Barry enough to go to bed with him? Because she'd instinctively known that he was a man she could trust with her heart?

Ever since her first night with him, Mikki had been asking herself how she could sleep with him, because it was so out of character for her to just jump into bed with someone. But what if she'd slept with Barry because, even though thirteen years had passed, the friendship bond they'd formed had still been there?

Mikki exited the shower and wondered if her sister hated her. Chantal was probably already on the plane with Ken, heading to Hawaii for her honeymoon. Mikki wondered if she had questioned Ken about what he'd done or if she would pretend it had never happened.

The knock on her bedroom door had Mikki whipping her head in that direction. She thought she was alone in the house.

"Who is it?" she asked.

"Mikki, it's me. Chantal."

"Chantal?" She was still here? Maybe her flight was a little later. "Um, just give me a minute, okay?"

Mikki hurriedly got into a robe, then went to the door and opened it. Facing her sister, she said softly, "Hey. I thought you left already."

"Can we talk? Mom and Dad aren't here."

Chantal sounded serious, and Mikki couldn't gauge her mood. She didn't want to rehash the argument she'd already had with her sister, but she said, "Sure."

Chantal headed into the bedroom and took a seat on the armchair. Mikki followed her, taking a seat on her bed.

"What you said about Ken—"

"Chantal, I know I hurt you, and I'm sorry. But you have to believe me—I was trying to protect you."

"Well, as you know, I was supposed to leave for my honeymoon today."

"You're not going? I . . . I'm sorry," Mikki repeated.

"I realized something," Chantal went on. "Last night, in the honeymoon suite with Ken, I thought about your comment. The warning not to make the same mistake as Mom. And it got me thinking that maybe I've been living a lie, just like she did for so many years. Here I was with a wealthy, gorgeous guy, and I can't deny that I thought I'd hit the jackpot. I overlooked a lot of things because on paper, Ken was a woman's dream. I forgot about all the things that were really important."

"Chantal," Mikki began, sighing heavily, "I didn't expect you two to break up. I just . . . I guess I just wanted you to know in order to make sure nothing like this happened in the future. Like maybe if you talked to him, he'd realize the error of his ways. I don't know."

"I confronted Ken, and at first he lied. Then he told the truth, blaming it on the alcohol. He thought he could simply apologize and I'd forgive him, but I told him that I can't go on a honeymoon. Not when I don't know if I still want to be married."

"No." Mikki shook her head. "Maybe I should have kept my mouth shut. Ken was drunk, and I probably overreacted."

"No, don't apologize. That's why I wanted to talk to you. I wanted you to know that I'm not mad at you. You did what any good sister would do, and I'm sorry I didn't appreciate that right away. I got really angry with you, but the truth is, I was angry with myself. Because Ken cheated on me before. And like Mom did with Dad, I forgave him. I forgave him because, like I said, on paper, he was every woman's dream man. He told me he'd never do it again, and I wanted so badly to believe him, even though in my heart I wasn't sure I could."

"Is it over?" Mikki asked softly.

"I'm not saying it is. Not necessarily. But I need to take some time and see what I want. Maybe we'll go to counseling and everything will be fine. All I know is that I don't want to settle, and I won't settle. I hope things will work out, but that can happen only when I'm convinced that Ken isn't going to break my heart down the road."

"I'm sorry."

"No," Chantal said. "Don't apologize, because you talking to me about what happened was a wake-up call for me. If need be, we can get the marriage annulled now. And like I said, I woke up realizing that I deserve better. I deserve a man who loves me whole-heartedly. A man who's crazy about me. If that's Ken, great . . . but I need to take time to figure it out."

Chantal got up and walked over to Mikki, and Mikki stood to meet her. Then Chantal wrapped her in a warm embrace, one that erased all of Mikki's doubts about whether she had done the right thing.

"Where are Mom and Dad?" Mikki asked as they pulled apart.

"They're with Ken and his parents, discussing the situation. As you can imagine, Mom is beside herself. And warning—she's not happy that you told me. But, given her own history with Dad, that's no surprise."

"I'm sure."

"I'm sorry I said you were jealous of me. I . . . I feel real bad about that."

"It's okay."

"I also said something about working it out with Alex. That was the anger talking. I don't think you should. In fact, I can't help thinking that something special is sparking with you and Barry." Chantal's voice rose on a hopeful note.

"Barry?" Mikki asked, her heart immediately beginning to thump.

Chantal grinned at her. "Come on. I think it's been obvious to all of us that you two are hot for each other. Being in a room with you two . . ." Chantal fanned herself. "Talk about smoldering."

"What are you talking about?"

"The way you both look at each other? All. The. Time. It's intense." Chantal paused. "And maybe it's love."

The next morning, Mikki awoke to the sound of knocking at her door. Glancing at the clock, she saw that it was almost nine-thirty.

More knocking. "Yes?" Mikki called.

"Can I come in?"

Her mother's voice. Mikki sat up, wondering if her mother wanted to come in for round two. She'd already given Mikki a good talking-to about causing problems between her sister and Ken.

"All right," Mikki said.

The door opened, and her mother entered. "You have to get up, sweetheart. Alexander is here."

Mikki's eyes nearly bulged out of her head. "What?"

"He's here."

Alexander was here? Mikki didn't know how to respond. She only knew that she was beyond shocked.

She said to her mother, "When you say he's here—"

"I mean he's at the door," her mother told her, a look of definite excitement on her face.

Good Lord, Alex was actually here, in her parents' home.

"Go talk to him," her mother said, speaking in a gentle tone. "Hear him out."

And then she quietly exited the room.

Hear him out. Her mother had done exactly that with her father, stayed in a relationship that she shouldn't have for the sake of appearances. Or perhaps she had done it for the children, but the only thing she had accomplished was to create two daughters willing to put up with bad behavior, instead of ones who had the guts to walk when the going got bad.

But thinking about her past wasn't going to solve anything. So Mikki got up, got dressed, and then headed out of her bedroom. She found Alexander sitting in the living room. When he saw her, he rose, a small smile lifting his lips.

This moment was odd, eerie almost. Seeing Alexander now was beyond surreal. It seemed as though a lifetime had passed since she had seen him, even though in truth it had been only just over a week.

But what an amazing eight days.

A life-changing eight days.

"Hey, babe," Alex said softly.

"What are you doing here?"

Alex started toward her. "I'm sorry. Sorry for being a royal jerk."

Mikki's eyes widened slightly, but she said nothing. In her silence, he went on. "I shouldn't have broken up with you. I was . . . I was confused. I was scared. My feelings for you were so strong that they terrified me."

Mikki didn't want to have this conversation in the living room, where her parents could overhear what they were saying. So she said, "Let's go in here."

She gestured to her father's study and then led the way inside. Once in the room, Mikki closed the door and wandered over to the window.

"I'm confused," she said, turning to face him.

Alex crossed the room until he was standing right in front of her. "I needed to see you. That's why I got on a plane and came down here yesterday. I got in too late to come here last night, but I had to see you bright and early today."

"Why didn't you leave me a message, give me some warning?"

"I tried to call you, but you didn't answer. And then I just knew I had to come down here, see you face-to-face. Make you understand."

"Just last week—"

"I know, it's crazy. I broke up with you, and now here I am. I guess . . . I guess the idea of a wedding terrified me. I knew you wanted to get married, and suddenly I was very scared of the idea." He paused. "But I'm not scared anymore."

Mikki wondered if she had been zapped into the twilight zone. "I don't understand."

Alex chuckled softly. "I love you, baby. You know that. Even though I tried to deny it, even though I broke up with you as a way to avoid facing my deepest fear, I realize that I can't live without you. I couldn't let Christmas pass with us being apart."

This was freaky, him being here. But it was also weird how a week could change everything.

One week ago, Mikki would have reveled in the idea of having Alex come to her the day after he'd broken her heart and say exactly these words. Instead, she felt strangely liberated.

And in total control.

"You told me that I was boring in bed. How do you take that back?"

Alex's eyes widened. Then he steeled his jaw and said, "I wanted to push you away. I was hurting you before you had a chance to hurt me."

"Me? Me hurt you?" Where was this coming from?

"My mother left my father. I know I never told you that before, but I guess it affected me more than I ever thought it would. I'm afraid of getting hurt," he said with a casual shrug.

"You said I was boring in bed," Mikki stressed.

"I know, and I'm sorry. Can you forgive me for being a jerk?"

The small smile on Alex's face said that he thought he only need flash his charming grin and all would be forgiven. It wasn't that simple.

Because Mikki was suddenly immune to his charms. And she was actually excited about what she was going to say next.

"A lot can change in a week."

"I know," he told her. "And that's why I have this."

Suddenly, he reached into his jacket pocket. Mikki's breath stilled.

He wasn't . . .

He couldn't be . . .

He produced a small Tiffany box.

Oh God. He *was*.

"Marry me," Alex said. "Marry me and make me the happiest man on earth."

Mikki stared at him in utter disbelief. To think that two weeks ago she would have easily said yes, but she knew now that had she said yes, heartbreak would have awaited her in the future.

"You want to marry me," she stated without emotion.

"Yes." He handed her the box, grinning like a fool.

"But what about Sandra?" Mikki asked, faking a tone of exaggerated concern.

"Sandra?" Alex asked, but she saw the way his jaw tightened.

Then he chuckled nervously. She knew he was about to lie, absolutely knew it in her soul.

"Sandra . . . The only Sandra I know is the assistant DA."

"Yes, her. The one you're sleeping with." Mikki crossed her arms over her chest, trying to keep her lips from twitching.

Again with the nervous chortle. "I'm not sleeping with her. W-what are you talking about?"

"Someone once told me that if a man isn't sleeping with you, he's sleeping with someone else."

Alex narrowed his eyes. "I don't—"

"I didn't want to believe it," Mikki went on. "But it

makes sense. Four months ago, when you pretty much stopped sleeping with me, I couldn't understand why. I didn't know what I'd done."

"Mikki, baby. I don't know what you're talking about. You're the one for me. You and you alone."

Mikki remembered being in the bar with her friends, devastated over the fact that Alex had broken up with her, that she had expected him to propose over the holidays. Now she couldn't believe just how lucky she was.

Everything had changed. And yet Alex was looking at her as though nothing had changed. As though his smile still had power over her. The power to make her melt. The power to make her his.

"I know you were sleeping with her," Mikki told him. "I can't believe you thought something like that wouldn't get back to me."

"All right," Alex said. "I admit I got involved with someone I shouldn't have. I'm not proud of that. But it was just a brief fling. Something meant to test my love for you," he added, looking at her earnestly. "And now I know, without any doubt. You're the one for me."

"But you're not the one for me." Mikki spoke simply, no emotion. She didn't want him to think that this was about her being angry about his affair, which she hadn't even known about until after the fact. This was about her realizing that she had been spared from making the biggest mistake of her life.

"W-what?" Alex sputtered, his smile promptly dying.

"It's too late," Mikki said. "For us."

"Sandra meant nothing to me."

"But Barry means everything to me."

Now Alex's eyes narrowed in confusion. "Who's Barry?"

An odd feeling came over Mikki, like tiny prickles of heat bursting on her skin. A slow breath oozed out of her as she realized what she'd said.

"Who's Barry?" Alex repeated, louder this time.

"He's someone I met."

"Since we broke up?"

"Someone who doesn't think I'm boring in bed."

"So that's what this is about," Alex said. "You're angry about that one comment."

"No," Mikki said simply. "It's about the fact that I met someone who made me realize I deserve better. Someone with whom things in the bedroom will never be boring. Because we click the way a man and a woman are supposed to click. On every level—emotional and physical."

As Mikki said the words, she realized that she was conveying to Alex a sentiment she had not even conveyed to Barry. Instead, yesterday she had basically told Barry that they'd been having fun, nothing more.

She had been scared, terrified of the idea of making another mistake. So fresh off the heels of her breakup with Alex, she hadn't wanted to trust that her heart was leading her in the right direction.

And the other hurdle, one she had considered last night as she'd lain in bed, was that Barry lived in Chicago while she lived in New York.

But suddenly, Mikki realized a glaring truth. Time and distance didn't matter. Not when you were dealing with Mr. Right.

She began to move now, one foot in front of the other fast. She headed to the study door.

"Where are you going?" Alex asked. "We . . . we haven't finished our discussion."

Mikki opened the door, then turned to face him. "There's nothing to discuss. Nothing you say will make me change my mind. Because I'm in love with someone else."

And then Mikki hurried into the foyer, slipped into her sandals, and grabbed the keys for the Chevy Malibu that were on the hall table.

She heard Alex saying, "Eight days? How did this happen in eight days?"

Mikki didn't answer. She simply opened the door and ran outside, knowing that Alex was completely baffled as to how any woman could possibly resist him. Especially her.

Thank God Barry's flight was later this afternoon. Because that meant he should still be at the hotel. Mikki had to get to him, tell him that she loved him.

It was amazing how crystal clear that realization suddenly was. Then again, maybe a part of her had always loved him.

Love was the reason they had connected in such an explosive way in the bedroom, because of their mutual bond from the past. A past in which they had forged a solid friendship over two years of high school. Barry had been the one she had turned to then, for laughter and comfort. And yet she'd thought he'd been in love with Tiffany, so she'd never dared to think past the idea of the two of them being friends.

Yes, it was all so clear now.

Mikki had so easily trusted Barry with her body the first night, because she had known that she could trust him with her heart.

As she pulled out of the driveway, she looked in the rearview mirror and saw Alex exiting the house and coming toward the car. Mikki turned right, and then Alex disappeared from her view—and her life—forever.

Chapter 16

Mikki drove all the way to the Marriott hotel with a lead foot and was elated to arrive there having avoided any cops. She parked, hurried into the hotel, then went upstairs to the fourth floor. Reaching Barry's door, she knocked on it.

No one answered.

Barry had to be in the shower. Mikki pounded on the door this time, hoping that he would hear her from within the bathroom.

Again, there was no answer.

She listened for sound inside the room. Hearing none, she frowned. Certainly Barry hadn't left for the airport already.

Mikki went back downstairs, suddenly terrified that she was too late. Stupidly, she'd left her cell phone at home, having simply rushed to her parents' car and started driving.

"Barry," Mikki said to the woman at the reception desk. "He was staying in room 402, and now he's not there. Has he checked out?"

The woman looked confused. "Barry? Can you give me the guest's last name, please?"

Of course. "Sanders. Barry Sanders."

The woman typed the information into her computer, and a moment later confirmed, "Yes. Mr. Sanders checked out. Not too long ago, actually. He mentioned something about being able to get an earlier flight."

Mikki's heart sank. No, she couldn't be too late. Not now that she had figured out exactly who she was meant to be with. She would never have guessed that Barry, her old friend from high school, would end up being the man of her dreams. But there was a certain serendipity to it.

Maybe something would have sparked with them earlier if Mikki hadn't had a knack for picking all the wrong guys to obsess over in high school. Or maybe if Barry hadn't headed off to Chicago for college. In a pre-Facebook era, they'd both lost touch.

Fate. She heard Isabel's word in her mind, and as Mikki got back into the car, she smiled. Her friend had been right after all.

Mikki started up the car and headed for Miami International Airport, knowing that it didn't matter how long it took to get love right. It only mattered that you did.

Mikki raced to the airport. She didn't know which flight Barry was taking, only that he would be heading back to Chicago. She was grateful that her parents had a pile of change in the car, money that allowed her to park.

Hurrying inside the airport, Mikki checked the boards for flight departure information. She saw that an American Airlines flight was leaving for Chicago in an hour and a half.

Was that Barry's flight? And if it was, how could Mikki get beyond the gate? She didn't have a ticket. She wasn't flying. You couldn't get past security unless you were booked on a flight.

Without her phone, she couldn't call him. How stupid she had been to leave it behind. Her goal then had simply been to get out the door as quickly as possible.

As Mikki pondered her quandary for a moment longer, she decided that she would have to ask security to page Barry. She would come up with an excuse. Something desperate.

Like what? That his mother was sick? No, that wouldn't be good. Then what? What could she say?

Because she had to reach him. She couldn't let him get on a flight to Chicago without letting him know how she felt.

Mikki's stomach tightened as she began to move across the airport floor, trying to figure out what she could possibly say to security in order to get them to page Barry. She scanned the area, looking for an information desk . . . and then her heart slammed hard against her rib cage.

It was Barry. She would recognize those broad shoulders anywhere, that smooth, bald head. He turned, allowing her to see his profile. Relief rushed through her when she got a glimpse of his goatee.

Yes, it was him!

Mikki began to rush through the crowded airport.

He was in the security line, heading toward an agent. Barry must've stayed outside to either get a bite to eat or do something else. It was her good fortune that he hadn't yet gone through the security line.

Fate.

She moved her feet quickly, muttering, "Excuse me" several times as she brushed past people. Barry was getting ever closer to the front of the security line. If he got past the agent, it would be too late.

"Excuse me," she said, and physically bumped a woman out of the way. She didn't mean to, so she said, "I'm sorry."

And then she was running. She could see from her vantage point that Barry was just about to reach the agent.

"Barry!" she yelled.

Barry was reaching for what she assumed was his identification to pass to the security officer.

"Barry!" she yelled again, louder this time.

He turned. His eyes scanned the area, but he didn't see her.

She kept going, now waving her hands frantically above her head. "Barry, it's me."

She saw the moment he saw her. His eyes narrowed in question, and his lips parted.

"Barry, please don't leave yet."

He had already handed his documents to the security agent, but now he took them back and stepped to the side.

Mikki went to the black rope cordoning off the security line, moving to get as close as possible to Barry. He stepped toward her, letting the people behind him pass.

"Mikki, what are you doing here?"

"I . . . I had to see you."

"But . . . why?"

"I couldn't let you leave."

"Yesterday you said—"

"I know what I said. And I . . . I was lying."

Barry's eyebrows shot up.

"Not really lying to you, but lying to myself," she clarified. "I found something with you that is real. Eight days ago, I was involved with someone else. Someone I thought I would be with for the rest of my life. I couldn't accept that I could so easily fall for you. You were supposed to be a fling to get over Alex."

Mikki was aware that people were gazing at her and Barry, watching their interaction with interest. But she didn't care.

"You told me we were only having fun," Barry said.

"I know. That's what I was lying about. Because it wasn't just fun, Barry. It was more."

Barry said nothing, just stared at her, and Mikki began to worry that he would respond to her the way she had only an hour ago responded to Alex. That he would tell her it was too late. Maybe her rejection of him had already caused him to decide that he was better off moving on without her.

She reached for him, taking fistfuls of his shirt into her hands. She couldn't let him walk out of her life the way she had just walked out of Alex's. Because what she had found with Barry was more than she had ever had with Alex. She was 100 percent certain about that.

"Barry, I love you. That's what I'm trying to tell you. I love you. I think . . . I think maybe I always loved you. But you were my high school buddy, and even though you were perfect for me, I never saw past that. Partly because I thought you were in love with Tiffany, but that's neither here nor there. I just didn't expect you to come into my life out of the blue. I didn't expect that everything I always wanted would be handed to me on a platter. So I was scared, and I was running from that." Mikki finally took a much-needed breath. "But I'm not running anymore. I know what I'm feeling, and I'm not afraid of it. I want you. Please tell me that you want me too."

The seconds that passed seemed like hours, the uncertainty threatening to overwhelm her.

But then a slow smile formed on Barry's sexy lips. He wrapped his arms around her and whispered hotly, "You know I want you."

Relief bubbled through Mikki. "Oh, Barry."

And then he brought his mouth down on hers and kissed her. Right there in the crowded airport, in the security line.

Cheers erupted around them. Oohs and aahs filled the air. It was Christmas Eve, a time when people were heading home to be with those they loved.

And Mikki was with the man she loved. He was the best Christmas present of all.

"I love you," Barry told her.

"I love you too."

"I know you're in Chicago, and I'm in New York, and I was worried about us not being able to make it work—"

"I'm moving to New York," Barry told her.

That stopped Mikki cold. "What?"

"I told you I was in New York because I'm heading up an advertising campaign. What I didn't tell you is that my firm was contemplating transferring me to the New York office."

"You're kidding."

Barry shook his head. "I think it's a go. I'm almost certain it is."

Fate. Everything was falling into place for them.

"And if it isn't a go, I can move to Chicago," Mikki told him. "There's nothing holding me in New York. Not anymore."

Barry framed her face. "We'll work it out."

"Yes, we will."

Because whatever it took to be with this man, Mikki would do it.

It may have taken nearly thirty-one years, but she had found the man she knew she was meant to be with forever.

A man with whom life would never be boring.

Her Holiday Gifts

Deborah Fletcher Mello

Chapter 1

"Well, I'll be damned!" Malisa Ivey cussed out loud as she tried for the umpteenth time to finagle the latch inside the small compartment she found herself trapped inside of. She couldn't believe this was happening to her, nor could she believe that whoever was suddenly moving the unit couldn't hear her screaming at the top of her lungs. She heaved a deep sigh, took a deep breath, and yelled once again. "Hello! Can anyone hear me?"

As she, and the crate she was stuck inside of, were being shuffled from side to side, the only sound that responded to her cries was the loud *THUMP THUMP THUMP* of someone's obnoxious music vibrating like thunder from the outside.

That does it! Malisa thought. She was banning music from the kitchens, no ifs, ands, or buts about it. She knew the culprit blasting the stereo was her new hire, her seventeen-year-old cousin Darryl, and when she got out of her current predicament and managed to get her hands around his scrawny neck, he was surely going to be her first casualty.

Malisa cussed again as she was slammed hard against the side of the wood structure, the knock making her hit her forehead. Hard. She could already feel a major lump beginning to swell from the violation.

This was not how Malisa had intended to spend her Christmas Eve. She gently rubbed at the bruise she was sure would have her face looking like she'd gone three rounds with a heavyweight contender.

Shaking her head, she suddenly wished she'd packed up her knives and had gone home with the rest of the staff when she'd had the opportunity. The morning hours in the bakery had been brisk, customers racing to pick up their holiday treats before the business's three-o'clock closing time.

The counters were now completely bare of the assortment of cakes, breads, and pastries her restaurant, Sweet Tea and Grits, was renowned for. Malisa had been done for the day when Junior O'Malley had come for the last confection, a sweet-potato cheesecake he'd ordered for his mother. And she should have gone home then. But *no!* Not one to ever be satisfied, Malisa had decided to get an early start on the biggest order she had for New Year's Eve.

Just days earlier, a senior staff member with the Whitman Investment Corporation had come to place an order for the company's end-of-the-year black-tie soiree. The massive New Year's Eve cake she'd designed included a multitiered platform that a company employee was supposed to pop out of. Her brothers, Bryson and Zachary, had constructed the base, and

Malisa had tested the structural integrity herself when she'd climbed inside to ensure there would be no problems the night of the event. *Clearly, though,* she thought, *there is a slight problem!*

The musical interlude suddenly ceased, and she called out again, banging at the walls with a tightly closed fist. "Hello? Hello? Darryl Ivey, you better let me out of this thing! Darryl? Darryl? Darryl!" The quiet was short-lived as the music sounded again, only louder and even more obnoxious.

Malisa couldn't believe this was happening to her. She should have been at her parents' home with the rest of her family eating roast pork and her mother's mango salsa; instead she was beginning to think her twenty-eight years were coming to an end inside a cake box on Christmas. Wondering when her nightmare was going to be over, she closed her eyes, wrapped her arms tightly around her torso, braced her feet and back against the wooden walls, and fought back tears.

Thirty-seven-year-old Gabriel Whitman reclined his lean body back against the leather executive's chair and lifted the length of his legs atop his desk. Clasping his hands behind his head, he heaved a deep sigh. Business never ended for the high-profile business tycoon. Not even on Christmas Eve when he needed to review the final details for his latest acquisition. Not until the last *i* had been dotted, and the final *t* crossed, would he be locking the doors of Whitman Investment Corporation for his holiday vacation.

Finally satisfied, he closed the manila folder,

reached for the glass of brandy that rested in front of him, and took a sip. Taking a quick glance at the Breitling watch on his wrist, he noted the time. He had just over an hour to spare before his ex-wife would be making an appearance at his home, having taken their fifteen-year-old son, Trey, shopping for the holiday.

Much like when they'd been married, the woman had planned out his next twenty-four hours, supposedly for the sake of their child, and then he and Trey would be left to their own devices. Knowing the drama his ex-wife was sure to bring had Gabriel anxious for their "family" time to be finished so that he and his only child could enjoy the rest of their holiday in peace. He gulped the last of his drink and heaved a deep sigh. Rising from his seat, he pulled on his leather jacket, shut off the lights in his office, and headed out the door.

Like he did every year, he slowly strolled the halls of the large offices. He'd purchased the building five years ago, as the company had grown to be a formidable competitor among the many investment companies around the nation. Financial wheeling and dealing had always been Gabriel's strong suit, and he took quite seriously his responsibilities to the many investors who trusted him with their money. Those investors had put him at the very top of his game, and the rewards had been a true blessing.

Walking those halls, reflecting on the year's accomplishments and contemplating what was to come, kept him centered and fueled his spirit. He stopped in the reception area and peered out the expanse of glass that walled the building. The views of the Blue Ridge Mountains were engaging, and with the prediction of snow falling over the holiday, he imagined the sight to come would surely be magnificent.

Looking out over the empty parking lot, he couldn't help but notice the white-paneled truck that pulled into the drive and circled around to the building's receiving area. When the driver backed his way to the loading dock and stopped, Gabriel couldn't begin to imagine what was being delivered at such a late hour on Christmas Eve.

Chapter 2

Gabriel arrived at the back of the building just as the driver was climbing into the truck, preparing to pull off. Not missing the large crate sitting at the end of the loading dock, Gabriel shouted for the young man's attention. Watching the kid's head bob up and down to the music screaming from the truck's interior, Gabriel knew that he couldn't hear a thing. He shook his head as the young man pulled off, his tires screeching.

Walking a wide circle around the large box, he noted his company's name and address stenciled along the structure's side. Not one shred of paperwork was affixed to the container to indicate where it had come from or who it was being delivered to. Gabriel was perturbed by the display of incompetence, making a mental note to reprimand whoever had arranged for the delivery on his end.

Reaching for the iPhone in the breast pocket of his jacket, he thought briefly about calling his executive assistant to come handle the problem. Noting the time, he dismissed the idea, not wanting to pull her from her family. He didn't believe that whatever was inside was of any great importance, since it had been left so casually. He figured that no harm could come for allowing it to sit until the day after Christmas when one of his employees could see to it.

Making the decision, he was just about to do an about-face and leave when he heard a faint cry and knocking coming from the structure's interior.

From inside, Malisa was screaming at the top of her lungs, kicking and banging against the walls. Her voice was just about hoarse from her shrieking and yelling. That last jostle had slammed her hard inside the confines of the container, and now she was beyond the point of being mad. She was furious, and she pitied the soul who'd dumped her wherever she now rested. She knocked harshly, and when a faint voice suddenly responded, her eyes widened with relief.

"Hello? Is someone there? Please, help! I'm trapped inside. Somebody, please!"

Gabriel was momentarily stunned. "What the hell?" Certain that something inside was crying for assistance, Gabriel knocked on the exterior wall, and that something knocked back. His first instinct was to call the police. He was just a fingertip away from dialing 911 when a side panel on the structure suddenly gave way and a high-heeled, black suede boot attached to an obviously feminine leg pushed its way free.

"Hello?"

"What are you doing?" Malisa shouted. "Help me out of this thing!"

"Who are you?" Gabriel asked, his curiosity further piqued.

"Who are *you*?" Malisa responded, suddenly nervous, not recognizing the voice on the other side of the wall.

"I asked first."

"So!" Her tone was indignant.

"So, I'm not the one looking for help to get out," Gabriel said, amusement tinting his words.

There was a pregnant pause as Malisa reflected on his comment. "Can you at least tell me where I am, please?" she finally asked.

Gabriel nodded into the cold evening air. "You're at the loading area of Whitman Investment Corporation."

Stunned, Malisa rolled her eyes skyward as she clutched the front of her blouse. Her cousin Darryl was definitely going to be one dead relative when she got her hands on him. She inhaled deeply and held it, fighting to calm her nerves.

"My name is Malisa Ivey," she finally said, her seductive tone causing a quiver of curious heat to ripple across Gabriel's spirit.

He raised an eyebrow at the familiar name. "Any relation to Judge Gattis Ivey?" the man questioned.

Malisa paused, heat flooding her cheeks. Her head waving from side to side with embarrassment, she answered, "He's my father."

Gabriel chuckled warmly. He had only recently made Gattis Ivey's acquaintance, the two men sitting on one of Asheville's public safety committees together. The patriarch's stellar reputation had preceded him, and Gabriel had much respect for the district court judge. He could just imagine the father's reaction to his daughter's predicament.

"So explain to me how you managed to get trapped in a container on Christmas Eve?" he asked.

"It's a long story," she said, "but would you please just help me get out?"

"I should probably call the police," Gabriel offered, a smug smile pulling at his lips.

"No!" Malisa shouted, her eyes bulging at the thought of any further embarrassment. "Please, just see if you can get the top to open. There's a handle on the side. I can't budge the latch from the inside. It's stuck. Please!" she pleaded.

Gabriel laughed again as he quickly searched the container for the handle she'd described. With a quick pull, the top of the box suddenly swung open. With a little wrangling, Malisa managed to pull herself upright so that she could stand on her feet, and then just like that, she was free.

As she popped anxiously out of the container, Gabriel's smile widened. The seductive voice belonged to an even more seductive body, the attractive woman inside teasing his sensibilities.

Malisa Ivey was a stunning caramel beauty with wide doe eyes that gave her a look of innocent wonder and belied the full pouty lips that begged to be kissed. Over black patterned tights she wore a form-fitting black cashmere sweater dress that just covered her assets, meeting those black suede boots thigh-high. She was lusciously curvy, and her sex appeal was heightened by her obvious spirit.

"Surprise?" Malisa said, amusement painting her expression as she glanced around her. Her sultry gaze fell on the handsome man who stood staring at her curiously.

The dark stranger was simply gorgeous. He was exceptionally tall, his height imposing. He was also nicely built, clearly hard-bodied. He was fastidiously dressed, a leather jacket complementing wide shoulders and a broad chest. His closely cropped haircut was freshly edged, and the meticulous line of his blue-black beard and mustache nicely highlighted his chiseled features, dark complexion, and light-colored eyes. A sumptuous shiver vibrated down the length of her spine.

Gabriel extended his hand to help her step out of the container, and when his hand touched hers, the contact took her breath away. Malisa felt herself gasp for air as he laughed warmly.

"So, now are you going to tell me why you're locked in this box?"

"Are you going to tell me who you are first?" she queried.

"Do you always answer a question with a question?"

"Your name?"

He chuckled heartily, "Gabriel Whitman."

"Whitman?"

He nodded. "Yes, ma'am. And it's a pleasure to meet you, Malisa Ivey."

Malisa could only imagine how red her face was, heat raging through her cheeks. Of all people to know of her predicament, why did it have to be the owner of the business she had hoped to impress.

"It's nice to meet you, too, Mr. Whitman."

"Please, call me Gabriel. I think under the circumstances we should be on a first-name basis. So now are you going to tell me how you came to be delivered to my door on Christmas Eve in a box?"

Malisa sighed. She wrapped her arms around her torso, the gesture drawing attention to the fullness of her bustline. "I will, but it's cold out here and my mother is probably having a fit about where I am. Do you think I can use your telephone to call myself a ride? I don't have my purse or my cell phone on me."

"I'll do you better than that," Gabriel answered. "Come on. I'll give you a ride home."

He gestured with his head for her to follow him. As he turned around and headed back inside the building, Malisa eyed him from head to toe and back again. She couldn't help but notice the fit of his denim jeans around an extraordinarily high behind that bubbled firm and hard and had her thinking about squeezing each cheek in the palms of her very small hands to see how they fit.

Her breath caught in her chest as she found herself imagining such a thing about a perfect stranger, and when Gabriel tossed her a look over his shoulder, she hoped her decadent thoughts weren't showing on her face.

She followed him back inside the building, watched as he secured the doors, then walked with him to the only car in the employee garage, a Range Rover.

Moving to the passenger side door, Gabriel opened it widely to allow her inside. As she settled her petite frame down against the leather seat, her gaze met his and held it. There was something in the look that he gave her that sent an obvious shiver down the length of her spine. Goose bumps rose like a raging rash on her arms, and she was grateful for the length of sleeve that hid her limbs from view.

Gabriel found himself strangely in awe of the young

woman who had toned down her hostile banter. She had reined in her spirited personality, and nervous tension had risen like morning mist between them. He still had more questions than she was willing to give him answers for, but he was pleasantly intrigued by her mysterious air.

As he pulled on his seat belt and started the ignition, she reached to turn off his radio. He was amused by her boldness and said so. "Don't you know you're not supposed to mess with a man's radio?"

She laughed heartily. "Had a man not been blasting his radio, I wouldn't be here right now. Let's just say I am not in the mood for music."

He nodded. "So are you going to tell me what happened?"

Malisa shook her head, the annoyance of her experience returning to her face. She blew a deep sigh. "I own the restaurant and bakery Sweet Tea and Grits. Your company hired me to do the cake for your New Year's Eve party. That box was the base that you are supposed to pop out of. I was testing it to make sure it worked and somehow got locked inside and delivered."

Gabriel cut his eye at her. "You're telling me I'm supposed to fit inside that thing?"

"It's actually quite roomy for a very brief period of time, but definitely not roomy enough for someone to travel inside of, obviously. And of course the latch jammed."

"I'm glad it jammed on you and not me."

"Me, too, but I wish you hadn't found out about it."

Gabriel laughed. "I can keep a secret if you can!" He smiled sweetly, meeting her stare a second time.

Malisa smiled back. "I appreciate that."

"So, are you better at making cakes than you are boxes?"

She nodded, her smile widening. "My cakes are on point," she said. "They're the best you will ever taste."

"I'm going to hold you to that," he said.

"What's your favorite flavor?" she questioned.

Gabriel thought for a quick moment. "I have a weakness for coconut and pineapple, if that helps."

"I would have thought you'd be a chocolate or a caramel man," Malisa teased.

He laughed. "Only my women need to be chocolate or caramel," he said smugly.

Fighting back the temptation to ask about the women in his life, she found herself giggling as she gestured with her index finger for him to make the turn onto Elk Mountain Scenic Highway. "It's the house at the top of the incline," she said, still pointing.

Pulling into the driveway, Gabriel came to a stop behind a long line of vehicles. The stone-and-wood-sided structure was well lit, and it was obvious family and friends had already begun to celebrate the holiday.

"Well, this has been an interesting evening. I look forward to seeing what your final cake looks like," Gabriel said, turning in his seat to face her.

"Please, come inside," Malisa said. "I really appreciate your kindness, and there's a ton of food. I at least owe you dinner for rescuing me."

He looked at his watch. He knew that it would be mere minutes before his ex-wife would be calling to ask where he was and why he wasn't home. But he wasn't ready to bid the beautiful woman good-bye.

"I don't want to intrude," he said, the look on his face expressing what he really wanted to do with her.

Malisa was taken aback by the intense stare he was giving her. She found her breathing coming heavily, a knot tightening in her abdomen. She stammered, "It . . . no . . . it's . . . you . . . you wouldn't be intruding. My parents host an open house every year for their friends and family. People from the community come and go all evening long. Plus," she said, daring to lift her eyes to his, "I owe you."

The car's interior was suddenly heated. It was on the tip of Gabriel's tongue to tell her how he would have liked to be repaid, suddenly wanting to taste her, to kiss her mouth and discover how she felt in his arms.

Malisa felt moisture beginning to puddle in places it had no business being. She desperately needed to put some distance between her and that man, so she pushed her door open anxiously. "Come on in," she said hurriedly, rushing out of the vehicle. Turning only briefly to ensure he was following, Malisa headed for the home's front door, Gabriel following not far behind her.

Chapter 3

Entering the home, every one of Gabriel's senses was assaulted by the noise and laughter that rang through each room. Malisa led him from the foyer to the formal dining room where adults were seated around an oversized wooden table. Children could be heard racing about in the background.

Malisa dropped her hands to her lean hips, her head shaking from side to side as her mother, Etta Ivey, sat in the center of the dining room laughing with the town's mayor. Malisa instinctively knew the two were sharing folktales that should have been left untold as far as she was concerned.

She shook her head again and whispered to Gabriel, "Don't take anything they say personally," she said, her eyes brimming with mortification. Malisa knew that anything was liable to spill out of her mother's mouth. Before he could respond, an uproar of laughter vibrated off the walls, everyone gathered breaking out into cheer.

Baylor Ivey bumped into her older sister as she

slipped into the room. "You're late and your mother is completely out of control," the seventeen-year-old girl whined, rolling her large brown eyes toward the ceiling. "Just listen to them. They're all crazy. And she keeps calling my name and telling them stories about me!"

Malisa shook her head as her brother Demetrius stepped in behind the girl. "Leave your mother alone," he said. "You know she likes to tell a good story." He chuckled under his breath. "And where have you been?" he asked, cutting his eye at Gabriel and then Malisa.

"It's a long story," she whispered back. "Where's Darryl?"

The man shrugged as he extended a hand in Gabriel's direction. "Hey, I'm Demetrius," he said, introducing himself.

Malisa eyed the two of them. "This is Gabriel Whitman," she said. "And the young lady over there pouting is my baby sister Baylor."

"Nice to meet you both," Gabriel said softly, not wanting to interrupt the conversation playing out around the table.

"Well, you know, insanity ran on her side of the family, so it wasn't a surprise when her girls dove right off the deep end of good sense and landed smack dab into the middle of never-never land," Miss Etta was saying.

Mayor John Lovett was swiping at his eyes with a cloth napkin, stifling a loud laugh. "They were close in age, those girls were, weren't they, Miss Etta?"

"Stair-step siblings. Could barely tell one from the other, they were so close. It was only them perfumed

names their mama gave them that let you know which
one was which."

The woman sitting with the mayor waved her hand
as if seeking approval to speak. "I met Miss Rose a
few years back. She wasn't that crazy."

Miss Etta and the mayor both shook their heads.

"Oh yes, they were," the man chimed heartily.
"Crazy as loons and it started with their mama and her
mama before that."

"Sure did," Etta interjected. "Hazeline's mama was
a plum fool, and her daddy didn't have much good
sense either, so poor Hazeline didn't have an ice
cube's chance in hell from the get-go. Then Hazeline
walked her own daughters right to the edge of sanity
and pushed them off the side. Once they'd dropped
into the pit of that psychosis, wasn't a thing that could
pull either of them back."

Malisa was cringing as she thought about the stories folks would one day tell about her mother and
some of her more glaring antics. She cut her eye at
Gabriel. The man stood with his arms crossed in front
of him, clearly amused by the goings-on. Malisa was
suddenly taken aback by the sheer beauty of him. His
facial features were crisp, with a chiseled jaw, cleft
chin, high cheekbones, deep dimples, and breathtak-
ing eyes. She found herself staring, unable to take her
gaze off the man.

Another roar of laughter pulled her back to the conversation. Her mother continued to tell the whole
room about Hazeline and her daughters, Rose, Lily,
and Iris.

"Hazeline James was born on the wrong side of

the moon. Most of her kin was. It was February the eighteenth, 1922, a Tuesday morning, in the backwoods of Cumberland County. Hazeline had been an only child. Not long after she was born, her daddy got killed sitting down on the train tracks that ran over Route Eighty-six. Some people think he must have fallen asleep, but Otis James heard that train," Etta said emphatically, taking a deep breath and then a sip of her drink before she continued. "Damn fool just didn't want to get up. Then when the thought finally possessed him to get out of the way, it was too late. A man the size of Otis couldn't move but so fast to begin with. When you have to lift more than four hundred pounds of overweight up off the ground, you sure 'nuff can't do it fast."

Malisa shook her head. "Heaven help us!" she exclaimed under her breath. "Where's Daddy when you need him?"

Demetrius gave her shoulder a quick squeeze before moving back out of the room. "Just let your mother be. Folks love Mom's stories, and no one remembers this old town and its people like she does," he said as he made a quick exit.

The mayor's companion, a woman with a porcelain-white complexion and flaming red hair, was fanning herself, gasping for breath from having laughed so hard. "Did Hazeline ever have any sons?" the woman asked.

"Oh, heavens no!" Etta exclaimed. "Hazeline used to say that if her husband had been a slow-stroking man instead of a wham-bammer, them little swimmers of his might of had some time to make her some sons," she said with a robust laugh.

Everyone around the table burst into another round of glee, and the mayor's friend laughed until her cheeks were flaming a brilliant shade of red like her hair. Etta lifted her body from the seat she was sitting in, leaning to give the mayor a quick hug.

"I will be at the next town meeting, John. And I want to see some control this time. You let folks get out of hand last month arguing over foolishness."

"Yes, Miss Etta," he said, his tone contrite. "I plan to speak to the town manager about that very thing."

The older woman smiled. "Bring Darius over to the restaurant for lunch sometime. You know how much he loves my daughter's catfish and corn bread. I'll set him straight."

The man grinned. "Yes, ma'am. I'll make sure to do that."

Moving toward the doorway, Miss Etta was still chuckling to herself, her gray head fanning from side to side. She cut her eyes toward Malisa, who was beet red with embarrassment, and then turned her full attention to Gabriel, noting the amusement that danced across the good-looking man's face.

"Malisa, you're late, baby, and you didn't tell me you were bringing a young man with you." She smiled broadly, extending her hand. "Hello there. I'm Etta Ivey, Malisa's mother. Merry Christmas to you!"

"It's a pleasure to meet you, ma'am. My name's Gabriel Whitman."

"Well, Gabriel Whitman, welcome to our home." Etta clasped her arm through his. "Are you hungry, dear? We have plenty of good food," she said, guiding him back to the kitchen. Without pausing to take a breath, she asked, "How long have you and Malisa known each other?"

Behind them, Malisa was looking like she wanted to find a hole to fall into. Her younger sister was giggling with glee, delighted that their mother's focus has shifted from her to one of her other siblings.

Inside the home's massive gourmet kitchen, the rest of the Ivey family was gathered with friends. Gattis Ivey, who was seated at the kitchen counter, came to his feet when he recognized Gabriel. "Mr. Whitman, hello! Happy holidays to you!" he said as he reached to shake Gabriel's hand.

"Judge Ivey, sir, it's a pleasure to see you again. And, please, call me Gabriel."

"Gabriel came with Malisa, dear," his wife said, an eyebrow arched in her husband's direction.

Gattis looked from his daughter to her friend and back again. "I didn't know you two knew each other," he said, clearly pleased.

Malisa rolled her eyes. "We just met. And it's a long story." She gestured toward the last of her siblings. "You've met Demetrius and Baylor. My father's spitting image on the end there is my brother Zachary. Next to him is Baylor's twin and my baby brother Bryson. And the woman shoving food into her face is my oldest sister, Anitra. Everyone, this is Gabriel," she said, casually making the introductions.

Her siblings threw up their hands in greeting, everyone welcoming Gabriel to the family's home.

"It's nice to meet you all," Gabriel said politely.

"Where's Darryl?" Malisa questioned a second time.

"He had to take your uncle Bunny to the train station to pick up his mother." The matriarch gestured to the expanse of food that covered the stove, counters, and table. "Fix Gabriel a plate, Malisa. Get your new friend some food."

The look Malisa gave her mother made Gabriel laugh out loud. He didn't need her to say what she was thinking; the words were written all over her face. Although it was on the tip of her tongue to tell her mother that he had two good hands and was capable of fixing his own plate, she didn't. Miss Etta would not have appreciated her saying that he could help himself if he were hungry. Malisa met Gabriel's gaze and shook her head.

He smiled brightly. "I appreciate the offer, Miss Etta, but I really can't stay. My son is waiting for me and I need to be going."

"You have a son?" Malisa asked curiously.

He nodded. "Gabriel Whitman the third. We call him Trey. He's fifteen going on thirty."

"Well, you shouldn't keep your son, or your *wife,* waiting," Malisa said, emphasizing the word *wife.* The snarky dig was meant to seek out information.

Gabriel chuckled at her inflection. "My son's mother and I are divorced." He locked his gaze with hers. "I don't have a wife," he said, answering her curiosity.

Miss Etta didn't miss the exchange, her gaze swinging back and forth between them as though she were watching a Ping-Pong game.

Her husband laughed. "At least try the sweet-potato pie. My wife makes a mean sweet-potato pie. And there might be a slice or two left of Malisa's famous cheesecake. Now, that's some good stuff too."

"Not as good as my pie," Miss Etta said as she moved to the pie plate and cut him a slice. She passed the dessert and a fork to him and waved Bryson out of his seat so that Gabriel could sit down.

Knowing he was in good hands, Malisa politely excused herself from the room to make her rounds through the home, speaking to her father's associates, her mother's friends, and the many cousins who were celebrating the holiday. When she returned to the kitchen, she stopped short in the doorway to stare.

Gabriel was sitting comfortably in conversation with her father and brothers, his one dish of pie having expanded to a full plate of fried chicken, macaroni and cheese, green-bean casserole, and her mother's famous corn pudding.

Malisa stood peeking through the entrance into the family room and kitchen area when her sister Anitra came through the back entrance. She was only slightly startled by the woman's deep, alto voice whispering against her ear.

"What are you staring at?" Anitra asked, peering past Malisa's shoulder. "Oooh, never mind," the woman continued, a wide grin filling her face. "I see where you're staring. Your new friend is *foine*! So where did you find him?"

Malisa blushed, pushing Anitra out of the way before the two were caught peeking. "Keep your voice down before he hears you," she hissed.

Anitra laughed and whispered back, "He can't hear me."

"Who can't hear you?" Baylor asked her two sisters as she moved into the hallway to stand with them.

"Malisa's new boyfriend," Anitra answered.

Baylor nodded. "He's cute, and Mommy and Daddy seem to like him."

"So, I ask you again, where'd you find him?" Anitra repeated.

Shaking her head, Malisa recounted her experience, filling them in on the details of her meeting Gabriel. Neither woman could contain her laughter, the two of them chuckling heartily.

"That is priceless," Anitra exclaimed.

"I wish he'd had a camera," Baylor interjected. "That would be some funny mess to put on YouTube."

Ignoring them both, Malisa went back to her position at the doorway, peeking back into the room.

Gabriel was more than just cute. The dark stranger was absolutely captivating, she mused, studying him closely. He had nice height, measuring somewhere in the vicinity of six foot three. He had a slim but athletic build, his body nicely proportioned with wide shoulders, a broad chest, and long, muscular legs. He was a man who commanded attention the moment he stepped into a room, and she liked how nicely his jeans hugged the shelf of his high behind when he'd taken off his jacket to sit down.

He shifted his position in his seat, twisting his body ever so slightly as he focused on something Demetrius was saying to him. His eyes were pale, a shade of warm caramel, and they peered past dark lashes that were forest thick. With his warm, mocha complexion, Malisa couldn't help but ponder just how delectable he might be.

As the thought crossed her mind, the man looked

up, meeting her gaze, and he smiled, clearly amused. Brilliant white teeth shimmered like polished pearls behind full lips that begged for her attention. Malisa heard herself gasp as she stepped quickly out of view, tripping and almost falling to the floor when she bumped into Baylor and a tray of dirty dishes the girl carried.

"Hey, be careful," Baylor chimed, annoyance coating her words.

"Sorry," Malisa mumbled, blushing profusely.

Baylor brushed past her, moving into the kitchen to drop the contents of the tray into the sink. From the other end of the room, Anitra was laughing loudly.

"Oh, shut up, Anitra," Malisa fumed.

Her sister continued to laugh, shaking her head.

Gabriel chuckled, the easy laugh pulling his full lips into a wide smile. He'd caught the woman peeking from the kitchen for the third time since he'd taken a seat. This time, she'd been so flustered that she'd tripped out the door, almost falling face-first to the floor. Her recovery had been swift, and he was willing to bet her brothers and sisters would give her a hard time the minute he was out of earshot.

She avoided his gaze as she stepped back into the room. Crimson-red flooded her cheeks.

"Here, Malisa," he said politely, "come sit." He gestured to the empty chair at his side.

Knowing that it would be a waste of energy to argue, Malisa moved to sit down. As she did, Gabriel rose from his seat to pull out her chair. Miss Etta smiled, approval raining from her eyes.

Malisa was caught off guard as the man moved

behind her, his hand brushing ever so slightly against her arm as he reached for the chair. She inhaled swiftly, hoping that her discomfort would not be noticed. Her heart was suddenly beating too rapidly in her chest, perspiration rising to her palms. The light scent of his cologne billowed in the air around him. Malisa found it intoxicating as she took a deep breath and then a second.

As Gabriel sat back down, he glanced out of the corner of his eye to observe the young woman. The color had risen to her cheeks a second time, a hint of red brightening her face. He smiled again, clearing his throat slightly as he caught her eye, lifting his eyebrows teasingly.

He reached for his glass of ice water just as Miss Etta asked about refilling his plate.

"Miss Etta, I couldn't eat another bite," he said, patting his stomach. "And I hate to eat and run, but I really do have to be leaving." He glanced down at his iPhone, noting the five missed calls from his ex-wife. Although he'd been having a great time, ignoring her would prove to be a headache for him much later.

"Well, I hate to see you rush off, but it was nice to meet you, Gabriel. I hope that we'll be seeing much more of you," Miss Etta said, the comment directed more at Malisa than him.

Gabriel smiled again, turning to look at Malisa. "I certainly hope so, Miss Etta. I certainly hope so," he said, the warmth of his smile caressing her like a wave of heat.

Rising from his seat, he helped Malisa out of her own chair. He moved around the room and shook hands with Malisa's father and brothers, kissed Miss Etta's cheek, and wished everyone a very Merry Christmas.

"I'll walk you out to your car," Malisa said, ignoring the looks her family members were giving her. "Zachary, let me borrow your jacket," she said as she reached for the coat hanging against the back of the man's chair. She slipped it on without waiting for him to answer and led Gabriel back through the house and out the front door.

Gabriel's smile widened with each step as he watched her ease her way beside him. He'd been completely enthralled as he had sat staring at her. The woman seemed to radiate light, a glow of energy encircling her petite frame. The cashmere dress she wore hung casually around her feminine physique, complementing every inch of her lush curves. The fullness of rounded breasts peeked from the opened buttons at the neckline that stopped before too much could be exposed. Those large eyes, high cheekbones with just the hint of a dimple in her round cheeks, and full, pouty lips filled her round face. Gabriel suddenly wondered once again what it might be like to taste her mouth, to feel those lips against his own. His eyes widened excitedly at the thought.

Outside, Malisa apologized. "My family can be a bit much sometimes," she said.

"I like your family. And I had a great time. I appreciate you inviting me inside."

"I'm glad you could stay. And thank you again for rescuing me earlier," she said softly. She looked back at the light-filled windows to see if any of her family was watching. For a brief moment, she thought her mother might have been peeking from behind the bathroom blinds, and she shook her head.

"So, when can I see you again?" Gabriel questioned, turning around to face her. He leaned back against the fender of his car.

Beneath the darkened sky, Malisa met his stare, knowing that he was eyeing her intently beneath the dim lights.

"I'd like that," she said softly. "Maybe we can do dinner sometime."

"What are your plans tomorrow? Do you have any free time at all?"

Surprise registered in her expression. "But tomorrow's Christmas. I'm sure you have plans with your family. Your son . . ." She paused.

He nodded. "We're spending the day at home, nothing special. And once Trey opens his gifts, he won't be interested in anything until the food is ready. Then he'll eat and forget all about me again." Gabriel pushed his hands into the pockets of his jacket. "I was thinking that maybe if you're not busy, you could stop by for a little while. It'll be very casual, and since I met your family, I would love to introduce you to mine."

There was a moment of silence before Gabriel continued. He took a step toward her, moving his body closer to hers. His voice dropped two octaves. "I hope I'm not being too forward, but I would really like to spend more time with you, Malisa," he said as he stared down into her eyes.

Malisa couldn't deny the wave of wanting that had suddenly consumed her. The man had her breathing heavily, and she was grateful that he couldn't see how her body was responding to the nearness of him.

"Unless, of course, you have plans?" he finished.

She shook her head, her fists clenched tightly at her sides. "I'm just spending time with my family. And there will be a few friends I plan to visit in the afternoon. Why don't you give me a call tomorrow and we'll take it from there?" she said. She boldly reached for the iPhone in his pocket, accessed his address book, and entered her contact information.

Gabriel grinned as she gently tucked the device back into the pocket she'd taken it from, drawing her palm easily across his chest. She lifted her eyes to his and smiled sweetly.

"I will call you in the morning," he promised, still not moving from where he stood.

She nodded, shifting her eyes back and forth across his face. Heat wafted between them like a rolling tidal wave.

Malisa was feeling out of sorts, unable to explain the undeniable attraction between them. He felt like an old friend and not a new acquaintance, someone she knew well and wanted to know better. Gabriel was equally mystified by the depth of chemistry that had drawn him to her, but he liked every ounce of it, wanting to see where it might take them.

Above them, bright stars shimmered in the darkness. The first flakes of Christmas snow began to fall, billowing like flecks of glitter in the late-night air. Malisa looked up into the night sky, a wide smile flooding her face. Gabriel's gaze followed hers, his own smile deepening warmly. He held up the palm of his hand, the downy specks melting against the heat of his skin. He dropped his eyes to hers, desire dancing between them in the dark orbs.

"Merry Christmas, Gabriel," Malisa said softly.

"Merry Christmas," he answered. Then, without a second thought, Gabriel Whitman leaned in and kissed her, gently pressing his lips to her forehead.

When he pulled his car out of the driveway and disappeared from sight, Malisa was still standing in awe.

Chapter 4

The three sisters were snuggled down in Baylor's bedroom, the teen more than perturbed by the intrusion. Had she had her way, her sisters would have bunked together in the family guest room, and her aunt and uncle would have stayed in town at one of the many hotels. As her mother would have it, the aunt and uncle were taking up space and she was stuck with her older siblings.

She tried to ignore them as she skipped about on the Internet, flipping back and forth from a news site to her Facebook page when neither of them was paying any attention.

Malisa raised an eyebrow in her direction. "Santa's not going to bring you any gifts if you don't go to sleep, Baylor."

"Santa already stuck my gifts under the tree before she went to bed, thank you very much!"

Anitra laughed. "Good try, Malisa, but that stopped working when Baylor was fourteen."

"No, it stopped working when I was nine and found

out Mommy and Daddy were the ones buying all my toys."

"Who told you?" Anitra asked.

"Kenny Banes. A dumb boy in my gym class!"

Her sisters laughed. "All boys are dumb. Don't ever forget that," Malisa stated matter-of-factly.

"Is Gabriel dumb?" the girl asked, her eyebrows lifted curiously.

"Gabriel's not a boy. He's a man!" Malisa exclaimed.

"And a very fine specimen if I do say so myself," Anitra noted.

Malisa grinned. "Yes, he is!" she agreed.

"His son is kind of cute too," Baylor interjected. "How old did he say he was?"

"How do you know what his son looks like?" Malisa asked.

The girl pointed to the screen on her laptop. "His Facebook page. He has over a thousand friends."

The two older sisters sprang from their beds to peer over Baylor's shoulder. The girl pointed to a young man who had Gabriel's features but was darker in complexion, his skin the color of melted dark chocolate.

"What else is on his page?" Malisa asked, scanning the screen excitedly.

"Not much. Some pictures of him at various business functions, a couple more with his son . . ." She paused. "Here's a cute one," the girl said, pointing. "They were skiing in Colorado."

"Stop clicking so fast!" Malisa said excitedly, wanting to examine each of the online images of Gabriel.

Baylor sucked her teeth. "Tch! Go get your computer if you want to check out your new boyfriend,"

Baylor responded. "I'm trying to make my own love connections."

"He's not my . . ." Malisa started before changing her mind. Arguing with Baylor was hardly worth the effort.

"I'm sure Mommy will have much to say about any love connections you're thinking about," Anitra interjected.

"Not if she doesn't know," Baylor chimed.

Malisa and Anitra cut their eyes at each other.

"Mommy knows everything," Malisa laughed. "Don't be fooled into thinking she doesn't."

"I know that's right," Anitra said. "And if you're thinking it, trust that Malisa and I have already done it and been punished for it. You are not going to get much past our parents."

Baylor rolled her eyes skyward. "So you two say."

"So we two know!" Malisa said with a deep laugh. "But that's okay, try your luck if you want to." She was still laughing.

"Well," Baylor said with a shrug of her shoulders, "if he were my boyfriend, I'd have to break up with him."

"Why?" Malisa asked, her gaze still scanning Gabriel's profile page anxiously. "What's wrong with him?"

"Mommy and Daddy like him," the girl said, meeting Malisa's curious gaze. "How much fun can that be?"

There was a moment of pause as Anitra and Malisa reflected on their sister's comment. And then both women burst out laughing heartily.

Anitra nodded. "Like we said, been there, done that!"

Malisa shook her head as she returned to the warmth

of her fleece coverings. "I'm going to sleep so Santa won't skip me this year."

"I think Santa brought you your gift already," Anitra said as she climbed back into her own bed. "He's over six feet tall, employed, educated, and has the body of a Mandingo warrior. The only question is, are you going to keep him or return him for an exchange?"

Malisa grinned as she pulled the covers up beneath her chin. Her thoughts wandered momentarily. She had thoroughly enjoyed Gabriel's company. The man had incredible presence, and Malisa liked a man who commanded attention by simply stepping into a room. He'd also been sensitive to her situation, allowing his jokes about her predicament to stay between the two of them, and the man had had many jokes.

But she liked his sense of humor. In fact, there was much about Gabriel that she liked. And even more that she wanted to learn about the man. She sensed that when she was completely educated with the ins and outs of Gabriel Whitman, she would not be disappointed.

Mulling over her sister's query, her grin widened even farther. "Sister dear," she said finally, "something tells me that Mr. Whitman is definitely a keeper."

Gabriel stood in the doorway of his son's bedroom, taking one last look at the sleeping boy. Quiet had finally consumed their home, his son having finally settled down for the evening. Trey lay sprawled across his bedspread, earplugs in his ears as he snored softly. He'd fallen asleep fully clothed, and knowing that his son's mother would be thoroughly annoyed by that fact, Gabriel opted to leave the youngster be.

Peering out the large bay window across the room, Gabriel saw that the falling snow had begun to cling to the landscape, a cushion of bright white decorating the tree limbs and grass. It would make for a beautiful Christmas morning.

He eased the door closed and moved down the hallway to his bedroom. Behind his own door, Gabriel undid the buttons on his shirt and pulled the garment off. He flexed his muscles as he tossed the top across a wingback chair that decorated the room. Moving to the desk and his computer, he settled down into the leather chair, switching the appliance on.

Before long, he was logged onto the Internet. Two clicks and the Google Web page filled the screen. He typed Malisa Ivey's name into the search engine and pushed ENTER. Sixteen seconds later, he was presented with a list of over six hundred fifty-five thousand entries. At the top of the page was the Web site link for the restaurant Sweet Tea and Grits.

An hour later, Gabriel had perused more pages and read as many articles about the renowned chef and bakery artist. Well respected in her field, Malisa Ivey had made quite a name for herself in the food industry.

Gabriel was surprised to discover that not only did she have a very successful restaurant in Asheville, North Carolina, but also one in Manhattan and another in Washington, DC. Malisa hosted two cooking shows on the Food Network, was the author of fifteen cookbooks, and was launching a new magazine called *Malisa Ivey's Good Eats.*

He was also intrigued to discover that the woman had homes in Tuscany, Italy; Lake Luzerne, New York; and Santa Barbara, California. In addition, she was an avid reader; loved to water ski and snorkel; and had dated a celebrity or two, the last being a star forward for the Miami Heat basketball team.

Every new photo that he found of the woman was even more intriguing than the last. The camera loved everything about her. Malisa Ivey looked like a top model for *Vogue*.

Gabriel was half tempted to print a few out when there was a knock on his bedroom door and his ex-wife pushed her way inside.

"Am I interrupting anything?" Delores Winn said, her tone sugary sweet. She didn't bother to wait for an invitation before entering the room abruptly.

Gabriel looked from her to his computer and back again as he pressed the machine's OFF button and shut the unit down.

"What's wrong, Delores?" he asked, fighting to keep his annoyance out of his tone.

Easing her way into the room, she closed the door behind her. "Nothing," she said as she struck a seductive pose, batting her eyelashes at him. "I just wanted to wish you Merry Christmas and say good night is all."

Gabriel nodded. There was no missing his ex-wife's intentions as she sauntered to the middle of the room and dropped down onto the edge of his king-sized bed. Delores was wearing lingerie, a see-through peekaboo negligee, the sole purpose of which was to tempt, tease, and thrill. It fit her nicely, and Gabriel would have been lying if he didn't admit to appreciating his ex-wife's well-toned body, melon-sized breasts, and dancer legs. But appreciating her from a distance was all Gabriel intended to ever do.

The chore was made even more challenging as Delores leaned back on her elbows and lifted her legs off the floor, gliding the manicured toes of her right foot up the length of his left calf. The woman drew the length of her fingers between her cleavage and smiled seductively in his direction.

Shaking **his** head, Gabriel blew a deep sigh. He had grown tired of Delores's antics while they'd still been married. The two had met in college, at the University of North Carolina–Chapel Hill. Delores had been a sophomore, Gabriel a freshman. The woman had been a vulture the way she'd hooked her claws into him and had refused to let go.

Trey had been born just weeks before his graduation, and to satisfy both sets of parents and preserve the family honor everyone kept bullying him about, he'd married the child's mother. Even as they'd stood in front of the justice of the peace at the county clerk's office, Trey cradled in Delores's arms, Gabriel had known he was making the mistake of a lifetime.

For ten years he had tried to make sense of it, to do the right thing, and no matter what he did or tried to do, Delores had never been happy. And the more unhappy Delores was, the more she tried to ruin everyone else's good time. Eventually, Gabriel knew that the very best thing he could ever do for his son, and the child's mother, was to file for divorce, fight for joint custody of his son, and write Delores a sizeable settlement check. Even his mother, who had never had a negative word for anyone, had pushed him to put his marriage to rest and rid all of the family from the misery that was Delores Winn.

And even now, almost five years later, Delores remained intent on making their lives as miserable as she could possibly manage. He met her gaze and shook his head vehemently.

"That was very nice of you, Delores. You have a good night now," he said as he rose from his seat, crossed to the other side of the room, and swung the bedroom door wide open. "Merry Christmas."

The woman's expression shifted from coquettish to venomous, her stare abrasive enough to cut ice. Her tone was harsh as she voiced her displeasure. "You don't have to be so hostile about it, Gabriel. It is Christmas and we were married. It's not like our being together would hurt anything."

He didn't bother to respond, the expression on his face voicing his displeasure. He had no intentions of having casual sex with his ex-wife, no matter how much temptation she tried to throw his way. She persisted before he finally said, "I'm sorry, Delores, but it's not going to happen."

She lay back against the mattress and spread her legs, her hand cupping her crotch. "It's Christmas, Gabriel. Come get you some Christmas pudding," she said, trying to entice him to her.

Gabriel grimaced, the involuntary muscle reflex moving Delores to frown, her ire rising. He bit his tongue, willing himself not to say how he really felt about her offer of her holiday treat. Closing his eyes, he took a deep breath and counted to five. Opening them again, he focused his gaze on the opposite wall behind her head, not wanting to meet the woman's raging stare.

"Let's not fight, Delores," he said finally. "I don't want to ruin Trey's holiday. Please don't make me regret allowing you to stay the night so that you can see your son open his gifts in the morning. You can give me a hard time if you want, but it's still not too late for you to go home. It's your choice."

Delores jumped off the bed in a huff. She stopped short in the entranceway, her eyes narrowed to thin, angry slits. "When all you have is your hand, you'll wish you had some of this," she hissed, and then she stormed down the hall to the guest room. Once Gabriel heard the door slam shut, he closed his own and locked it behind him.

Chapter 5

Morning sunshine was gleaming off the bright white landscape outside the oversized window. The light pouring into the room pulled Gabriel from a deep slumber. He'd rested well when he'd finally drifted off to sleep, and as he stretched his body against the mattress, he felt completely renewed.

He glanced at the digital clock on the nightstand. Noting that it was almost nine o'clock in the morning, he smiled. Years earlier, Trey would have had the whole house up at the crack of dawn to see what Santa Claus had brought him. Since he'd become a teen, it took an act of nature to move him from his bed before the noontime hour.

Sitting up, Gabriel leaned his naked torso back against the headboard. He reached for his iPhone and pushed the speed dial to access his only child. Gabriel Whitman the Third answered on the fourth ring, sleep still tinting his words.

"Huh?"

"Merry Christmas!" Gabriel said cheerfully.

"Merry Christmas, Dad," the boy answered with far less enthusiasm. "What time is it?"

"Time for you to get up out of that bed. I'm sure we both need to get downstairs to run interference between your aunt and your mother."

Trey laughed. "I hope one of 'em's cooking pancakes and bacon. I'm hungry!"

"You just woke up. How can you be hungry?"

"I was hungry in my sleep."

"I just bet you were, kiddo! Well, brush your teeth, toss some clothes on, and meet me down in the kitchen."

"Hey, what did Santa get me for Christmas?" Trey asked smugly. "Is it worth getting up for?"

Gabriel shook his head. "I actually don't think he got you anything. I got a letter from one of the elves, something about you being a spoiled brat and not deserving Christmas this year."

"I'm thinking that elf was writing about the wrong Gabriel Whitman. He might have been thinking of the other one, Gabriel *Junior*. Like always, Gabriel *the Third* has been perfect this year."

Gabriel laughed. "Get up, kid!"

"Love you, too, Dad!"

As the line disconnected, Gabriel shook his head. He and his son had a wonderful relationship. Although he and Delores had joint custody, Trey had moved in with him just after his twelfth birthday. Preteen angst had made him difficult to deal with, and Gabriel had decided that a firm paternal hand had been in the boy's best interest. Delores had balked the first few months, finally yielding when Trey's grades had gone up and his disposition had shifted to the right side of pleasant. Now Gabriel balanced Trey wanting to be a teen, doing what teens weren't supposed to be doing, and spending quality time with his mother when the opportunities presented themselves.

As a thought crossed his mind, Gabriel redialed his son.

"I'm up! I swear I am!" Trey said, laughing.

Gabriel laughed with him. "I just had a quick question for you. I was thinking about inviting a friend of mine to the house this afternoon. Will you have a problem with that?"

The kid paused. "What's her name?" Trey asked, smirking into his cell phone.

Gabriel chuckled softly. "Her name's Malisa. Malisa Ivey."

"The chef? The one with the cooking show?"

"You know her?"

"Who doesn't know her, Dad? She's hot! And she cooks!"

The father laughed again. "I hear she does."

"Is she cooking Christmas dinner?"

"No, Trey. She's our guest. Your aunt Naomi is cooking dinner. And I'm sure she's already started on it by now."

"Okay."

"So you won't mind?"

"No. I think it's cool. I'll get to take a picture with her so I can show the guys at school, right?"

Gabriel shook his head. "Good-bye, Trey!"

"Hey, Dad!"

"Yes?"

"I have a quick question for you. What do you plan
to do about Mom? You know she's going to have a
problem with your new friend."

"If you hurry up and get downstairs for breakfast
and open your gifts, your mom will be gone by the
time Malisa gets here. So get a move on it."

Trey laughed. "You hope she's gone. I'll pray for
you, Dad. In fact, I'm saying my prayers right now!"

As his son disconnected the call, Gabriel thought
about his ex-wife's behavior the night before, and he
couldn't help but think he might need to say a prayer
or two of his own.

"Merry Christmas! Merry Christmas, everybody!"
Malisa chimed as she moved through the family room
and into the kitchen. She reached for an empty coffee
mug and the decanter of freshly brewed coffee that
rested on the center island.

"Merry Christmas, daughter," her father said as he
moved to her side and kissed her cheek.

"Santa got me an iPad!" Baylor gushed, her eyes
glued to the digital screen of her new device. "It's so
pretty!"

Malisa met her mother's gaze as the woman shook
her head.

"It was pretty expensive," the matriarch muttered,
cutting an eye in her husband's direction. "Santa should
have known better."

Malisa laughed. "Santa never did stuff like that
for us."

Her big brother nodded in agreement. "I remember one year all Santa brought us was a bag of oranges. You remember that year, don't you, Anitra?"

Anitra, who had just come into the room, shrugged her shoulders. "You boys got oranges. I got apples. Malisa, you weren't born yet."

"Y'all didn't have any complaints back then," Gattis said with a hearty chuckle. "Every one of you got the best of the best for the times."

Malisa was still grinning from ear to ear as she took a sip of her coffee. Her mother was eyeing her suspiciously.

"Malisa, you look like the cat that caught the canary. What are you cheesing about?"

Anitra interjected without being asked, "That man called. The phone ringing woke me out of a perfectly good sleep. And then, Mama," she said, her eyebrows raised high, "Malisa put on that syrupy-sweet voice she gets." Anitra dropped her hands to her hips and mimicked her sister, the pitch to her tone rising. "Gabriel! Merry Christmas! What a surprise!" Anitra tossed her sister a look, amusement painting her expression.

Malisa laughed. "I did not sound like that!"

"Yes, you did," Baylor interjected. "You sounded desperate."

"Now, I know I did not sound desperate. I have never been desperate for any man," Malisa stated, tossing a look of annoyance toward her baby sister.

Anitra continued, "And you know good and well you weren't surprised. You've been waiting for him to call you ever since he left last night. Lord knows what would have happened if you hadn't gotten your phone back. If Gabriel Whitman hadn't called, you would be having a fit. Might even be thinking about poisoning his New Year's cake."

"What happened to—" their brother Bryson started, joining Malisa at the counter.

Malisa stopped him midsentence, pointing her index finger in his direction. "Do not ask me about that man. All you want is season tickets to the games, and that is not going to happen."

Bryson smirked, raising his hands as if in surrender. "Sheesh! I was just asking. You don't have to be so sensitive."

"I'm not sensitive," Malisa said. "I just will not have you ruining my Christmas Day."

Their mother interjected. "I was quite impressed with Mr. Whitman. He's an outstanding young man."

"He'd make you a fine son-in-law, Etta," Malisa's father said, trying to instigate. A wide grin blessed the senior's face. "Yes, indeed!"

Malisa shook her head. "Please don't start, people! I barely know the man."

"And what time *are* you planning to see him today?" Anitra asked, much emphasis on the question.

Malisa's family turned to stare in her direction, everyone waiting with bated breath for her to answer.

She shook her head. "I don't recall saying I had plans to see Mr. Whitman any time soon," she said, trying to sound disinterested.

There was a pregnant pause, and then her siblings and parents all burst out laughing.

"If that's your story, baby girl, you stick with it," her father said. "It's none of our business anyway."

"Speak for yourself, Gattis," Etta stated. She cut her eyes at her daughter. "So, will you be here for dinner tonight or not?" her mother questioned.

Malisa blushed, color filling her cheeks with heat. She shrugged her shoulders. "Gabriel invited me to his house, so I may eat there. I'm not sure yet," she said.

A wry smile pulled at Miss Etta's lips. The matriarch crossed her arms over her chest as she continued to eye her daughter. She hadn't missed the looks that had passed between Malisa and Gabriel when neither had thought anyone was watching. Every time Malisa had crossed the length of the room, Gabriel's stare had followed her footsteps. Her child had feigned disinterest, but her face had been flush with color, her eyes skirting briefly toward the table each time she stole a glance in the man's direction.

Miss Etta had watched them both with much interest. There was definitely something about Gabriel that she and everyone else had liked. From their brief conversation, she'd gleaned enough information to know that he'd make a good catch for a young woman if she were so inclined. Miss Etta mused that Malisa might actually be so inclined with a little motherly prodding in the right direction. Her smile widened as she nodded her head slowly, a low chuckle easing past her lips.

"My people, my people," she chorused softly, the rest of the family chuckling among themselves.

"What?" Malisa queried, curious to know what her mother found so amusing.

This time Miss Etta shrugged. "Not a thing," she said, waving her head from side to side. She set her cup onto the countertop, cutting a quick eye at her husband, who was eyeing his family curiously, just taking it all in. The man could tell exactly what his wife was thinking, and if his daughter didn't, she was surely going to be in for one big surprise.

Malisa looked from one parent to the other, then cleared her throat and changed the subject. "Isn't it Christmas? Don't we have some presents to open?"

Chapter 6

The drive to the Whitman family estate took longer than Malisa anticipated. The roadways were a challenge with the light snow and ice that had come during the night and early morning.

The night before, as her parents' holiday gathering had wound down, her brothers had driven to the restaurant to retrieve her personal items and her four-wheeled vehicle, saving her the trouble of having to do so before going to meet Gabriel.

Malisa was excited at the prospect of seeing the man again. They'd spoken on the telephone for almost an hour before he'd been pulled away by his family. Speaking with him had reminded her of just how much she'd enjoyed his company the night before. It had also brought back the memory of his kiss, his lips still feeling like they were burning against her forehead. She took a deep breath, air catching in her chest at the memory of his touch.

Pulling onto Hilltop Road, Malisa couldn't help but be impressed by the large estate that loomed in the distance. The home was renowned in the Asheville area, having been built by John Sprunt Hill, whose family had been benefactors and board members of the University of North Carolina for over one hundred years. The prestigious patron had founded North Carolina's largest bank and had built the illustrious Carolina Inn in Chapel Hill.

Much had been written in the local newspapers about the renovations the massive Tudor Revival–style home had undergone since Gabriel Whitman had acquired it. Malisa had put a bid in for the catering job when he'd had his housewarming to showcase the meticulous restoration, but she'd been outmaneuvered by an overly enthusiastic new kitchen in the area.

For what the family had asked for, Malisa knew her competition had seriously underestimated his costs for the project. She'd been unwilling to do so, not even for the recognition. At the time, it would not have made for good business, and she'd been too focused on doing what was in her growing company's best interest.

She maneuvered her Ford Expedition into the parking area of the massive driveway and shifted the transmission into park. Stepping out of the vehicle, she took in the views before her. The home sat on seven acres of immaculately manicured land. It looked as if every tree and bush had been perfectly designed to complement the home's stone and stucco façade.

Malisa's attention was drawn to the front of the home and the large front door that had opened. Gabriel stepping out of the entrance, waving excitedly in her direction, made her smile, a full grin blossoming across her face. She waved back, then reached into the backseat of her vehicle for her contribution to her host's holiday meal.

"Merry Christmas!" the man chimed, meeting her midway. He wrapped his arms around her shoulders and gave her a welcoming hug. The soft scent of her perfume tickled his nostrils. He was suddenly distracted, consumed with thoughts of her small waistline, her curves, and the length of leg that stood in fire-engine-red rubber boots.

His grin was wide and full, complementing the deep dimples that filled his dark cheeks. Malisa found herself wanting to linger in the embrace, but she stepped away when a teenaged version of Gabriel stepped out to greet her.

"Hey! I'm Trey," Gabriel's son said, his enthusiasm painted on his face.

"Hi, Trey. My name's Malisa."

"I love your show. I watch it all the time," the young man said excitedly.

Malisa's eyebrows rose as she smiled. "Do you? Well, thank you very much." She extended the large plate in her hand toward the young man. "I wanted to thank you and your father for inviting me, so I baked you both a cake. It's one of my favorite desserts," she said as she handed him the covered dish.

Trey bubbled with excitement. "Hey, do you think you and I could take a picture together with it? The guys at school will bust!"

Malisa laughed. Gabriel shook his head.

"Trey, do you think we can let our guest inside the house first? It is cold out here, son."

Trey nodded, gesturing with his head for Malisa to

follow him inside. Gabriel's arm was still wrapped around her shoulders as he guided her into his home.

"This is beautiful," Malisa said as she took in the expanse of woodwork and ornate details of the home's interior.

"Thank you. I'm very proud of it."

"You should be. You've done a beautiful job."

Gabriel nodded, a slight blush blossoming across his cheeks. "Trey and I were back in the family room," he said, his hand cupping her elbow. He paused for a moment, his voice dropping to a loud whisper. "I hope you won't be uncomfortable, but Trey's mother is still here. She's been saying she's going to leave for the last hour, but we haven't been able to get rid of her."

Malisa smiled, meeting his gaze. "I'm sure I won't be, as long as I'm not intruding on your time together."

He shook his head vehemently. "Not at all. It's like I told you over the telephone, she is only here for Trey. We try not to shuffle him back and forth between us over the holidays, so she stayed here last night so she could see him open his presents this morning, but she's headed to her mother's house this afternoon. My sister's been running interference to keep us from killing each other." He chuckled softly.

Malisa shook her head, wondering what she might be getting herself into. She followed as he led the way to the rear of the home. Stepping through a wide entrance into an expanse of space, Malisa was completely taken by the massive chef's kitchen that sat adjacent to the family room. The off-white cabinetry accented by maple-toned flooring, a coffered ceiling, and top-of-the-line stainless-steel appliances was a dream come true for any cook. Her wide-eyed expression did little to hide her excitement.

"Do you like it?" Gabriel asked as he studied her intently.

"It's divine!" Malisa exclaimed. "How could you not love it?" she said, moving in the direction of the large center island.

The woman standing at the kitchen stove greeted her warmly. "You should have seen what he wanted to put in here," she said, smiling warmly at Malisa. "It's a good thing he had a great interior designer, thank you very much!" The woman took a slight bow.

Malisa laughed. "Hi, I'm Malisa," she said, extending her hand to a female version of Gabriel. "And I need to hire you to do some work at my house."

The other woman nodded. "Anytime, Malisa, and I'm Naomi, Gabriel's little sister. It's nice to finally meet you. Gabriel and Trey have been talking about you all morning. We even watched your show on holiday desserts this morning. I was tempted to try those chocolate bourbon cookies. They looked so easy."

Trey interjected, holding the cake tray out in front of him, "Malisa made me a cake."

Gabriel scoffed. "Um, that was made for *us,* thank you very much."

Trey rolled his eyes skyward. "You say tomato, I say tomahto!"

Naomi took the tray from the boy's hands. "I'm sure this will be better than anything I could have cooked." The woman peeked beneath the plastic cover. "Mmmm!" she hummed.

Malisa nodded. "It's a seven-layer pineapple cake

with a coconut and buttercream frosting," she said. She met Gabriel's gaze and smiled sweetly.

"When did you have time to whip that little concoction up?" he asked, his own mouth lifting into a wide smile. "I know you were tied up yesterday," he said smugly.

She returned his smirk. "I baked it this morning after I got your invitation. I didn't want to come empty-handed."

Naomi was eyeing the two of them, amusement filling her face at the repartee between her brother and his new friend. There was no denying the attraction between the two as they bantered back and forth.

From the doorway, a loud cough interrupted the laughter. Delores cleared her throat loudly as she made her way into the room. Malisa smiled as the woman's stare wafted from the top of her head to the bottom of her feet and back up again.

Delores moved to Gabriel's side, sliding one arm around his waist as she pressed her other hand to his chest. "Gabriel, aren't you going to introduce me?" she said.

Taking a deep breath, Gabriel stepped out of her grasp, moving to the other side of the island. "Trey, why don't you introduce your mother to my friend?" he said, his eyes meeting Malisa's, an apology shining in his eyes.

Trey moved to the spot his father had just vacated, dropping a heavy arm against his mother's shoulder. Malisa couldn't help but feel as if this were a dance the two men had done many times before.

The boy smiled. "Malisa, this is my mother, Delores Winn. Ma, this is Malisa Ivey."

Delores lifted the ends of her mouth in a slight smile. She cut her eyes at Gabriel before settling her stare back on Malisa.

"It's very nice to meet you," Malisa said politely.

There was a pregnant pause, Delores saying nothing for a moment. "Same here," she finally muttered. "Do you live here in Asheville?" Delores asked, feigning interest.

Malisa nodded. "Asheville is home for me. Do you? Live here, I mean."

Delores's eyes widened. She ignored Malisa's curiosity, turning her attention to Gabriel. "Well, I guess I'll be leaving. Gabriel, I'll call you and Trey later." She lifted her hand in a quick wave. "Naomi, hon, I'll give you a call and we'll make plans to get together sometime soon. Okay?"

Delores turned abruptly, almost rushing out the door.

Naomi shook her head, muttering under her breath as she leaned toward Malisa. "Now, she knows damn well she is not going to call me and we are not going to get together. She can pretend we're best buddies if she wants to, but I will hurt her feelings here this afternoon!"

Gabriel shook a finger at his sister. "Be nice, please." He rested his eyes on Malisa. "Malisa, if you'll excuse me for a minute. Trey, come say good-bye to your mother," he said, gesturing for the boy to follow his lead.

Trey tossed Malisa a deep smile.

In the distance, Malisa and Naomi could hear the unhappy murmurings between Gabriel and his ex-wife. Clearly, Delores was not happy about Malisa being there.

Naomi laughed loudly. "Ignore her," she said, not

bothering to drop her voice. "That woman will get right on your nerves if you let her."

"I didn't mean to cause any friction for anyone."

"You haven't. We're all glad you're here. Me especially. It's been a long time since my brother brought anyone home. I just wish my mother were here to meet you."

Naomi noted Malisa's confused gaze. "Mom and Pop are traveling through Europe, a twelve-city tour. It was Gabriel's gift to them. They celebrated their fiftieth wedding anniversary this year, and it's the first vacation our father has been willing to take since forever. Mom really wanted to go."

"That's so exciting," Malisa responded.

Naomi smiled. "Trust me when I tell you that Gabriel dating someone is even more exciting."

Malisa laughed. "I don't know if you can define what we're doing as dating. Not yet, anyway."

Naomi nodded. "Well, if nothing else, him inviting you here for Christmas is a good start."

Malisa nodded her head in agreement. She liked Gabriel's sister, and his son. She sensed that she and Naomi would soon be fast friends. Her instincts also told her that she and Delores Winn would not be, and from the obvious disagreement still flowing from the front of the family's home, Delores was clearly no fan of hers either.

As if reading her mind, Naomi gestured for her attention. "Don't pay them any mind. This is typical Delores behavior. The woman is never happy, and she is a complete monster when she thinks Gabriel is. None of us can stand the beast!"

Malisa heaved a deep sigh as Naomi quickly

changed the subject. "What do you know about making gravy?" she asked as she opened the oven door to peer at the large turkey cooking inside. "'Cause I don't have a clue."

Malisa laughed. She reached for the apron that Naomi was passing to her. "I think I can do gravy," she said, turning her attention to what she loved best.

Gabriel savored the last bite of his pineapple cake, the decadent flavors flooding his taste buds. His eyes rolled skyward as he purred his satisfaction. "Mmmmm . . . this is so good!" he murmured, using his finger to sweep up the last remnants of buttercream icing. As he pulled his finger into his mouth and sucked it slowly, Malisa felt a shimmer of energy cut through her abdomen.

Shaking her head to stall the sensation, she smiled brightly, her smug expression saying that she'd told him so. "I'm glad that you enjoyed it, Mr. Whitman."

He nodded, meeting her stare with his own intense gaze. "You outdid yourself. I feel very special."

They sat together in his private office. Gabriel leaned forward in his seat, dropping his saucer to the coffee table before them. Malisa sat at his side, nibbling on a chocolate bourbon ball that she and Naomi had made together.

"I can't believe my sister had you cooking. You were supposed to be our guest."

"Your sister and I had a great time. It was a lot of fun."

Gabriel shifted his body closer to hers. "I'm glad you came. I'm sorry we got off to such a rough start, though," he said, referring to his ex-wife and the drama that followed her like a shadow.

Malisa shrugged her shoulders. She'd been only slightly bothered by the woman and she said so, questioning the relationship between the two of them. "How long have you two been divorced?" she asked.

"Five, almost six years now."

"I get the impression that she hasn't truly moved on yet. Maybe she's still hoping the two of you will get back together. How about you? Have you moved on?"

Gabriel took a deep breath. He dropped back against the cushions, resting on the wealth of pillows that decorated the upholstered furniture. "I can only speak for myself, but I assure you, Malisa, I am completely over my marriage to Delores. There is absolutely nothing between us other than our commitment to our son."

"I don't get the impression that your ex-wife would agree with you," Malisa said.

Gabriel blew a deep sigh, warm breath washing over his full lips. He turned to stare at Malisa. "If someone had asked me two days ago about starting a new relationship, I would have told them that I had no interest in doing so. I've had a few dates since I divorced, but to maintain peace for my son, I've avoided getting serious with anyone. In fact, I was really determined to *not* get involved with anyone until after Trey turns eighteen and graduates from high school.

"I didn't think it would be fair of me to pull anyone into my mess, and I know that dealing with my ex can be extremely difficult." He paused, his gaze dropping down to her manicured fingers. "I know that Delores and I still have some issues between us, but that is not a relationship I'm interested in going back to. I have no love for my ex-wife. Absolutely none at all," he emphasized as he reached for her hand.

He clasped her fingers between his own. "Like I said last night, I really like you, Malisa. I would like to get to know you better. I'm curious to know where we might take this, so I hope Delores hasn't scared you off."

Malisa dropped into deep thought. Men with baby-mama drama were at the top of her list of things she didn't want in her life. She was also a woman who required a lot of attention, and she didn't take kindly to any man who was distracted by a family that took that attention away from her. Kids and ex-wives tended to need even more attention than she did.

But there was something about Gabriel that excited her. The man was intoxicating, his sex appeal leaving her drunk with wanting. Heat rushed through her, and she knew that nothing and no one, not even a bitter ex-wife, could stall the desire that had surged with a vengeance and had her wanting Gabriel Whitman the way she'd never wanted any man before him.

Malisa smiled, lifting her eyes back to his. "No, Delores doesn't scare me."

However, wanting you scares me to death, she thought to herself, fighting not to say the words out loud. She studied the long length of his fingers. His hands were slightly calloused, feeling like a working-man's hand. She was surprised as she drew her index finger across the weathered flesh.

Gabriel read her mind. "I have an extensive car collection. I like to spend my time working on the engines. My hands tend to get beat up a bit. It's probably time for me to get myself a good manicure."

Malisa laughed. "You have great hands." She lifted her eyes to his as she pulled his palm to her lips and kissed the center of it. There was a lingering moment when neither of them spoke one word, the two of them focused on the wave of wanting that seemed to wash over them.

Gabriel pressed his hand to the side of her face, his fingers caressing her profile. His touch was heating her too quickly, and Malisa was suddenly in desperate need of cool air to blow between them. Her heartbeat thundered beneath her breast. Her palms began to perspire. She pulled her hand from his, brushing the rise of moisture against her black silk pants. She spoke his name, then paused, words catching in her throat as her thoughts suddenly became muddled.

His name on her lips suddenly had Gabriel's insides melting. There was no denying that something was brewing between them. Gabriel felt it intensely, the urgency of it lengthening a rock-hard erection in his slacks. Despite wanting to maintain a semblance of control, Malisa's presence reminded him that he was wholeheartedly a hot-blooded male.

He got to his feet, hoping to hide the telltale sign of his desire. He moved to the other side of the room to stare out the windows that overlooked his rear yard. The nearness of her was making him think of nothing but pure, unadulterated pleasure, and he desperately needed to regain sense of his mind and his body.

Outside, there was no evidence of the Olympic-sized swimming pool that connected to the back patio. Snow covered the pool's top and the grass, a winter-white carpet of cold fluff decorating the landscape. As Gabriel focused on the lingering flakes that still blew outside, Malisa moved behind him, drawing her hand against his lower back. Her touch surprised him, and he closed his eyes for a quick minute, the sensation of her caress like a bolt of lightning flooding through him. His erection hardened even more, and Gabriel was unable to stall the hunger that seemed to suddenly consume him. His gaze washed over Malisa's thoughtful expression.

Moving in front of him, Malisa wrapped one of his arms around her waist, and then she wrapped the other, moving him to clasp his fingers together at the small of her back. She snuggled her pelvis tight to his. Feeling his desire as it stirred with a mind of its own between them brought a coy smile to her face. Gabriel smiled back, his seductive stare stirring a longing deep in the core of her feminine spirit. She lifted her arms around his neck and pulled him to her, reaching up on her tiptoes to lift her mouth to meet his. She wanted to be kissed, and she wanted Gabriel to kiss her right then and there.

Needing no coaxing, he held her tightly, his large hands skating the length of her back and buttocks. His fingers curved against the round of her bottom as he pulled her tighter against himself, feeling the steel between his legs pulsing against the soft core of her pubis. His mouth danced like silk against hers, his tongue snaking past the line of her teeth. Her breath was sweet, her tongue warm and darting. The kiss was intense and deep, and it was like nothing either of them had ever experienced before. Gabriel couldn't deny that he wanted more.

The duo was so lost in the embrace that they didn't hear the door opening behind them. It wasn't until Trey cleared his throat, calling for his father's attention, that they pulled away, widening the space between them. Gabriel held her gaze for a moment, something he didn't understand shifting through his emotions. She smiled and nodded her understanding, sensing that she, too, was feeling what he was feeling.

Gabriel turned toward his son, who stood in the entranceway with a smug grin on his face. "Yes, Trey?"

"Sorry to interrupt, but Mom's blowing up both of our cell phones. She says it's important and that you need to call her right now."

"Why didn't she call the house phone?"

"Aunt Naomi took it off the hook. Something about not wanting to be annoyed on Christmas Day."

Gabriel took a deep breath. His gaze fell back on Malisa as he studied her intently. He leaned to give her one last kiss, a quick peck against her closed mouth. Then he politely excused himself and followed his son out of the room.

Chapter 7

It was almost three o'clock in the morning, and Gabriel was wide-eyed and awake, unable to stop thinking about Malisa Ivey. Thoughts of the woman still had him hard, his desire refusing to subside. He heaved a deep sigh as he cupped a heavy palm over his crotch, adjusting the length of himself in his briefs.

Malisa had said her good-byes shortly after he'd finished his telephone conversation with Trey's mother. Delore's intrusion had left him annoyed and frustrated, most especially because she hadn't wanted him for anything important. He had also sensed that Malisa had not been happy about the interruption either. But then why should she be? No woman wanted drama at the onset of a new relationship, and he certainly didn't want Malisa to have to deal with his mess. His son had been the only one to find any humor in the unnecessary drama. Gabriel heaved a deep sigh.

Still thinking about Malisa and the look in her eyes when she stared at him, the way her lips curved into a coquettish smile, had him breathing heavily. His member was throbbing for release, the engorged organ tenting the fabric of his briefs. He gently caressed the line of his penis beneath the cotton undergarment.

Thinking about the beautiful woman had him horny as hell, unable to shake the yearning from his mind. Gabriel slid his hand into the front opening, wrapping his hand around the length of his manhood. He gripped the shaft with a tight fist and squeezed. His fingers gently stroked the sensitive underside, toying with his testicles. With his other hand, he adjusted the pillows beneath his head, reclining back to make himself more comfortable. His legs sprawled open as he pulled his erection free, beginning to slowly stroke the length of hard flesh.

With his eyes closed, he thought of the beautiful woman and the kiss they'd shared, her lips sweetly dancing against his. She'd felt good in his arms, her softness molding nicely against his hard lines. Gabriel was stroking himself more vigorously, imagining Malisa's touch, her perfectly manicured nails caressing his flesh, teasing and taunting as she wrapped her delicate hands around his throbbing organ.

He fell into the fantasy, imagining himself making sweet love to her, teasing her sensibilities with his mouth as he drew a line of easy kisses in the inner curve of her neck, between the cleavage of her full breasts, his tongue lapping at her belly button. He imagined himself tasting her, his mouth meeting her flesh in an intimate kiss, pleasuring her most sensitive spot, Malisa pleading with him to never stop.

He imagined her riding the length of him, her petite frame rocking rhythmically against him. He wanted to feel her, to dance inside the softness that made her female. The wanting was intense, building with frenzy as he continued to pleasure himself. He rubbed himself harder and harder, images of Malisa flashing through his mind.

His ministrations became more urgent as he stroked himself more furiously, his fist flying up and down his shaft until his toes curled and his back arched. Then suddenly his legs trembled, and his buttocks tightened and clenched as a wave of intense pleasure washed over him. Gabriel stifled a cry as he climaxed, Malisa's name on the tip of his tongue.

Lying there, waiting for his breathing to return to normal and his body to stop quivering from aftershocks, Gabriel was completely focused on wanting to make Malisa Ivey his. Minutes passed before he finally reached for the box of tissue that rested on the nightstand, wiping the remnants of his orgasm from his fingers and palm. He readjusted himself back into his briefs.

He hoped Malisa was thinking about him as intensely as he was thinking of her. Malisa Ivey had his nose wide open, the stirrings in his spirit reminiscent of his first crush and love, only ten times stronger. It had been some time since any woman had him playing with himself as he imagined the two of them together. And although he knew there were many females in his little black book who would have been delighted to provide him with some sensual companionship, he suddenly couldn't imagine himself with any other woman but Malisa.

* * *

With most of her relatives gone, Malisa had slept alone in her parents' guest room. But she'd hardly slept, having tossed and turned most of the night. Gabriel Whitman had consumed every one of her thoughts. She'd fallen asleep thinking about the man, had dreamed about him, and he'd been the first thought that had come to her when she'd wakened.

The evening hadn't ended at all the way she'd wanted. His conversation with his ex-wife had been drawn out and frustrating. By the end of it, he'd clearly been perturbed, and the annoyance of it had spoiled his mood and their good time. It had also pissed her off, irking her one bad nerve, and Malisa had been reminded of all the reasons she'd sworn off men with baggage. By the time she'd said her good-byes, she'd been more than ready to leave.

After she'd wished him and his family a Merry Christmas and made her way back down the snow-covered roads to her parents' wintery retreat, she found herself wishing she was still with him, still lost in his embrace, his arms and lips still wrapped around her. She found herself wondering if she'd overreacted, if instead she should have stayed longer. She found herself yearning to have stayed just a wee bit longer, because once she'd left, she'd missed him like she had never missed any other man before.

Malisa rolled onto her back. The digital clock on the nightstand read five twenty-five. She needed to get up. She'd promised her mother that she'd go to the country club for an early morning swim and a water aerobics class, and then she needed to get to work. With Christmas Day having come and gone, her holiday was officially over. She needed to get the restaurant open and functioning for those intent on getting out and about for the after-holiday sales.

Swinging her legs off the side of the bed, she reached for her cell phone on the nightstand. She hoped that Gabriel had called or texted her, but there was nothing, her screen void of any new messages.

Thinking of the man suddenly had her hot with wanting, desire surging through her feminine core. She shook her head, wishing that Gabriel were there to put out the fire that was burning for some male attention. Malisa pressed her knees tightly together, trying to stall the shimmer of heat between her legs, moisture beginning to rise down in her core. Her nipples hardened beneath the T-shirt she wore, and she crossed her arms over her chest, tweaking the rock-hard candies beneath her palms.

None of it made an ounce of sense to her, she thought as she rose from the bedside and headed into the bathroom for a cooling shower. Just the mere thought of the man had her craving his touch.

Turning on the shower, Malisa dropped her T-shirt and panties to the floor, then stepped into the spray of lukewarm water. She closed her eyes, allowing the flow of water to rain down over her face and shoulders. The cooling liquid felt good against her skin, and she welcomed the flow that seemed to stall her sudden cravings.

Thinking of Gabriel yet again, Malisa found herself imagining the two of them in a shower together, her hands gliding suds over his hardened muscles. She couldn't stop herself from fantasizing about Gabriel's hands kneading and caressing her own sinewy muscles, teasing her flesh with each pass of his fingers.

She found herself lost in thought as she wished for those hands to glide between her thighs to stroke her most private place.

Malisa reached for the shower massager, lifting the instrument from its harness. Adjusting the water spray, she set the device to pulse, then aimed it at the apex of her crotch. The sensation was overwhelming as the spray danced against her clit, making her knees quiver uncontrollably. As Malisa manipulated the device over her body, she imagined every touch was Gabriel's touch.

She saw Gabriel in her mind's eye. Gabriel holding her hand. Gabriel stroking her hair. The lift of Gabriel's smile as he leaned in to kiss her lips. She imagined his hard, wide shoulders and broad chest, his thick neck, athletic legs, round behind, and the length of steel that had pressed against her when he'd held her touch. Every perverse thought of her and Gabriel together flashed like photographic images through her mind.

Malisa bit down on her bottom lip to keep from crying out with pleasure. Her head was thrown back against her shoulders as she strummed her clit, the spray of water tap-dancing over her sensitive flesh. She clutched her inner thigh with her other hand as the first wave of her contraction pulsed from deep inside her.

When her body erupted in pleasure, Malisa grabbed at the wall behind her to steady herself. The sensations swept over her spirit with a vengeance. As the tremors slowed down to a gentle pulse, Malisa knew that she wouldn't be fully satisfied until she could press her naked body against his and have Gabriel bring her to orgasm.

* * *

Gattis nuzzled his lips against Etta's neck one last time before lifting his naked body from the king-sized bed. The woman rolled to her side to watch him as he searched inside the walk-in closet for a suit and shirt to wear. Outside, the sky was still dark, no sign of a morning sun visible.

Sitting up, she swung her legs off the padded mattress, inching her buttocks to the edge of the bed. As Gattis moved back into the room, he eased his way to her side, posing in front of her. A wry smile pulled at Etta's full lips as she took in the magnificence of him. With abs that were still taut, a broad chest, and muscular arms indicative of physical strength, and thick, solid legs like the trunk of an ancient tree, her husband was an extraordinary specimen of a man.

Etta dropped her hands against his waist, pressing her mouth against the line of his belly button. When she trailed her tongue into the hollow sink, Gattis inhaled swiftly, a current of energy surging into every muscle.

"If you keep that up, woman, we're not going to get out of this bed today," the man said, his tone husky.

Etta chuckled softly. "We both have things to do today. We'll get up."

"We really don't have to, you know."

"And what would we do if we stayed?"

Gattis pushed her gently, easing her back against the mattress. He lifted his body above hers, kneeling as his knees cupped the sides of her thighs. His manhood surged eagerly between them. He leaned to kiss her mouth, both hands palming the lush tissue of her full breasts.

"I think we can find something to do to entertain ourselves with," he murmured, his lips still caressing hers.

Etta purred. "Mmm. That sounds tempting, but you have some paperwork to wrap up, and I need to get to my swim class before I go help Malisa at the restaurant."

"Did Malisa ask you for help, or are you doing that mommy thing that you do? Gettin' all up in your children's business?"

Etta rolled her eyes, pushing a palm against the man's chest to move him off of her. Gattis rolled back against the bed.

"Gattis, I do not get up in our children's business. Sometimes, though, they need a little motherly advice. Like right now, Malisa is already having issues with Gabriel." Etta's thoughts raced back to the conversation she'd overheard between her daughters, Malisa sharing details of her time with Gabriel and his son, and specifically her encounter with Gabriel's ex-wife.

It had been obvious from the look on her daughter's face that she was quite smitten with the man. It was also clear that she was frustrated about something she chose not to share, and her mother didn't need to be a rocket scientist to figure out what that was. "Mark my words, Gattis, Malisa is going to need my advice," Etta pronounced.

Gattis shook his head. "Sometimes our children have to learn things on their own, Etta."

Etta heaved a deep sigh. "Malisa needs to focus on something other than business all the time. She already has a successful career but that is not going to keep her warm at night. She's met a nice man who will not only be good to her but who will also be good *for* her. She needs to be thinking about her future and how to make that happen."

"And that's for Malisa to decide, Etta, not us. The problem our kids have is you trying to dictate what they should and shouldn't be doing."

"The biggest problem with our children is they want to treat us like we are past our prime and need to be put out to pasture. They forget that we still know what we're talking about," Etta concluded.

"That's not true, Etta."

"And you're doing a good job of trying to make me feel obsolete too. I've got a few good years left in me, Gattis Ivey."

Her husband laughed, moving to kiss her cheek. "Well, I certainly hope so."

"In fact," Etta said, nuzzling her body against his, "why don't we start the day late so I can show you what I've got left."

Gattis nuzzled her back. "Now, see, that's just what I wanted to hear. You can worry about them kids later."

Chapter 8

Waiting for the water aerobics class to begin, Etta sat on the side of the athletic club's pool, Lycra pretending to be a bathing suit stretched over her ample frame. Much to her chagrin, her daughters made her do this each week, and she imagined that in her new bathing suit, a Lane Bryant half-priced special with a bold floral print, she was probably a sight to behold.

From her perspective, and the one that looked back at her from the club's many mirrors, her thighs were flapping thick like two sides of ham, her expansive chest pushed up and out like large watermelons threatening to burst free and flap in the wind. She had curves and then some, and it was all that extra somethin'-somethin' that kept her husband begging two or three times each week.

Malisa seemed to read her mind. "That new swimsuit looks good on you, Mama. I saw the way Daddy was eyeing you before we left," she teased.

Miss Etta smiled ever so slightly. Her focus was elsewhere as her daughter made small talk.

Dark shades covered her eyes so no one would know who or what she was watching. But Malisa knew her mother had her eyes on someone's child doing something he or she didn't have any business doing. What each of the children hoped was that Miss Etta would not single them out to be disciplined, but instead would tell the tale to the child's parent as soon as Miss Etta could get to a telephone or, even worse, to their front doorstep.

On this particular day, Miss Etta had her eye on sixteen-year-old Jasmine Pines. Her youngest daughter, Baylor, and Jasmine had been best friends since forever, but they had fallen out with each other over Asheville High School's star quarterback. He was a big, beefy boy named Sanford James, and Miss Etta thought he resembled a chipmunk with his round, chocolate face and bubbled cheeks. Baylor had been hot to trot after some Sanford James.

Baylor hadn't been the first of her daughters to be guilty of lusting after some teenage boy who played ball on the football field and the basketball court. Malisa and Anitra both had acted the fool over some little boy pretending to be a man and not knowing a thing a real man needed to know. And just like with her older daughters, Miss Etta had put Baylor's raging hormones on ice, squashing any notion the girl may have had about overstepping the boundaries she and the judge had laid down for her.

Miss Etta could see that Jasmine needed a little more parental intervention, her behavior on the other side of the pool leaving much to be desired. The string bikini that was more string than fabric needed to be addressed as well. She heaved a heavy sigh, air rising from deep in her midsection and swelling through her chest before blowing hotly past her full lips. Miss Etta made a mental note to give the girl's mother a phone call as soon as she reached home later. She also voiced such out loud.

"Remind me to call Shirley Pines when we get back to the restaurant," she said to Malisa, gesturing in Jasmine's direction.

Malisa rolled her eyes skyward. "Mama, you need to leave that child alone. She is not hurting a soul. Let her have a good time."

Miss Etta cut her eye at her daughter. "One day you might have a daughter of your own, and then I will remind you of this conversation," she said.

Malisa laughed. "One day."

Her mother cut an eye in her direction. "Speaking of, how did your evening go with Gabriel? He's such a fine young man," she noted.

Malisa grinned broadly. "I had a very nice time. Thank you for asking."

"Even with his ex-wife?" Miss Etta questioned, her eyebrows raised ever so slightly.

Malisa shook her head. "Does anything ever get past you?"

Her mother laughed. "No."

The younger woman shrugged. "He's got some family issues, but they really aren't my concern."

"Don't you believe that," her mother responded. "His relationship with his child's mother will last until graduation and child support are finished and not one minute before. If you become involved with him, then his issues will be your issues."

Malisa paused to reflect on her mother's words. She

turned her focus to the clear blue water shimmering in the Olympic-sized pool. There was no denying that she'd been thinking the very thing her mother had spoken out loud. But wanting Gabriel had her ignoring any challenge that could potentially come between them. She twisted against the vinyl lounge chair, the plastic leather sticking to the flesh along the backs of her legs and across her shoulders. Her mother was still giving her the hundred-dollar version of her two cents.

Miss Etta sighed again, reaching to pull her bathing suit out of her posterior cavity, the material starting to rise up into her crack. She lifted her body up from her seat and threw herself into the pool with a large splash, quickly immersing herself beneath the icy water.

"Hot damn!" she cursed, swimming back to where Malisa now stood. "When are these people going to put some heat in this water?"

Malisa laughed. "You know it's cold for only the first few minutes. They'll have you sweating up a storm before you know it."

Miss Etta grunted, rolling her eyes. Before she could comment further, the familiar faces that made up the early morning class dropped into the water to join them.

Malisa and her mother both smiled and nodded their hellos as people began to greet them. Both women didn't miss that Irene Hill was the only one who didn't have anything to say, not even bothering to look in their direction. Miss Etta had had just about enough of Irene's rude behavior, and it wouldn't take much more for her to say so, she thought.

"Let me tell you a story," Miss Etta started, leaning against her daughter's shoulder. "Now, we done told you a dozen or more times about how your daddy and I met up, but I don't remember if I ever told you about me and Beau Hill."

Malisa shook her head. "No, I don't think you did."

"Well," the woman started. "Before I met and married Gattis, Beau Hill used to chase after me like a chubby kid chases cake. This was before he was married to Miss Irene over there." She gestured at the woman with her head and a raised eye. "Wasn't my fault old Beau was all worked up over me. I just had it going on like that!"

She grinned and winked at Malisa as she continued. "But it didn't take me long to figure out that Beau wasn't worth my energy, so I had to let him go. Hard! You would have thought I'd broken up with Irene the way she be actin'. The woman still burns hot with spite that I had him before she did!"

Malisa chuckled, her head waving from side to side. "And then you met Daddy?"

"That's right. See, what Beau had to offer didn't amount to more than a bland frankfurter with no bun. Two bites and you were done with it, the taste not even lingering against your tongue. I like a man who comes with the works: chili, spice, onion, and slaw. A man who leaves you wishing you had ordered just one more of him with a side of fries and a thick milkshake. Your daddy was like that, a full meal with leftovers!"

Malisa laughed heartily.

"And Gabriel Whitman, well, daughter, know it when I tell you, that man is an all-you-can-eat buffet special with free sweet tea and banana pudding for dessert. He'll keep you fed and fed well for a good long time," she said with a wink of her eye. "This is not an opportunity you want to pass up, Malisa."

She started to move toward the center of the pool as she tossed one last look in Irene's direction. "Irene's problem," Etta concluded, laughing softly as she propelled herself through the water, Malisa trailing behind her, "is, she needs to slip out and get herself a real meal instead of settling for that snack she's married to."

The kitchen was suddenly warmer than usual, and Malisa knew it had nothing to do with the heat wafting off the large, black burners or coming from inside the oven where fresh biscuits were starting to rise in their pan. Her temperature had risen with a vengeance the moment Gabriel and his son had walked into the restaurant for breakfast.

Since she'd first laid eyes on the man, every thought of him caused her temperature to rise, and this time was no exception. She shook the sensation, taking another deep breath. Her mother had greeted him, the older woman excited to race back to the kitchen to let Malisa know he was there and wanting a moment of her time.

After brushing her flour-stained hands against a clean dishtowel and double-checking her requisite apron, she made her way to his table, greeting the father and his son warmly.

"Good morning, you two! What brings you here so early in the morning?"

"Trey and I thought we'd come get a great breakfast this morning," Gabriel said, trying to contain the excitement in his tone.

Trey laughed. "And Dad wanted to see you!" the boy chimed teasingly.

Gabriel tossed his son a look, his head waving from side to side.

Malisa laughed. "Well, I'm glad you both did."

Just then, Brenna, the waitress on duty, arrived with pen and paper in hand to take their breakfast orders. After convincing them both to try her infamous breakfast casserole and sweet-potato biscuits, Malisa sat with them briefly, chatting easily about the previous day, Trey's gifts, and his plans for the New Year. When Brenna returned with orange juice, a carafe of hot coffee, and a basket of hot biscuits and pastries, Malisa politely excused herself and almost ran back to the security of her kitchen.

As she passed her mother, the woman chuckled softly. "Yes, yes, yes, daughter! A whole darn buffet!"

Malisa heaved a deep sigh as she turned the stove down low. She placed a cover on a pot of simmering grits, satisfied that they were thickening properly. She reached for her coffee, enjoying the last few sips remaining in the cup.

Anxious to take her mind off the man seated in her dining room, she sat down at her desk, pulling pen and paper in hand to make a list of things she wanted to accomplish during the week. As she sat pondering, her cousin Darryl came in through the back door. Contrition painted his expression as he lifted his hand in a slight wave.

When he'd first arrived for his shift, Malisa had reamed him good, still furious about her impromptu ride on Christmas Eve. After giving him a good piece of her mind, docking his pay, and threatening to send him straight to the unemployment line, her mother had interceded, reminding Malisa that Darryl wasn't the sharpest knife in the silverware drawer. The boy's saving grace was that Malisa was still flying high from having met Gabriel.

"You still mad at me, Malisa?" Darryl asked, his gaze flitting over the floor.

Malisa shook her head, gesturing in his direction with a ballpoint pen. "No," she said, a bright smile spreading across her face as she rose to her feet.

Darryl leaned in to kiss his cousin's cheek. "You know I'm sorry, right, Malisa?"

She nodded. "Yes, Darryl. Now you need to go help the girls out front so I can get some work done. I need to start prepping for the New Year."

Darryl nodded. "I went and got the box back like you said, and it was still sitting on the loading dock! It's in the van."

"Well, you need to bring it inside, please. Put it back in the bakery."

Darryl nodded, turning an about-face. He laughed warmly as he went out the door. "Malisa got locked in the box! Hahahaha!"

Malisa rolled her eyes skyward, still tempted to cut all ties with the kid.

From behind her, Gabriel's familiar voice chimed warmly. "Well, it was funny. You have to admit that."

With her hands perched atop the curve of her hips, Malisa spun around to face him, Gabriel having made his way into the kitchen area.

"You're starting early, I see."

He grinned broadly. "Figured I would get your day started on the right note."

She nodded. "Did you enjoy your breakfast?"

"I did," he said as he stepped in closer, moving his body against hers. "And since you're hiding back here in the kitchen, I figured I'd come get dessert myself. Your mother told me it would be all right." He eased an arm around her waist and pulled her to him. His seductive smile seared heat straight through her.

Malisa pressed her palms to his chest, clutching at the front of his T-shirt. Gabriel leaned in as if to kiss her, then paused, drawing back as he stared into her eyes. He did it a second time and then a third, moving Malisa to hold her breath in eager anticipation.

When he finally kissed her, his touch was easy and gentle, a light brushing of flesh against flesh. When he drew back, he hummed his appreciation. "That was very sweet," he whispered, leaning his forehead against hers as the two stood holding each other tight.

Malisa nodded. "You're going to make me burn my biscuits," she said after a few minutes. Stepping out of his arms, she hurried back to the ovens to peer inside.

Gabriel chuckled, leaning his back against the counter, his arms crossed over his chest. "So, do you plan to be here all day?" he queried, his expression eager.

As she lifted the pan of baked goods from the oven, setting it atop the counter, she met his questioning stare. "I was planning on it. I need to start prepping my New Year's orders. We're only open for breakfast and lunch this week, and then I need to be in the bakery during the afternoons."

"Can you play hooky?"

"I . . . well . . . it . . . ," she stammered, pondering whether she could change her schedule for an impromptu afternoon with the man who had her wishing she were buck naked beneath him on top of the stainless-steel counters. She took a deep breath. "What did you have in mind?" she finally managed to answer.

"Trey wants to go spend the afternoon with one of his friends, and I thought that maybe we could spend some time together after I dropped him off—that is, if you *want* to spend some time with me?"

Knowing that she *needed* to stay and work, despite *wanting* desperately to disappear with the man, had Malisa completely discombobulated. It was on the tip of her tongue to say so when her mother and sister both came into the kitchen, Anitra waving hello. Her sister's grin was all-knowing.

"Your sister and I can handle the restaurant," Miss Etta said as she pointed Anitra to the stove. "Go have yourself a good time!"

Gabriel laughed. "Thank you, Miss Etta."

Malisa's mother winked at the man, pushing her daughter toward the exit. "Go on, Malisa. You deserve a break. We've got this handled."

"But . . . but . . . ," Malisa stammered.

"But nothing, daughter," Miss Etta said, her sly grin pulling at the edges of her mouth. She leaned to whisper into Malisa's ear. "Go get you some buffet, child!"

Chapter 9

"Miss Etta's cool!" Trey chimed as the trio pulled out of the restaurant's parking lot.

Malisa laughed. "My mother definitely has her moments," she said.

"I like your mom," Gabriel interjected. "She reminds me of my own mother."

"Nana's cool, too," Trey agreed. The boy went back to texting on his iPhone.

With one hand on the steering wheel, Gabriel reached with his other to brush his fingers against the back of Malisa's forearm. He smiled sweetly. "I'm glad you could get away," he said.

Malisa nodded. "Me too," she whispered softly.

Two right turns and an extended pause at an intersection put them in front of a modest two-story home. As Gabriel pulled into the parking lot, a young man about the same age and size as Trey rushed out the door, waving excitedly.

Gabriel rolled down his window and waved back. "Did you have a good Christmas, Michael?" he asked.

Michael nodded. "Yes, sir. I got the Wii console and a few new games."

"Nice!" Gabriel chimed. The man looked over his shoulder as Trey jumped from the car, tote bag in hand.

"What's all that?" his father asked.

"Stuff, just in case."

"Just in case what?"

"In case I spend the night."

"I don't remember you asking anyone for permission to spend the night."

"Mom said I could."

Annoyance creased Gabriel's forehead as Trey stood at the car window waiting for his father to send him off to join his friend.

"Let me remind you," Gabriel started, his tone firm. "You live with me, Trey, and that means you need my permission, not your mother's. As your custodial parent, if something happens, I'm responsible."

The boy rolled his eyes skyward.

Gabriel's eyebrows arched high. "We'll discuss this later. I'll call and check on you this afternoon. Go have fun!"

Trey nodded, tossed Malisa a quick wave good-bye, and rushed to join his friend. The couple watched as the two boys greeted each other eagerly, then rushed back inside the home.

Gabriel cut his eye at Malisa before shifting the car in reverse and backing his way out of the drive.

Malisa smiled. "The joys of parenthood," she said, chuckling softly.

Gabriel laughed with her. "I'm sure it's not nearly so difficult when parents are on the same page," he said. He heaved a deep sigh. "But I don't want to spend the afternoon complaining. I've actually made plans for us, but is there anything special you'd like to do?" he asked.

Malisa shrugged, her shoulders pushing skyward. "I'm riding shotgun today, big guy. You're the party planner on this one, and you better make it good," she said teasingly.

Her new friend laughed. "Well, then," he said. "Since you put it like that!"

She grinned broadly. "You've left quite an impression, Mr. Whitman. I'd hate to see you crash and burn now, because I would have to talk badly about you."

Gabriel laughed heartily, his head tossed back against his shoulders. "Now I'm scared," he said. "I'm going to have to get it right, aren't I?"

"Yes, you are," Malisa answered. "Yes, you are!"

Minutes later, Gabriel pulled the car in front of one of the cutest log cabin homes Malisa had ever seen. The A-frame retreat was complemented by cedar tongue-and-groove logs, a rustic stone chimney, and a deep wraparound porch.

"This is adorable," Malisa chimed, her gaze skating over the details of the home's structure.

"My father and I built it. It was my very first house," Gabriel said proudly. "Dad and I cut and fit every last log in place."

He exited the vehicle, crossed in front of the car to the passenger side door, and extended a hand to help Malisa out of the automobile.

"It's impressive," Malisa said as he held her hand, pulling her along beside him as they made their way up the front steps. "How long did it take you?"

"Three years of some serious father-son quality

time. Best experience of my life. I really got to know my father during that time."

Malisa didn't miss the echo of pride in his tone as he talked about his parents, the wealth of it vibrating through his whole spirit. The love between him and his family was palpable, much like with her own family.

Without a key, Gabriel pushed open the front door. Malisa's curiosity rose tenfold as they were greeted by two women who stood waiting in the home's sizeable living room.

"Good morning, Mr. Whitman!" the tall blonde chimed cheerily.

"Felicia, Bernadette, hello," he answered, gesturing with his head at both women. "This is Ms. Ivey," he said, making a quick introduction.

Malisa smiled her hello, her gaze racing between them. Curiosity pulled at her eyes, moving Gabriel to chuckle softly.

"Are you ready for us?" he asked, still not letting her in on what he had planned.

Felicia nodded. "Yes, sir. When you two are ready, so are we."

"Ready for what?" Malisa asked, confusion washing over her expression.

Gabriel laughed heartily. "You're riding shotgun, remember? That means you just get to ride, no questions."

Malisa cut her eye at him. It was on the tip of her tongue to give him a snappy comeback, but instead she bit back the words. Gabriel was acutely aware that she wanted to say something smart, and her holding back amused him.

He slipped an arm around her waist, guiding her

down a short length of hallway into the home's family room. Two massage tables draped in white sheets sat room center. A fire burned invitingly in the oversized fireplace. Candles blazed strategically around the room. Soft music played on the stereo system, a mix of soft jazz and blues caressing the wood walls.

"I get a massage every week. I thought a couple's massage might be a nice change this week. And since I know you have so much on your plate, I was hoping that you might enjoy an hour of relaxation."

Malisa smiled. "Well," she said softly. "Looks like you're off to a nice start, Mr. Whitman. I might not be able to talk badly about you after all."

Gabriel grinned broadly. "Did that sound like approval?" He blew against the back of his fingers, then brushed them across his broad chest. Malisa rolled her eyes, smiling widely.

Behind them, the other woman held out a white cotton robe, a plush white towel, and slippers. Gabriel took them from the woman's hands and nodded his gratitude.

"There's a bedroom on the left where you can change," he said, passing the garments to Malisa.

"Thank you," she responded as she headed in the direction he pointed.

Minutes later, Malisa lay facedown on the massage table, a white cover draped over her nakedness. Gabriel lay on the table beside her, the man so close that their shoulders were just millimeters from touching. Heat wafted between them with a fury, it taking everything the duo had between them not to toss their coverings aside. Allowing herself to fall into the sensations, Malisa closed her eyes, her thoughts focused on

Gabriel's deep breathing beside her. Each inhale was slow and steady as the man fought to contain his rising excitement.

Malisa lay like that for some time, hot stones pressing against her pressure points as the licensed massage therapist began to slowly loosen her muscles, the woman's touch both relaxing and restorative. As the masseuse folded the sheet back to expose the length of her leg and the outer curve of her buttock, she opened her eyes. Gabriel had been eyeing her intensely, and his gaze shifted down the length of her body, eagerly examining every line and curve. When he lifted his eyes to hers, meeting her stare, he smiled sheepishly, only slightly embarrassed at being caught.

Malisa smiled back, her own gaze skirting the length of the table and his exposed flesh. She took a swift inhale, awash with excitement by the beauty of his hard lines. Reaching toward her, Gabriel brushed his fingers down the length of her profile. Malisa's smile widened as she closed her eyes a second time, savoring the sensations sweeping through her.

The hour sped by and before either of them knew it, their massage was finished.

"How are you feeling?" Bernadette asked her, leaning to whisper into Malisa's ear.

Malisa smiled. "Wonderful," she said. "I feel wonderful."

Gabriel sat upright on his table. "Ladies, thank you both very much. We both greatly appreciate your services."

"You're very welcome, Mr. Whitman." Felicia nodded. "Will you both be having massages next week, sir?"

Gabriel looked toward Malisa, his expression hopeful.

She shrugged ever so slightly. "I'll have to get back to you on that one," Malisa said. "I have to fly to New York after the New Year so I may not be here."

A flash of disappointment shone in Gabriel's eyes. "We'll get back to you, Felicia," he said.

The woman nodded. "Yes, sir."

He turned to Malisa. "Excuse me for a moment while I show these ladies out," he said, rising from the table. He adjusted the large towel around his waist, being mindful to not expose himself unnecessarily. Malisa didn't miss the look the two other women exchanged between them. She was certain that neither would have minded seeing even a hint of what the beautiful black man might be working with.

As the trio disappeared from sight, she lifted herself off the table and slipped back into the robe that rested across an upholstered chair. When Gabriel returned, she was standing, anxiously waiting.

"I usually spend a few minutes in the sauna when I'm done," he said, "and we can also take a plunge in the hot tub, if you like."

"You have a sauna?" Malisa asked.

"This was my pleasure retreat when I built it," he responded. "My bachelor haven before the ex-wife and the kid."

"I'm sure," Malisa replied, just imagining the kind of pleasures he might have enjoyed there.

"So," Gabriel questioned, "what will it be, sauna or hot tub?"

Malisa met his intense stare, and it was on the tip of her tongue to say she wanted him to take her to bed and make love to her instead. She couldn't believe how aroused the man had her, his presence igniting a torch deep in her core. Her nipples had hardened beneath the terry robe, the soft fabric brushing sensuously against her skin. She would have gladly replaced the touch of fabric with Gabriel's hands.

Gabriel shifted his stance, trying to hide the rise of his rock-hard erection. He'd been hard ever since she'd come into the room in her white robe, his imagination gone wild at the thought of her being naked and so close to him. When he'd seen the hint of bare skin, the curve of her behind melding into the long length of her leg, and the honey-silk skin, he'd been no more good. He'd been ready to toss his staff out the door so that he could take the exquisite woman right then and there. And now she was standing before him looking even more delectable as she bit down on her bottom lip.

When she still hadn't spoken, seemingly unable to answer his question, Gabriel reached for her hand. With her fingers entwined in his, he guided her toward the back of the home and the wooden structure adjacent to the master bedroom.

The sauna could have easily held three or four people comfortably. Benches lined three walls and the music echoed from speakers built into the walls. Gabriel pushed the digital controls to turn up the heat. He gestured toward Malisa to make herself comfortable.

Within minutes, the temperature had risen considerably, the radiant heat beginning to penetrate each and every pore in their bodies.

Gabriel didn't miss her rising discomfort, never

taking his eyes off her. "That robe is a little heavy," he said as he passed an oversized towel to her. "This might be more comfortable." He turned around in his seat. "I won't peek. I promise," he said with a soft chuckle.

Malisa giggled. "Sure you won't," she said.

"Really, but you need to hurry up," Gabriel replied, pressing both of his hands over his eyes. "If you take too long, I might have to break that promise."

By the time he'd finished the sentence, Malisa had already dropped her robe to the floor and was tucking the towel closed around her torso.

"Well, then, I guess you should turn back around," she responded.

Gabriel smiled his approval as he turned back toward her. "You look very relaxed," he said as she lifted her legs and stretched them out on the bench before her.

"I am," Malisa answered. "Do you always come here for your massages?"

He nodded. "I love this place. I have great memories here, and usually it doesn't take any time at all for me to relax once I get here. When I need to think things through, I come here."

"Interesting," Malisa said as she swiped at the moisture that had risen across her forehead.

"Why's that?"

"It just is. Everything about you is interesting, Gabriel." She smiled sweetly. "So, do you always bring your dates here?"

Gabriel laughed. "Actually, I don't. You are the very first woman to come here since before I got married. My ex-wife has never been here. In fact, Delores doesn't even know I own this place."

Malisa's expression was one of disbelief. "How did you manage that if you two were married?"

He shrugged his broad shoulders. "Our relationship was complicated. Her not knowing simply made things easier."

He paused, a flash of something Malisa didn't quite recognize washing over his expression. Sensing that he didn't want to go into detail, she changed the subject.

"So, tell me something about you that no one knows." Her gaze met his.

He smiled, the wealth of it lifting his eyes widely. He paused in reflection. "Don't you dare tell anyone," he said as he leaned toward her, almost conspiratorial. "But I'm afraid of spiders."

Malisa grinned, breaking out into a low laugh. "Really? You?"

"Yes, ma'am. Screaming-like-a-girl terrified! It's some serious arachnophobia."

"I'll have to remember that," Malisa responded, her head bobbing up and down.

"And you? What don't people know about you, Malisa Ivey?"

"Are you any good at keeping secrets, Gabriel?"

He grinned. "I think so," he said, his tone everything but convincing.

"If you ever say a word, Gabriel Whitman, I will hurt you," Malisa continued, pointing her index finger at him. "But I have a tattoo."

"A tattoo? That's your big secret?"

"Yes. But only four people know it exists. Me, the tattoo artist who did it, my last boyfriend, and my gynecologist. You make five."

Gabriel was suddenly intrigued. "And where is this tattoo?" he questioned in a deep, husky tone.

Malisa stared into the man's eyes. He was staring back just as intensely, and there was no mistaking the look of desire in his eyes. Her pulse began to race ever so slightly, a low throbbing beginning to beat between her legs. She dropped her gaze to the floor as she slid her fingers through her hair and down the side of her face. She cleared her throat, then lifted her eyes back to his.

The man was grinning widely. "Oh, now I have to see this tattoo," he said. He inched his way closer to her, dropping his hand against her calf.

"My tattoo is for select eyes only," Malisa said, pulling her leg back and tucking it beneath her bottom.

"So you're going to tease me and not let me look. That's not right," Gabriel laughed.

"I didn't say I *wasn't* going to let you see it," Malisa intoned. Her seductive voice dropped to a loud whisper. "I just said it's for select eyes only."

Gabriel paused, waiting anxiously. Malisa laughed heartily. She rose from her seat, holding her towel tightly around her petite frame.

"Where did you say that hot tub was?" she asked.

Gabriel pointed. "On the other side of the master bedroom through the glass doors and onto the enclosed porch."

Malisa moved to exit the room. Unable to resist, she leaned forward and placed a gentle kiss against his lips. She felt her blood sizzling through her veins, and then he reached one large hand up to press his fingers against the side of her face as the other slid easily around her waist. His touch was almost too much for her to bear.

Drawing back, Malisa moved to the sauna's door. With her hand on the doorknob, she turned slightly to face him. "I'm going to grab a quick shower and then I'll meet you there," she said. Her seductive expression moved Gabriel to sit upright, stirring heat deep in his core.

As she closed the door behind her, disappearing from his view, he thought about the kisses they'd shared. He'd give anything to keep kissing her lips, never wanting to stop making the lush pillows his. It was becoming harder to maintain control, temptation winning the battle he was trying to fight.

He reached beneath his towel to release the concrete appendage that had risen with a vengeance beneath the covering. His erection bulged anxiously for attention. Gabriel stroked himself gently, willing the protrusion away. When nothing happened, he heaved a deep sigh. The desirable woman had him hungry for her flesh. He would need a cold shower to stall the heavy rise of wanting. Lifting himself from his seat, he headed down the hall to the other bathroom, hoping to rinse away his craving for Malisa but knowing the chances of his doing so were slim to none.

Chapter 10

The spray of cool water felt good against Malisa's skin. It had become quite heated in the small enclosure, the rise in warmth having nothing to do with the sauna's temperature. Being near Gabriel kept her heated, even when they were standing knee-deep in snow.

She'd been surprised by her boldness, her desire to kiss the man completely out of control. Never before had she felt the way kissing Gabriel made her feel, intense sensations firing through every fiber in her body. Somewhere in the back of her mind, there was a very tiny voice telling her she might need to step back and slow it down, and then there was that louder voice whispering that she needed to take control and enjoy the buffet that was everything Gabriel.

Malisa sighed, blowing warm breath past her lips. Even beneath the spray of water, she was becoming heated at the thoughts of him, her nerves completely on edge. She wanted Gabriel and she wanted him to want her just as badly.

Gabriel beat her to the hot tub, the man already

ensconced beneath a bubbling flow of water. His eager eyes followed every one of her footsteps as she moved from the entrance to the edge of the large pearlescent tub. He swallowed hard as she stood staring at him, her hands playing with the belt that held her robe closed tight. He was rendered speechless at the sight of her, blood shooting straight to his groin. He swiped a wet hand across his face.

Her hair was damp from the shower she'd just taken, ringlets of water trickling down her face and neck. An ample amount of cleavage peeked from beneath the robe, her firm breasts sitting high and firm. Everything about her was steeped in sensuality, the beautiful woman everything fantasies were made of. Gabriel clamped his legs tightly together, his hand cupped over his crotch in an attempt to hide the telltale sign of his wanting.

He took a deep breath, trying to regain his composure. "Did you find the swimsuits in the bedroom? They were supposed to leave a few for you to choose from."

She nodded. "I did," she said softly. "But"—she slowly pulled at the belt tightened around her waist— "if I put on a swimsuit, you wouldn't be able to see my tattoo."

A teasing smile pulled at her lips as he shifted forward in his seat. As if she were in slow motion, Gabriel watched the belt fall to the floor first, the bathrobe falling right behind it. His gaze slowly shifted upward from the garments on the floor.

Dressed in absolutely nothing but her birthday suit, Malisa's seductive pose stirred something deep in the core of Gabriel's body, every muscle and vein hardening like steel. Her caramel complexion glistened from the heat, a smooth, silky confection that had his mouth watering for just a little taste of her decadent delights.

And that tattoo! Never before had he seen anything like it. His eyes flitted back and forth over the details, then looked to her face and back again. Malisa chuckled, his reaction exactly what she'd expected. The body art had been the result of a bet, a wager between herself and a former lover who she had at one time thought would be with her forever. Forever had lasted only two years, when the man suddenly decided that his interests lay elsewhere. The tattoo, however, remained with her, a reminder that some rash decisions might not always be in her best interest.

Her neatly cropped patch of pubic hair served as the foundation for her tattoo, creating the base of a bird's nest. Just a few single branches coiled up toward her stomach. Rising out of the nest were three baby birds craning their necks upward, and perched protectively on one of the tree limbs was the mommy bird. It was not at all what he expected, but it was one of the most beautiful designs he'd ever seen.

"Why birds?" Gabriel asked, smiling up at her.

"Because if you stroke me the right way, they'll sing for you," she said, her smile teasing.

Gabriel nodded, excitement gleaming from his expression. His desire raged like wildfire in his eyes, his wanting so acute that nothing and no one could have put out the flames. He wanted her. He knew she wanted him. She was his for the taking. He didn't want for anything more. He moved himself forward, his erection pressing against the front of his swim trunks, his attempt at modesty belied by the engorged organ begging for her attention.

As Malisa stepped into the pool of water, one slow step and then another, she reached her manicured hand toward him for his support. Clasping her fingers, Gabriel helped her down into the whirling pool, the woman coming to stand before him. Without a second thought, Gabriel pressed his mouth to her abdomen, planting a damp kiss against her belly button. He gently rubbed his cheek against her stomach and drew his fingers over the line of her tattoo.

When he touched her, Malisa inhaled swiftly, air catching somewhere deep in her chest. She felt the heat of her desire deep between the center of her legs and all the way to her toes. Wrapping her arms around him, Malisa drew him closer to her, his touch fueling something so deep within her that the wealth of it was almost frightening. No man had ever moved her like Gabriel moved her. No man had her wanting him as much as she found herself wanting Gabriel. She couldn't imagine not opening herself up to him, allowing herself to lose complete control in all that he had to offer. She'd given herself permission to let him in the moment he'd said hello.

Malisa leaned in to kiss him, and he felt the weight of her body slide down his chest and lower against his lap. He opened his mouth to her, her tongue gliding in sync with his as he wrapped his arms tightly around her torso. Drawing back, she smiled, her seductive expression igniting a wealth of heat through his groin. Her breath held as Gabriel stared deep into her eyes, every ounce of desire shimmering in the dark depths.

She pressed her palm to his chest as she nestled herself against him, her knees clasping the sides of his torso. Her delicate hands caressed his chest, gliding around to his shoulders and to his back as she pressed her bare breasts against him.

"If you want me to stop, you need to say so now, Malisa," Gabriel whispered, nuzzling her neck. "Because I want to make love to you. I *need* to make love to you," he murmured against her skin, trailing kisses over every inch of skin that he could reach.

With no intention of stopping, wanting to make love to him just as desperately, Malisa kissed his mouth. Snaking her tongue past his lips, the kiss was urgent and demanding. Clasping his cheeks between the palms of her hands, their tongues danced nicely together. When she finally pulled away from him, they both gasped hungrily for air.

Shifting her body back, Malisa met his gaze, holding the lingering stare. There was no need for words. They knew what they wanted, and they knew that nothing was going to keep them from it. The passion rising between them was like nothing they'd known before. It had taken on a life of its own, the wealth of it corporeal.

Beneath her, his manhood pressed hard against her bottom, the enormity of his erection tattling the degree of his arousal. He was large, thick, and raging hard. Malisa was suddenly desperate to nestle herself around him, to feel him deeply connected to her. She wanted to touch him, to hold his hard flesh in her hands. And she wanted most to mold her body around his. She slid her hands down into the water, caressing the outside of his thighs and then drawing her palms back to the waistband of his cotton trunks.

As she gestured for him to rise, Gabriel lifted his hips, with her still sitting in his lap. His erection shifted even more between her legs, and he inhaled swiftly at the sensation. He was desperate for release. Malisa pulled at his shorts, her touch demanding as she pulled them down. As they tangled around his ankles, he kicked his feet free. His erection stood at full throttle, every ounce of his excitement pulsing through the rock-hard tissue with a vengeance.

Sliding her hands between their bodies, Malisa grasped him with both palms. His flesh was warm in her hands as she stroked him boldly, her fingers gliding up and down the length of him. Her gaze shifted to his face, and he smiled, a slow, easy bend of his mouth. Malisa moaned his name as he leaned forward and captured her mouth. The frenzied sensations had her stomach clenched.

"You're driving me crazy!" Gabriel roared into her neck, his words a deep growl from someplace deep in his throat. His heart was beating like a steel drum in his chest, and he felt as if he might explode at any moment.

Clasping her buttocks, he settled her around his waist and settled himself up from the whirlpool of water. He wanted her in his bed, and she wrapped her arms around his neck, surprised by how easily he had lifted her into his arms. Before she realized it, Malisa was lying on her back against the king-sized mattress in the master bedroom. She watched as Gabriel pulled a condom from the bed table and stretched the prophylactic over his engorged member.

Just as quickly, his hands were drawing a slow path over her shoulders and down to the twin peaks of her breasts. The caress was slow and easy, and when he reached her nipples, he caressed the hard buds with amazing skill, his touch followed by his tongue as he outlined each tip before sucking them gently into his mouth. As he suckled her easily, Malisa knew that it would take very little more for her to orgasm.

"Gabriel!"

Reaching farther down, he dropped his fingers between her legs. She was hot and wet and needy, both their emotions raw and intense. He towered over her, his masculine frame easily finding its place. Staring into her eyes, Gabriel knew there was no turning back for either of them. Their gazes still locked tightly together, he gripped her hips and raised them toward him. When he entered her, the joining brought tears to his eyes.

Malisa had never known anything sweeter. Her body instinctively gave in to him, her inner walls stretching eagerly. Heat flared, muscles quivered, their bodies trembled, and then he began moving, pumping into her with painstaking precision. He hovered between her legs possessively, each stroke deliberately making her his one and only.

As if she'd been hit with something akin to an electrical shock, Malisa felt her muscles clench tightly around his. She drew him deeper inside her, waves of pleasure consuming every fiber of her being as she devoured him hungrily.

Gabriel screamed her name. Their orgasms hit at the same time, and he dropped his mouth to hers, the warmth of her breath on his lips as they both fell off the edge. Sensation rippled from his core, hot and consuming as every bit of his soul shot deep inside of her, collapsing above her as she drained everything he had to offer. The moment exceeded every one of their expectations.

Malisa didn't have a clue how long they lay together. She felt as if she'd just gone through an out-of-body experience, every coherent thought she could muster lost in another hemisphere. Beside her, Gabriel was lost in his own world, completely drained and whole-heartedly satisfied. Neither had ever known a time when making love had them feeling the way they were both feeling.

She sucked in a trembling breath, wanting him to do to her again what he had just done. She closed her eyes, her body temperature starting to rise once again. As if reading her mind, Gabriel pressed a kiss against her neck and then nibbled at the soft flesh, biting her gently. She purred beneath his touch, his hands starting to glide like warm butter over her heated surface. Wrapping her limbs around him, she hugged him tightly, welcoming his weight above her body.

Gabriel was in awe of what was happening between them. His erection had barely subsided, blood still surging for attention. He rested just at the entrance to her secret garden, wanting back inside. He dropped his gaze to her face, his eyes locking with hers. Neither spoke, having no need for words. "I want to be inside of you," he whispered, his words cutting through her thoughts of wanting him there.

Malisa closed her eyes, a throaty sigh spilling out

of her mouth. Her lips were swollen from his kisses, lush pillows that had been well serviced. Her mouth fell open ever so slightly, and she bit down against her lower lip. His body grazed hers intimately, and then he was inside her again, a slow, easy grind filling her deeply. He thrusted in and pulled out, in and out, the motion methodic and steady as he savored each stroke. With each thrust, his erection expanded inside her, marking the walls of her inner lining as his own.

With an unwavering grip, her muscles tightened around him, drawing him in deeper and deeper. Emotion suddenly shook him to his core as an electrical current spurted through him. Every part of his body was impacted by the scorching release.

Calling out as if in prayer, Malisa reveled in the pure pleasure of the moment. Everything about Gabriel felt wonderfully right, like destiny had put her in the right place at the right time with the perfect partner. Opening her eyes to him, she found herself lost in his dark eyes. His stare was engaging, his expression completely captivating.

Gabriel knew that whatever was happening between them had taken on a life of its own. The intensity of it had rendered them both speechless, lost in the sheer beauty of its magnitude. This Christmas gift was wholeheartedly the best present he had ever received.

Chapter 11

After making love one last time, they had fallen asleep, only to wake up and make love yet again. The warmth of his touch on her skin sent shivers down the length of her spine, and Malisa couldn't begin to imagine him never touching her again.

At that moment, he was still dozing, his head resting comfortably on her tummy. She drew her fingers across his brow, following the line of his precision haircut. The curls of his closely cropped mane swirled ever so slightly, the dark strands complementing his chocolate complexion. He was beauty personified, and Malisa had to wonder what she had done to have gotten so lucky. A smile pulled at the corners of her mouth, lifting her face in glee.

Across the room, his cell phone vibrated against the dresser top, the device tapping for attention on the hardwood. It had been ringing on and off for the last few hours. Once Gabriel had ensured that it wasn't his son and that all was well with Trey, he'd ignored it, turning it on silent while they lavished in each other's company. Malisa hadn't thought anything about it until that moment, when the annoying tone cried out for attention.

As she shifted against the wealth of pillows that decorated the bed, Gabriel shifted with her, opening his eyes. His gaze flitted back and forth before resting on her face.

"Hey, beautiful." He smiled.

"Hey, yourself! Did you get a good nap?"

He stretched his body, snuggling closer to her as he wrapped his arms around her torso. "I had a very good nap. How about you?"

Malisa nodded. "Someone is anxious to reach you. Your phone has been ringing off the hook," she said, gesturing toward where the appliance lay on the dresser top.

"Trust me when I tell you it is no one important."

She smiled, chuckling softly. "Your ex-wife might not agree with that. I'm sure she thinks she's very important."

Gabriel couldn't help but laugh with her. "Let's not talk about my ex-wife."

Malisa heaved a soft sigh, raising an eyebrow slightly.

"At least not right now," Gabriel concluded, sensing that Malisa was not happy with his dismissing her comment.

She shrugged. "Actually, I'm thinking that I need to be heading back to the restaurant. I still have work to do, and you have completely distracted me today."

Gabriel reached up to kiss her mouth. "Distractions are good."

"Your distraction was great, but that doesn't change

the fact that I have ten parties to prepare cakes for, including your office party."

"That's right! My special cake that someone is supposed to jump out of . . ." Amusement painted his expression. "If it works, that is!"

Malisa laughed. "Precisely why I need to get back to the bakery, smart-ass!"

Gabriel nuzzled the soft spot beneath her chin, licking a slow line up to her mouth to kiss her lips. "Well, then," he whispered, "I had better get you back, but first"—he kissed her mouth one more time—"I need some attention."

Malisa smiled brightly, kissing him back. "And what kind of attention might you be in need of, Mr. Whitman?"

Gabriel grabbed her hand, drawing her fingers down his chest. He wrapped her palm around the rod of steel between his legs. He lifted his eyes to stare into hers. He shifted his eyebrows up and down suggestively, his grin spreading full across his face.

Malisa laughed as she began to gently stroke the long length of thick flesh. "Well," she said, shifting her body closer to his. "I think the bakery can definitely wait."

"Where is your father?" Delores Winn hissed as her son slammed the car door.

The boy tossed his tote bag onto the rear seat. "I don't know," Trey said, attitude registered in his tone. "I didn't put a leash on him this morning."

Delores cut her eye in the boy's direction, her annoyance masking her face. "What is your problem?"

"You said I could spend the night."

"Well, I changed my mind. I thought it was a better idea for me, you, and your dad to spend some quality time together."

"Well, when he didn't answer his phone, why didn't you change your mind?"

Delores gnashed her teeth together, fighting not to rage at her young son. She took a deep breath, filling her lungs before blowing breath back out.

"Did he say what he had planned?" she finally asked.

Trey shrugged. "He was with Malisa. He didn't say anything about where they were going."

"Malisa?" The woman had a death grip on the steering wheel.

Stealing a quick look at his mother, Trey shrugged, not bothering to respond. He focused his attention on his iPhone, knowing that he needed to warn his father that his mom was on the warpath.

Gabriel had just kissed Malisa good-bye and stepped back into his car when his phone chimed that he had a text. Pulling the device into his hand, he quickly read the message.

OMG . . . Mom spitting mad . . . made me leave Michael . . . sorry, told her about your date.

Gabriel shook his head. It was always something with those two, but he was determined that neither's antics were going to spoil his good mood. He texted his son back.

No problem. See you home.

As Gabriel started the ignition, Trey texted him back.

About to blow a MAJOR blood vessel!!!!
Take cover . . .

He shook his head. He should have known that things were going too well. Something had to blow up sooner or later.

"I think it's totally irresponsible of you!"

Gabriel rolled his eyes skyward, his gaze returning to the big-screen television in his home's family room. He flipped the channel, focused on the remote in his palm.

"Do you hear me talking to you?" Delores screamed.

Gabriel cut his eye in the woman's direction, then returned his gaze to the NBA game playing on the TV.

There was no need for him to respond. How could he not have heard her? Delores had been raging and ranting for the last twenty minutes. He imagined that whether they wanted to or not, the entire state of North Carolina had been able to hear her.

Exasperated, Delores tossed her hands into the air. "Why do you do this to me, Gabriel? What did I do to deserve such disrespect?"

Gabriel heaved a deep sigh. He flicked off the television and slowly turned in her direction.

Delores was eyeing him intently. "Well?"

"Delores, you're obviously upset, and I know that there is nothing I can say or do that is going to change that. But I still don't know what it is you have a problem with. And I seriously have had just about enough of this foolishness."

"Why didn't you answer my calls?" Delores persisted.

"I was busy, Delores."

"Doing what? I needed you. It was important."

"No, it wasn't. It was you wanting to dictate to me how I needed to be spending my time."

"You were supposed to be spending time with Trey."

"Trey was fine and enjoying the day with his best friend like he wanted."

"Well, we should have been spending family time together."

There was a very pregnant pause before Gabriel finally responded. "We are not a family, Delores. What part of that don't you get?"

Delores huffed, her hands clutching angrily at her full hips. Rage filled her face as she sputtered like a fish out of water, opening and closing her mouth as she searched for a comeback.

"So, some tramp comes into your life and suddenly your son and I don't mean anything to you?"

"What the hell are you talking about?"

"You know exactly what I'm talking about. Malisa Ivey," she spat, her face skewing with displeasure as she said the woman's name. "She's got you sniffin' behind her tail, and you just toss me and Trey to the side."

Gabriel rose from his seat and moved toward the front door. "You really need to check yourself, Delores. We are not married. What I do with my time and who I do it with is my business. All that you and I have to concern ourselves with is our son and his welfare. Now, if you're done, I have some paperwork to finish."

Livid, Delores stormed behind him. "You'll regret this, Gabriel. I promise you that," she screamed.

Gabriel sighed as he held the door open. "I have no doubts, Delores," he said as she brushed past him, still ranting as she headed to her car. Closing the door behind her, Gabriel repeated himself. "I have no doubts."

Delores didn't even bother to turn the lights on in her small apartment, opting instead to sit still in the darkness. It had been just over an hour since she'd stormed into her home and had thrown herself down across the living room sofa. She was still fuming over the afternoon's events.

Gabriel had always been easy to manipulate. And she had gotten her way with him more times than not. Their only child had always been enough leverage for her to justify her actions, Gabriel's love for the boy having no limits.

When she'd risen that morning, determined not to spend the day alone and wanting to spend it with Gabriel and Trey, she hadn't fathomed Gabriel not acquiescing. It was the holidays, after all, and she'd wagered that her insisting they needed to share that time with Trey would have been enough to move him to do so. She hadn't figured Malisa Ivey into the equation, or Gabriel ignoring her in favor of that woman.

Delores heaved a deep sigh, blowing stale air past

her lips. "I need to put that woman in her place," she spoke out loud, her mind beginning to race.

Rising from her seat, Delores moved to the laptop computer that rested on her dining room table. Making herself comfortable in one of the cushioned chairs, she powered the unit on, her arms crossed over her chest as it flickered light. When she was logged onto the Internet, she pulled up a search engine and typed in Malisa Ivey's name. Her eyes widened at the numerous entries that suddenly filled the page.

Delores shook her head. Moving into her kitchen, she filled a ceramic mug with water and popped it into the microwave. When the water began to bubble, she made herself a cup of instant coffee. It was going to be a long night. Something, somewhere, in that long list of information about Gabriel's new friend was going to give her an idea on how to bring her down. Malisa Ivey would soon be a nonexistent problem for all of them.

Trey stood in the doorway of his father's room, leaning on the wooden frame. He disconnected the call on his cell phone and sighed.

"She's still mad," the boy said, reflecting on the conversation he'd just had with his mother.

Gabriel lay relaxed across his king-sized bed, leaning back against the headboard and pillows that supported his head as he read a stack of reports that needed his attention.

"Well, I'm sorry about that," he said, lifting his eyes to look at the boy. "But that's not my problem and it certainly isn't yours."

Trey shrugged, his thin shoulders reaching for the high ceiling.

"Why does she get like that?" he asked, knowing that his father knew who 'she' was without him having to say so.

Gabriel stared off, reflecting, thinking about what made Delores Winn do the things she'd been known to do. His gaze shifted to the boy who was waiting for him to answer. "I don't know, Trey. Your mom isn't very happy, and I think she sometimes acts out because she's frustrated and hurt that her life isn't going the way she would like."

"Was she always like this?"

This time Gabriel shrugged. "Not always."

"Do you still love Mom?"

He met his son's curious stare. "I care about your mother because she's your mother. We both love you."

The boy smiled. "I'll take that as a no."

Gabriel shook his head. "It's hard to explain, Trey. I want your mother and I to be friends because that would be best for you. Sometimes, though, that's hard to do. I don't hate your mother, and I don't want to be mean to her, but I do have to draw the line at some of her behavior. And that puts us at odds with each other."

The kid nodded his understanding. "So, what's the deal with you and Miss Ivey? You like her a lot, don't you."

Gabriel couldn't keep himself from grinning. "I do like her. I'm hoping she and I will become very good friends."

"Did you kiss her again?"

Gabriel laughed. "Don't you have some homework to do, boy?"

Trey grinned, his wide smile filling his face with joy. "I'll take that as a yes!"

"Good night, Trey!"

"Good night, Dad. I love you."

Gabriel nodded. "I love you, too, son. I love you too."

Back in his own room, Trey turned on his stereo system, blasting rap music into the quiet space. He adjusted the volume just as his father called out for him to do so.

As he lay back against his mattress, sprawling his body crossways on the bed, he couldn't help but think that his mother was on a rampage and that his father didn't have a clue. He'd listened to her rant for almost an hour, knowing that if he feigned enough interest, it would pay off for him in the long run. He wanted a new pair of Nike sneakers, a limited-edition version that would run well into the range of a few hundred dollars.

Trey knew his father would never invest the funds in a pair of shoes he didn't need, but his mother could easily be cajoled into doing so if he played his cards right. Right then, his mother wanted to be angry and hateful toward Malisa Ivey. Trey reasoned that it wouldn't hurt if he went along with her, garnering some favor points with the matriarch to use later on. Playing one parent against the other for his personal benefit was easiest when the two didn't like each other, and right now his mother didn't much like his father.

The boy thought about his dad and the woman who had come so suddenly into their lives. He liked Malisa. She'd been a lot of fun, and he could see that she and his father liked each other. They'd been openly amorous with each other, and Trey had never before seen his father so smitten with any woman.

His mother had insisted that Malisa was an intrusion, that she was set on getting her hooks into his dad. She'd inundated him with stepmother horror tales, and Trey had to admit that a few of her comments had been cause for concern. For all of Trey's young life, he and his father had shared a bond that no one, not even his mom, could penetrate. Trey wasn't open to anyone interloping on that, no matter how pretty she might be. But Trey figured he only had to keep his eye on things, and if Malisa got out of hand, he could easily shut her down.

Chapter 12

As Malisa poured herself a third cup of coffee, she couldn't understand why her love life was the subject of conversation for her family. Her sister and mother stood in the restaurant's kitchen talking about her as if she were not even there. The moment was just shy of baffling, the young woman bemused by the turn of events.

"I've dated only one guy who had an ex-wife, and she was a major witch," Anitra was saying.

"You just came at the woman the wrong way," Miss Etta interjected. "It's one thing when you just have to deal with the man. It's something different when he has kids."

"Well, this guy didn't have any kids, and his ex was still a witch."

"That's because he was still doing her," Miss Etta stated emphatically. "That boy was lying to you and to her too. She had every reason to act a fool."

Anitra shrugged. "Well, I didn't know that then. Do you think Gabriel is still doing his ex-wife?"

Miss Etta paused. "No. I don't think he's that kind of man. I think when he says things are over, they are over. Now, I could be wrong, but usually I'm a good judge of character."

"Do either of you want to know what I think?" Malisa asked, looking from one to the other.

Anitra laughed. "No!"

Malisa rolled her eyes. "Well, something's not kosher. That woman called him at least twenty times yesterday. He insisted that she didn't want anything."

"Was the boy with her? Maybe there was a problem with him. He shouldn't ignore her if it might be about their son."

"No, his son was at a friend's house, and Gabriel called to make sure everything was well with Trey. The one and only time he did answer her call it was like the Inquisition. The woman gave him the third degree: Where are you? What are you doing? Who are you with?"

Miss Etta nodded. "Did he answer her?"

"No. He just asked her what she wanted. I don't know what she said, but he told her he was busy and would have to speak with her later, and then he hung up. She called back ten minutes later and she kept calling."

Malisa's mother continued to nod, the woman's gray head bobbing slowly on her thick neck. Malisa had moved to the counter and was cracking eggs into a bowl.

"So what do you think the problem is?" Miss Etta asked, wanting to hear her daughter's assessment of the situation.

Malisa paused, reflecting back on her time with

Gabriel. Everything about their afternoon together had been great. Nothing in his behavior had indicated he had any interest in his ex or what she thought or wanted. He'd been anxious to ensure that their good time hadn't been marred by the other woman's persistence, and Malisa had believed him when he'd said he was no longer interested in Delores Winn.

"I think she's just jealous," Malisa finally said.

Anitra hummed. "Hmmmm . . ."

Their mother smiled ever so slightly. "It sounds like more than jealousy, Malisa. If you're the first woman Gabriel has had in his life since they divorced, or the first she's found out about, then she's probably very unhappy about the situation. Trust me when I tell you that an unhappy woman can be a boil on everyone else's behind. And an unhappy woman, who is also jealous, can be unpredictable. Just be careful and watch your back."

Malisa shrugged. "What can she do? I'm sure if I leave her alone, she'll leave me alone too."

Anitra cut an eye in her mother's direction, the two women both turning their gazes back to Malisa. "Well, better safe than sorry," the older sister intoned. Never forget, baby sister, a jealous woman can be a crazy fool."

Malisa laughed. "I don't think I'll have any problems, but if I do, I'm sure Gabriel will take control of the situation. She is his problem, after all, not mine."

"Maybe," Miss Etta said, "and maybe not. Gabriel may not have the control you think he has," the woman said emphatically.

An hour later, Malisa was tossing her second batch

of chocolate fondant into the trash can. Her focus was seriously compromised, and she couldn't begin to understand why she was having such a difficult time perfecting a recipe that was her trademark. Chocolate fondant had always been as easy for her to make as pie, and for the first time, her efforts actually felt laborious.

Gabriel had called minutes earlier to see how her day was going. Their conversation had been easy and comfortable, and as they'd made plans to connect later that evening, Malisa had been feeling on top of the world.

Her conversation with her mother and sister had been all but forgotten as she'd remembered her time with the man, his touch still burning hot against her skin. As thoughts of him consumed her mind, Malisa found herself in want of his touch, anxiously looking forward to the prospect of him and her being intimate with each other again. And then she'd ruined her second batch of fondant, tossing salt into the mixture when she should have added sugar.

Malisa had to admit that she liked the prospect of them becoming a couple. What she was feeling for Gabriel was about far more than the sexual attraction they had with each other. Admittedly, their intimate connection was off the charts, the man having awakened her inner tigress with a vengeance. She'd never known just how powerful that kind of connection could be with a man, and her connection with Gabriel was like nothing she'd ever known before. A quiver of heat coursed from her feminine spirit at the thought.

Across the room, Miss Etta was eyeing her with

reservation. Malisa sensed there was something her mother wanted to say and that she was only waiting for the right opening. She met the older woman's stare but said nothing, not wanting to hear once again that she and Gabriel might want to be more concerned about how his child and that child's mother might be taking to their new relationship.

It was selfish of her, but Malisa didn't want to think about anything but her and Gabriel and what they wanted with and from each other. She wasn't interested in everyone else's opinion, especially if the couple was able to build something special between them. Malisa had begun to believe that what she was feeling was just short of love, and she didn't want anyone to spoil that for her. Malisa knew that loving Gabriel could be as easy as breathing if she let it be. And she couldn't imagine anyone who truly cared for the beautiful man not wanting him to be loved.

When Gabriel had asked her about her day, all Malisa could do was shake her head. The duo sat over dinner, enjoying a corner table at one of Gabriel's favorite eateries.

"Everything I tried to cook today failed. I had two cakes fall, ruined my buttercream icing, and put salt in the chocolate fondant. Today was not a good day!"

Gabriel chuckled. "What was going on with you?"

Malisa shrugged. "Thinking about you. I told you that you were a distraction," she said, tossing him an easy smile.

Gabriel smiled back. "I'll own that. I had a little difficulty getting focused today myself. I kept thinking about dessert."

"Dessert? Were you planning on ordering something special tonight?" Malisa asked.

"What I plan to eat is not on the menu here," Gabriel said as he leaned forward in his seat, heat shimmering out of every pore. He raised his eyebrows suggestively.

A jolt of desire surged between Malisa's legs. She shifted back from him, fanning a hand in front of her.

"You're making it difficult to get through dinner," Malisa finally responded, reaching for her glass of ice water.

The look she tossed him was enticing, the honey-glazed salmon on his plate not looking half as delectable.

He nodded in agreement. "I'll try to do a better job of behaving," he concluded, drawing a forkful of risotto into his mouth.

"So, how is Trey? Is he enjoying his time off?"

Gabriel nodded. "He is. Naomi took him shopping today. It's their holiday ritual. She waits until after Christmas for the big sales and buys him twice what she would have purchased had she just gotten him a few gifts. It's crazy, but it works for the two of them."

"Sounds like she enjoys spoiling her favorite nephew."

"Too much! It makes me crazy because half the time he hardly deserves it."

"I bet he's not that bad. He seems like a really good kid."

There was no missing the gleam of pride that blessed the man's handsome face. "Trey *is* a good kid.

He can be quite a handful when he wants to be, but for the most part, I rarely have any trouble out of him. Like most teens, though, he is always trying to see how far he can push the boundaries. But then I'm sure you know. Your baby sister isn't much older than Trey, is she?"

"Actually, Trey and Baylor are the same age. And you definitely have to stay on your toes with her. She keeps our mother challenged."

Gabriel nodded his understanding as he took another bite of food.

"So, you pretty much know about my one and only other relationship," he said, placing his fork against his plate. "What about you, Malisa? Anyone I need to be concerned about?"

She chuckled warmly. "Uh, no! I've never been very good at dating. I've gotten it wrong more than I've gotten it right. I've had only one really long-term relationship, with my college sweetheart, and that didn't end well. Afterward, I put my full attention on my career. Building my empire has been my only focus for some time now."

"I know what that's like."

Malisa took a deep breath. "So, tell me about your ex. Why did you two break up?"

"Delores and I wanted very different things. Trying to grow my business required a great deal of my attention, and she wasn't very supportive. Eventually I felt like I was always coming home to a battleground, and that's not a nice feeling. I desperately needed some peace and quiet in my life, and leaving her was the only sure way I knew I could have that."

Malisa nodded ever so slightly. "I sometimes get the impression that you two still have a very significant connection with each other. Besides your son, I mean." She met his stare as he looked up at her.

"It's not like that—I can assure you. I had hoped that she and I could build a friendship that would be good for Trey, but that's been a challenge at best. And unfortunately, I now spend a great deal of time just trying to pacify her to keep the peace."

"And does my presence in your life now disrupt that peace?"

Gabriel smiled. "Why do you ask that?"

"I see the look on your face when your phone rings, and you answer her calls."

"I have a look?"

Malisa raised an eyebrow.

Gabriel lifted his hands as if he were surrendering. "I guess I have a look sometimes. I've just never been in this position."

"And what position is that?"

The man paused, studying the exquisite lines of her face and the intensity of her stare as she waited for him to answer. "It's like I told you before. I never planned on allowing myself to become involved with anyone until Trey was graduated and out of the house. Now I realize that I'm going to have to try to balance his needs and his mother's wants with what I'm feeling for you."

Malisa stared intently. "And what are you feeling for me?" she asked, her voice dropping to a low whisper.

Gabriel reached for her hand, pulling the backs of her fingers to his lips. His kiss was tender, a gentle brushing of her flesh. Silence filled the wealth of space between them as Gabriel gave her a sweet smile, not bothering to answer her question.

He didn't yet have the words for what he was feeling. None that he imagined would make an ounce of sense to a woman who still barely knew anything about him or he about her. As he stared into her eyes, though, Gabriel couldn't help but sense that Malisa knew exactly what he was feeling, because she, too, was experiencing the same waves of emotion.

Back at Gabriel's home, he and Malisa sat side by side on his living room sofa. The house was empty, no one else being expected home any time soon. With Naomi and Trey still out gallivanting through the malls, the duo had been making out like love-struck teens.

Malisa pulled away from the man's hold, coming up for a breath of air. "Are you sure your family's not expected?" she queried, panting heavily.

He laughed, nodding. "I swear! I told Naomi that you were here and asked her to call me before they came home. She'll call."

On his assurances, Malisa did nothing to stop the hand that eased beneath the hem of her skirt while his other began to play with her breasts. She reclaimed Gabriel's mouth, kissing the man hungrily as he fondled her unabashedly.

Boldly slipping his hand beneath her clothing, Gabriel eased his fingers beneath the line of her silk thong, his palm sliding over her downy pubic hair to cup her groin. Easing herself back ever so slightly in her seat, Malisa opened her legs to allow him easier access, and Gabriel pushed firmly against her moist flesh. Her pleasure increased tenfold as his index finger rested firmly between her labia. She responded by grinding her hips forward, thrusting gently against his fingers until they skirted the entrance to her privates.

Again and again, she thrust gently forward until she felt the sensation of his fingertip resting inside her, moving her to gasp with pleasure. Writhing in her seat, Malisa was consumed by the ecstasy, whimpering for more as Gabriel fingered her gently. Every erotic thought imaginable filled her mind, rendering her senseless.

As he kissed her, his tongue dancing in her mouth, Malisa was consumed by the vast sensations sweeping through her. She was completely lost in the moment when Gabriel pulled her thong from her body, ripping the thin strap that held the quadrant of fabric in place. She didn't have a clue when he had opened her blouse and had slid it and her bra from around her body.

All she could think of were his kisses as they gently rained down on her naked flesh, her breasts and nipples being tenderly lashed by his tongue. A loud moan rang through the quiet, and Malisa realized that sound was coming from deep within her. For Gabriel, the sound was pure joy to his ears.

His kisses moved across her torso and down toward her tummy. She sucked in air, her eyes widening at the prospect of him kissing her in such an intimate way. Gabriel slid his hands beneath her buttocks and pulled Malisa to him. He nipped at the flesh of her legs, gently biting and licking his way upward. Malisa rose up on her elbows, leaning forward to watch him as he crawled between her thighs.

She pulled her hand over his head, wanting to draw him closer to his target. She was eager for his touch, her desire obvious in her hardened nipples and slick wetness that coated his fingertips as he tapped at the door to her most private place.

As he stuck his tongue out, the tip of it easily licking the swollen nub, he met her passionate stare, his intent gleaming in his eyes. Malisa shuddered, her muscles quivering uncontrollably. His intimate kiss was mind-blowing, moving her to fall back against the sofa. Her legs spread farther apart, her knees bent as Gabriel continued licking and nibbling at her until she was just a second shy of coming, and then he stopped abruptly. Malisa's breath caught in her throat.

His voice hoarse, Gabriel's tone was commanding. "Turn around and kneel on the couch," he whispered.

As he guided her onto her stomach, Malisa did as she was directed, rising up onto her knees. Her skirt was still bunched around her waist, her bra lost somewhere on the floor, nothing in place but her high-heeled shoes.

From behind her, Gabriel kneaded the taut muscles of her buttocks, squeezing her flesh. His touch was urgent and wanting, his treaties burning like fire beneath the pads of his fingertips. He moved up close behind her, his left hand sliding between her legs from behind. His mouth followed his hands, biting and licking her hungrily as his fingers spread and stroked the damp spot between her legs.

Malisa had to fight to keep herself from collapsing from the intense pleasure. Gabriel's husky whisper rang through the air. "You like this? You like when I play with your kitty like this?"

Malisa nodded, her head bobbing eagerly. "Yes," she answered. "Oh yes!"

He continued to play with her, moving Malisa to push herself backward, pressing her behind against his hands. He toyed with her little button of pleasure-flesh, frigging her clit with rhythmic stroking, varying the speed and pressure, dipping down occasionally into the vaginal well to refresh his finger's lubrication. "Damn, woman! You are so hot and so wet." Gabriel groaned. "You know this makes me so hard!"

Malisa could only moan her assent, words completely lost to her. She was ready to explode, every fiber in her body raging a private war inside of her. And just as abruptly as before, Gabriel stopped his ministrations, sensing her need to come and come hard. Malisa groaned.

"Stop . . . stop teasing!" she pleaded. "I want to come!"

Gabriel chuckled ever so softly. "Turn back over," he directed, moving her to sit and face him. He pulled away from her, sitting back against the wooden coffee table. His erection peeked eagerly from the split in his boxers, his pants abandoned on the floor beneath his feet.

The man's expression was taunting. He drew the index finger that he'd teased her with into his mouth, sucking the appendage. The gesture was erotic and hot, and Malisa found herself holding her breath.

"Play with yourself," Gabriel said. "Spread your legs for me so that I can watch."

She hesitated momentarily. With his hands clasped together, his elbows resting on his knees, he leaned toward her, his stare compelling her to do his bidding.

He repeated his request. "I want to see you touch yourself, Malisa."

Doing as he instructed, Malisa slowly spread her legs wide open, leaning back against the sofa cushions. Her hands dropped to her thighs as she eased one and then the other along her inner legs. Timid at first, Malisa touched herself, stroking the brush of pubic hair against the back of her fingers. Gabriel leaned even closer, and she began to slowly finger the delicate labial folds. She tapped her thumb against her clit, stroking the nerve-laden nub in a slow, circular motion.

As she rubbed her pleasure spot, Gabriel's expression was priceless, the man completely consumed by the moment. He moved even closer to her, a hand dropping against her knee, his other hand wrapped around his manhood. "Pinch your nipples for me," he demanded.

Malisa's expression was coy as she did exactly what he wanted, pinching one candy-hard nipple and then the other. As he stroked himself more firmly, she lifted one breast to her mouth and sucked her own nipple, still fingering herself with her other hand. Her fingers dipped in and out, the man becoming even more aroused by the sight of her. Her eyes never left his, her gaze locked wholeheartedly with his as he watched her.

When neither of them could resist a moment longer, Gabriel came to his feet, shedding his T-shirt and his boxers as he tossed them across the room. Malisa slid forward on the couch. She wrapped her arms around his waist and kissed his stomach. She looked up at him as his hands groped her breasts, enjoying the sight of the large appendages against her skin. Gabriel put his hands behind her head and pulled her against him. Without any further guidance from him, Malisa clasped his engorged penis and sucked him in hungrily. Her lips slid over the crown and down the shaft. Her tongue sensually swathed the length of him.

The sensation was overwhelming, and Gabriel's body tensed, fighting not to explode right then and there. He lifted one foot up on the couch and pumped himself into her mouth. Thrusting his hips forward, he closed his eyes and let out a gasp of sheer pleasure. Wild with passion, Malisa lapped and sucked at him heartily, encouraging the man to feed her as much of himself as he wanted. She was in heaven, his clean, musky scent fueling every ounce of her desire.

Ready to combust, Gabriel dropped his hands to her shoulders and pushed her back, moving her to lie back against the upholstered cushions. Malisa lay back with her legs spread, watching as Gabriel dropped down between her thighs, rubbing his phallus against her until he was wet, and then he slid himself deep into her. He pushed as far as he could go, then stopped to revel in the rapture that shone in Malisa's face.

Lifting her hips, Malisa shifted her body against his. She needed him, wanted him so much that the wanting hurt. It was the sweetest pain imaginable. Driving in and out of her, Gabriel was suddenly overwhelmed by the realization that never again would he want any other woman. Malisa had him heart and soul, the magnitude of her possession rivaled only by his need for her.

Euphoria came in abundance, the couple reaching climax simultaneously. It was joy like neither had ever experienced before. As he spilled into her, Malisa cried out, calling his name over and over again.

Gabriel collapsed down against her as Malisa clung to him, wrapping every square inch of herself against his body. So lost in the moment, neither heard the front door opening and then closing. And they barely heard Naomi and Trey stepping inside, Delores following closely on both their heels.

Chapter 13

Gabriel pressed his index finger to his lips, his eyes bulging anxiously. Malisa was snatching her clothes on and tossing him his, both more than surprised by the sudden intrusion. From down the hallway, they could hear Gabriel's family in heated conversation, and both knew it was just a matter of moments before they were caught with their hands deep in the cookie jar.

"Yo, Dad!" Trey called out loudly.

Gabriel shook his head, meeting Malisa's nervous gaze. Delores's voice rang out loudly.

"I've been sitting out front for almost an hour now. He's not answering the door or his phone. Something is wrong, I'm telling you."

"Don't be so dramatic, Delores," Naomi responded. "He is probably just upstairs, sound asleep." There was no missing the annoyance in her voice as she dismissed Delores's concern.

"Trey, go upstairs and find your father," Delores ordered, rolling her eyes at her ex-sister-in-law.

"Dad!!!" Trey shouted loudly. "You home?"

They could hear the boy's heavy footsteps stomping up the flight of stairs to the second floor of the large home.

Malisa was mortified as she struggled to pull on her top, gliding her palms down her skirt to straighten it over her hips. There was no time to hook her bra, so she shoved it deep into her purse, knowing there would be no way to hide that she wasn't wearing one, her breasts swinging freely beneath the silk fabric.

Just as Gabriel was zipping up his pants, Naomi stepped into the room. Her eyes widened in surprise, and a slow grin pulled at her mouth. She tossed a quick glance over her shoulder, then gestured for the two of them to hurry. "Your shirt's on backward," she whispered, stifling a laugh as she pointed to her brother.

Malisa could feel a blush of embarrassment painting her expression, her cheeks turning a vibrant shade of red. Both were grateful that Delores had paused at the foot of the stairs, waiting anxiously for Trey to call down and report back to them.

Fanning her hands at them, Naomi pointed to the butler's pantry, gesturing for them to move into the kitchen. Peering down the hallway, she signaled when it was safe for them to pass behind her; then she returned to the front foyer and to Delores, who was still standing in wait.

She called out to her nephew, "Trey, is he there?"

"Is who there?" Gabriel asked, easing his way in their direction.

Naomi grinned. "There you are! Delores was sure that you were passed out dead or something, big brother."

"You didn't call me," he said, raising his eyebrows at his sister.

The woman giggled. "I knew I forgot something," she said, snapping her fingers.

"Why didn't you answer the door?" Delores asked, suspicion shimmering in her eyes. "I've been ringing the bell for an hour now."

Gabriel shrugged. "Sorry, we didn't hear the bell. The television was too loud, I guess."

Delores's neck snapped to attention. "We?"

Trey interrupted the conversation. "Hey, Pop!"

"Hey, son!"

"Whose car is that in the back parking lot? Something happen to yours?"

Gabriel's head waved from side to side. "I rode home in Malisa's car. We have to go pick up mine later."

"Where is she?" Trey questioned.

Gabriel nodded. "We were back in the family room watching television."

The muscles in Delores's face tightened, her jaw locked tight at the mention of Malisa's name. Glaring at Gabriel, she moved in the direction of the family room.

Gabriel called out her name. "Delores! You didn't tell me what it was you wanted."

The woman tossed him a look over her shoulder, her eyes narrowed into thin slits. "My family," she snapped, not bothering to pause.

Malisa was seated on the cushioned sofa, her legs resting atop the ottoman as she clutched a pillow to her chest. Her gaze was locked on the television set, and someone's reality show played across the screen. When Delores marched into the room, she lifted her eyes innocently and smiled.

"Delores, hello! It's nice to see you again."

Delores looked around the room, her eyes shifting anxiously to and fro. Naomi stepped past her, waving a hand in Malisa's direction.

"Hey, girl! How are you doing?"

"Better now," Malisa said with a slight laugh. "How about yourself?"

Naomi nodded. "Everything is good."

Delores cut her eye from one to the other, certain that she was missing something and not knowing what that might be. In the entranceway, Gabriel stood with his arms crossed over his chest. She turned in his direction. "May I speak with you privately, please?"

Gabriel met Malisa's stare and smiled. He turned back to his child's mother and nodded. "Sure," he answered, gesturing for her to follow him to the front of the home.

Back in the living room, he turned to face her. "What's the problem now, Delores?"

"I can see why you like her. She's got a big ass and she's trashy," Delores said snidely.

Before Gabriel could answer, Delores shook her head in disgust. She pushed past him, bending down to the floor by the corner of the sofa. When she stood back up, she was holding Malisa's thong between the tips of her two fingers.

"I can't believe you'd expose our son to your filth!" she hissed, throwing the garment at him.

Gabriel took a deep breath, catching the garment as it hit his chest. "Since you don't have a clue what you're talking about, Delores, I'd suggest you leave this alone. I pay the mortgage here. I don't recall you investing one red cent into my home, so you don't dictate what happens behind my doors." He pushed Malisa's panties deep into his pant pocket.

"Now, is there something I can help you with or not? I have company," Gabriel concluded.

Delores pointed her finger at him, shaking it feverishly. Her rage distorted her face, and Gabriel imagined that if it were at all possible, her head might actually explode. Without saying another word, Delores turned on her heels and tore out the front door, hell-bent on causing her ex-husband and his new friend as much hurt as she could possibly muster.

Malisa stood alone in the powder room, still in disbelief over the turn of events. Naomi found the whole experience humorous, and even Gabriel had been able to finally laugh at the moment. She shook her head, the humiliation continuing to shine in her eyes.

She'd been ready to head home right behind Delores, but she knew that to rush out so abruptly would have drawn Trey's attention to their predicament, and no one wanted Trey to suspect a thing.

For the last hour, she'd been engaged with stories of his latest antics, the kid having a keen sense of humor and ability to make them all laugh. But she was grateful when he had finally gone up to bed. Naomi had also wished them a good night, whispering to them both to behave. Now Malisa was waiting to take Gabriel back to his car and make her way home.

Drawing her hand through her hair, she took a deep breath, filling her lungs with much-needed oxygen and then sighed. Gabriel's light tap on the restroom door pulled her back to the moment.

"Malisa, is everything okay?"

Pulling the door open, she greeted him with a slight smile and nodded. "I am. Are you ready?"

Gabriel nodded, wrapping his arms tightly around her torso. "I am so sorry," he whispered in her ear. "We should have been more careful. I can't believe we were so reckless."

"I hope that doesn't mean you won't let me make love to you ever again," Gabriel said teasingly.

She smiled. "No, it just means that from now on, we go to my house, not yours."

The man hugged her tightly and then said the unexpected. "And then maybe, one day, my house will be *our* house?"

Lying alone in her bed, Malisa was still reeling from the night's events. She'd been so shaken by what had happened that she absolutely refused to share the details of her evening with her sister, feigning exhaustion when Anitra and Baylor wanted to chat.

But being caught with her pants down didn't compare to Gabriel suggesting that they might one day live together. He'd expounded on the subject as he'd driven her home, foretelling the future he was suddenly imagining for the two of them. Malisa had to admit to being caught up in the possibility of him and her together forever.

She rolled onto her side, pulling the sheet up and over her body. Everything about her and Gabriel together excited her. She loved the thought that he could be her good morning when she woke up each day and her sweet dreams when she drifted off to sleep at night. She was completely enthralled with the idea of being one with Gabriel Whitman.

As she lay there wishing he were with her, Malisa realized that love was exactly what she was feeling and that Gabriel was loving her back just as hard.

Exactly seven hours later, Malisa knew she was dreaming when Gabriel slid into the bed beside her, pulling her against his body as he slid his arms tightly around her. Certain that she was dreaming, she had no desire to ever wake up as she snuggled close against him, reveling in the warmth of his body heat.

The deep tenor of his voice pulled her abruptly out of her slumber.

"Good morning, sleepyhead. Are you planning on getting up anytime soon?"

Malisa's eyes opened wide, skating around the room as she took in her surroundings. "What? How? Gabriel?"

He chuckled softly. "Yes, ma'am, it's really me. Good morning!"

"What are you doing here?" Malisa asked as she wiped her face with the back of her hand.

"Your mother let me in. She said to tell you that she and Anitra will open the restaurant and that she is making Baylor work a shift too. Your dad said to tell you he'll see you later tonight. And here I am!"

"You mean we're here alone? Everyone's gone?"

He nodded. "Yes, but don't get any ideas. I'm not that kind of guy!" He smiled teasingly.

Malisa shook her head. "I need to get up. I have a ton of work to do."

"So do I," Gabriel said matter-of-factly. "But I had to see you this morning before I went to my office. I wanted to make sure that you were okay after last night."

She nodded. "I'm sure I'll get over it. I hope we didn't scar your sister."

He chuckled. "Trust me, it didn't faze Naomi in the least. Delores, on the other hand, was a bit perturbed."

Malisa eyed him suspiciously. "What do you mean?"

Gabriel reached into his back pocket and pulled out what was left of her thong. "Delores found these on the floor. She wasn't happy about it."

Malisa groaned, pressing her face into a pillow. Her cheeks were a brilliant shade of fire-engine red. She blew a deep sigh, shaking her head. "What about Trey?" she asked, peeking from behind the pillow.

"He doesn't have a clue."

Malisa blew a grateful sigh. "That's all that matters, then," she said. "I'd be absolutely mortified if he had caught us red-handed."

"Yeah, I would have had a hard time explaining how you managed to seduce me like that." Gabriel nodded, a blank expression on his face.

She laughed, pushing him back against the bed. "Very funny, Mr. Whitman."

Gabriel laughed. "I thought so."

Lifting her body from the bed, Malisa headed in the direction of the bathroom. She tossed him a glance over her shoulder.

"Are you sure there is no one home?" she questioned.

He nodded, amused as she lifted her nightshirt over her head and dropped it to the floor.

"Well, then," Malisa said as she stepped her naked body into the other room, "lock the door and come scrub my back for me, please."

Gabriel grinned. "Yes, ma'am!"

Gabriel was out of his clothes and in the shower behind her before Malisa could even think to ask him twice. Taking the bar of vanilla-scented soap from her hands, he began to rub it against her shoulders and down her back, heading toward the virgin territory that was the soft cheeks of her bubble-shaped behind.

He lingered there ever so briefly as he slipped the edge of his palm into her crack. Malisa responded with a light giggle and a shake of her hips.

"You need to behave," she giggled softly.

Squatting, Gabriel worked the rich lather down the length of her right leg, caressing and kneading her thigh and then her calf. He repeated the exercise in reverse as he moved up her left leg. When he reached the apex between her thighs, his fingers eased between the tight cavity, gently caressing her slit.

He chuckled softly when Malisa giggled, wiggling free from his touch. Continuing his mission, he massaged lather across her belly, pausing to pay homage to her belly button.

Malisa laughed. "That tickles!" she said as she pushed his hand away. Continuing his journey, he moved back up to her breasts, carefully kneading the nipples as they hardened beneath his touch. After devoting attention to the fleshy tissue, he finished his ministrations back at her shoulders.

Wrapping her arms around his shoulders, Malisa

hugged him close, rubbing the lather from her body against his broad chest. The steamy water cascaded down, rinsing soap into the drain. He felt good against her, and Malisa liked how her morning was starting.

Between them, his dick had hardened, seeking out her attention. Malisa lathered soap into both of her hands, then slowly glided her palm and fingers over the length of him. Gabriel inhaled swiftly, her touch shooting electrical currents through his bloodstream.

"Are you certain you locked that door?" Malisa questioned one last time, nipping at his Adam's apple.

He nodded, grunting his response, the intense pleasure of her ministrations muddling his thoughts.

"Then let's take this back to my bed," she said, sliding out of his reach and grabbing a plush white towel.

As she sprawled across the bed, Gabriel's excitement was urgent, his raging libido moving him to wrap his hand around his rigid penis. The woman was gorgeous, her skin shimmering from dampness, water still running in trickles across her flesh. The room was hot and humid, and all he wanted was to throw himself between her legs and love her like she'd never been loved before. There was no need or want of any more foreplay.

Standing at the foot of the bed, he gripped both of her ankles and pulled her to him, her buttocks just barely hanging off the edge of the mattress. Lifting her legs against his chest and shoulders, he drove himself into her with one harsh thrust, one deep stroke after another, hitting his target with perfect precision. Malisa clutched the bedsheet and comforter between her small hands. She felt every muscle in her body become increasingly rigid with the most delicious sexual tension. Pleasure fired like a missile from deep in her core. When he exploded with her, Gabriel cried out loudly, tears rising under his eyelids.

Their bodies clung together, wracked with spasms of pure, unadulterated pleasure. Their moans and incoherent verbalizations echoed loudly around the bedroom. And then they relaxed, exhausted, their hearts thumping in unison.

"My God! That was unbelievable!" Gabriel murmured at last.

Malisa nodded in agreement, her hands caressing the sides of his torso. "Oh, yeah!"

Rolling onto his side, Gabriel dropped his palm to her abdomen, caressing her gently. "I vote that we wake up together and do this every morning!"

Chapter 14

The secretary sitting at the desk was a temp from the agency, Gabriel's administrative assistant having the week off for the holiday. He greeted the robust woman warmly, humming to himself as he stepped past the glass-topped reception desk.

"Good morning, Mrs. Dade," he said.

The matronly woman nodded in greeting. "Good afternoon, Mr. Whitman," she responded, chuckling heartily. "The time got away from you this morning, I see."

Gabriel laughed, remembering how hard it had been for him and Malisa to tear themselves away from each other and out of her bed. "Is it afternoon already?" he asked, his tone incredulous. "Well, yes, ma'am, I guess it did." He laughed heartily. "Anyway, how are you doing?"

"I am doing quite well, Mr. Whitman. I didn't see my name in the obituaries this morning, so I have no complaints."

Gabriel laughed. "That's a good thing! Do I have anything pressing today?"

"No, sir. Your attorney called to say that he won't be available until after the New Year but that if you had an emergency, you know his private number. Also, Mr. Hodges from acquisitions left some reports for you to review. Oh, and you had a few urgent telephone calls. Your son called and asked that you call him as soon as possible. Your sister called and said that it's important that you call her, and Mrs. Whitman called. She asked that you call her back the minute you get her message."

Gabriel raised an eyebrow. "Mrs. Whitman?"

The woman passed him the pink message sheets. "She said she was your wife and that it was important she speak with you."

Recognizing Delores's cell phone number, Gabriel grimaced. "The only Mrs. Whitman I know is my mother, and she is out of the country. This is my ex-wife, Ms. Winn. But thank you."

The woman tossed him a quick smile. "Yes, sir. Have you had lunch yet? Is there anything I can get for you, sir?" she asked, rising from her seat.

Shaking his head no, Gabriel moved into his office and closed the door behind him. He searched the breast pocket of his jacket for his cell phone and then remembered that the last time he'd seen it was when he'd knocked it off of Malisa's nightstand to the floor. He'd have to get it back from her later, he thought, annoyed that he hadn't missed it sooner.

He had known that it would be only a matter of time before he would have to have a conversation with

Delores. He had hoped that it would have been much later, like closer to never, but luck was never on his side when it came to his ex-wife. He couldn't begin to imagine what was so urgent that both Trey and his sister had called for him at the office.

He reached for the phone on his desk and dialed his son's cell phone number. When the young man picked up, he was clearly upset, sounding like he'd been crying or was well on his way to teardom. Anxiety suddenly exploded in the pit of Gabriel's stomach.

"Trey, what's the matter, son?"

The first few minutes of their conversation were practically incoherent as the boy sobbed into the receiver. It took much prodding for Gabriel to understand that there had been some kind of encounter with the boy's mother, the two having butted heads. His anxiety dropped substantially, him being used to the bouts between Trey and Delores.

"Okay, Trey, you need to calm down, please. Where's your aunt Naomi?"

"Here."

"Let me speak with her, please."

Gabriel waited as the boy passed the phone to Naomi. He could hear his sister take a deep breath before suggesting to Trey that he go to his room until she called for him to come back downstairs. He heard her promise to return the youngster's cell phone as soon as she was done with the call. As Trey's footsteps faded off into the distance, Naomi said hello.

"Hey, what's going on?"

His sister's distressed tone reaccelerated his unease.

"That crazy beast is completely out of control!" Naomi almost shouted into the telephone.

"Who? What happened?"

Naomi took a deep breath, then gave her brother a blow-by-blow snapshot of what had happened in his home.

"Trey and I were having breakfast when Delores suddenly showed up. She was all sugar and spice, promising to take him to buy sneakers and saying he could drive her car if he spent the day with her. The next thing I know, the two of them are in your bedroom screaming at each other like they'd gone absolutely mad.

"Delores had asked to use the bathroom, and apparently, instead, she went up to your room to see if she could find any evidence that would prove you were allowing Malisa to spend the night here. Trey caught her and told her to stop, and she insisted that she could do whatever she wanted. That's when all hell broke loose. She tore up your room, threw stuff, broke stuff—you name it, she did it. It looks like a damn hurricane went through here. They exchanged words and she punched him in the face."

Gabriel could feel his blood beginning to boil. "She punched him?"

Naomi paused. "And Trey hit her back."

He pulled his hand over his face, his good mood having swooped right out the door. "Where is Delores now?"

"Gone, but not before threatening to press charges against Trey for assaulting her. He's been hysterical ever since."

"I declare, Naomi. What the hell is wrong with those two? That's her son for Christ's sake!"

"Delores couldn't care less about Trey," Naomi said emphatically. "She's a miserable beast and she uses that child. When she isn't trying to buy his affection, she ignores him. It's crazy and you know it. And you're crazy for continuing to allow it," his sister concluded, interjecting her opinion.

For a split second, Gabriel thought that his sister might be right. He had no understanding why Trey and his mother could not get along. From the moment the boy was old enough to express his own opinion, he and Delores had waged war with each other. The intensity of their conflicts had gotten so bad that before taking up permanent residence with his father, Trey had been kicked out of his mother's home on two separate occasions before he'd reached the age of ten. Her throwing the young boy's possessions into the street and screaming for him to get out had been the last straw for the entire family.

When Gabriel thought about the relationship he had with his own mother, the woman being his best friend in the whole wide world, he felt as if he had personally failed his only child. He sighed heavily.

"Okay, I'm coming home. I should be there in a few minutes."

"I'm sorry, big brother. I'm sorry that you and Trey have to go through this," Naomi said just before disconnecting the call.

As Gabriel stared off into the distance, he was sorry too. From day one, it had always been something with Delores. Had he listened to his sister and his mother back then, it was likely that he would never have gotten into a relationship with her at all. But headstrong and stupid, he thought he knew better than them all, and Delores had been making him pay the price ever since.

He dialed his ex-wife's number and waited for her to answer. When the call connected, there was a heavy pause, a lengthy moment of silence during which Trey's mother said absolutely nothing.

"Hello? Delores?"

"It's about time you called," she said finally. "Why does it take two days for you to return my calls?"

"What happened at my house this morning, Delores?" he responded.

She paused. "I don't know what you're talking about."

"You didn't get into an altercation with Trey?"

"Trey and I had a disagreement."

"You hit him."

"Trey needs to be disciplined. He is out of control."

"And you tore my house up."

"I did no such thing," she said, the blatant lie rolling off her tongue with ease.

Gabriel was suddenly disgusted with everything about the woman. His disgust was bordering on bitter hatred, and he didn't like the feeling at all.

"We need to sit down and talk," Delores said, breaking the silence that had risen between them. "I can come to the house later and . . ."

Gabriel shook his head, forgetting that she couldn't see him on the other end of the phone. "No," he said emphatically.

"Excuse me?"

"No. We don't need to talk, and you cannot come to my house. You are no longer welcome in my home. If you need to see Trey, I will bring him to you. You are welcome to pick him up if he wants to see you, but he'll have to meet you at the gate. You are *not* welcome back into my home or on my property ever again. Is that clear, Delores?"

On the other end, the woman sputtered, words like concrete blocks caught in her throat. The expletives that eventually came spewed through thin, empty air. Having already disconnected their call, Gabriel didn't hear one word.

Gabriel stood in the doorway of his room, assessing the mess that now adorned his quiet sanctuary. The bedclothes had been ripped off the bed. His clothes had been tossed from one side of the room to the other. A dresser drawer hung askew. The papers atop his work desk had been tossed to the floor, and his collection of cologne bottles were shattered on the floor.

Assessing the devastation, he couldn't begin to imagine what had moved Delores to be so destructive. As he stepped into his room, Trey came up behind him.

"Sorry, Dad. I tried to stop her. I really did."

Gabriel appraised his son's tear-streaked face. He cupped his fingers beneath Trey's chin and tilted the kid's face upward. There was a noticeable bruise tinged with a hint of red along his left profile.

"Does it hurt?" he asked, his gaze meeting his son's stare.

Trey shrugged. "Not much."

"And Naomi tells me that you hit your mother?"

The boy pushed his shoulders skyward a second time. His eyes dropped to the floor as he cast his gaze downward. "I didn't mean to," he said softly. "It just happened."

Still staring at the child, Gabriel nodded ever so slightly. It was moments like this one that reminded him of just how much maturing Trey still had to do. His tone was calm and even as he responded. "Nothing ever just happens, Trey. People make choices, and you made a really bad choice. So now you're grounded. You are not to come out of your room until I say you can. And you need to leave your iPhone on my dresser."

"But, Dad—" Trey started, intent on defending himself.

"But nothing, Trey. Son, I don't care what Delores does. She is still your mother, and you will not disrespect her. I don't know what you were thinking, but you don't put your hands on any woman, for any reason, ever."

Trey tried again. "But she hit me first!"

"And that puts her in the wrong too. You should have called me and let me deal with her. Better yet, you should have just let your aunt Naomi handle it. But you had no right to hit her. None. And I don't care if she is whaling on your behind just for the fun of it, don't you ever put your hands on her again. She is your mother! What you did is completely intolerable, and I will not put up with you doing it ever again. Do I make myself clear?"

Trey muttered under his breath.

"I didn't hear you," Gabriel admonished.

There was no missing the seriousness of his father's tone. He was angry and Trey knew he needed to tread lightly. "I said yes, you made yourself clear. I won't ever do it again."

Gabriel continued. "If it happens again, Trey, I'm going to wear your ass out. And don't get it twisted that I won't. You are not grown yet."

Trey took a deep breath, held it, then blew the air back out. "Yes, sir," he said.

Gabriel nodded, pulling his son into his arms. He kissed the top of the kid's head, gently caressing his back and shoulders.

"I love you," Gabriel said softly.

Trey nodded his head against his father's chest. "I love you, too, Dad."

Releasing his hold, Gabriel moved to pick up the mess strewn around the room. He gestured toward his dresser, tossing one last look in his son's direction. "Leave your iPhone over there," he said sternly.

Hours later, when Gabriel made it back downstairs, he found Malisa standing in his kitchen. She was wrapped in a floral-print apron, taste-testing a simmering pot of brown gravy that bubbled on the stovetop.

"Hey!" he said, the surprise of the moment echoing in his voice. "When did you get here?"

Malisa smiled as she reached up to kiss his mouth. "A while ago. Naomi called," she said, gesturing in his sister's direction.

"I called her," Naomi echoed from her seat on the sofa, her gaze focused on an episode of *Oprah*.

Gabriel smiled. "And you're cooking?"

"Dinner. Chicken smothered in gravy and onions, rice, collard greens, and corn bread, which reminds me," she said as she peered into the oven door. "Are you hungry?"

He nodded. "I could eat," he said, his head bobbing easily above his broad shoulders.

"How about Trey? Do you think he has an appetite?"

Gabriel smiled. "Trey always has an appetite."

"Good, then why don't you call him down for dinner. The food's ready."

Gabriel paused to watch as Malisa moved easily around his kitchen. As she pulled the corn bread from the oven, she tossed him an easy smile, the wealth of it warming his bruised spirit.

Moving to her side, he pressed his palm to the small of her back and leaned to kiss her forehead and then her cheek. "I'm glad you're here," he whispered softly, his gaze locking with hers.

Nodding her understanding, Malisa smiled back. "Go get Trey," she said, gesturing for him to move. "We're having brownie sundaes for dessert."

As he stepped out of the room, the two women resumed their assessment of Oprah and Gayle's lifelong friendship. Their comfortable banter made him smile. He felt exceptionally blessed in a way he hadn't thought possible. Trey was coming down the stairs as he was heading up.

"Something smells really good," the boy said, nervousness wafting over his expression. "I just came to see what was cooking."

"Malisa made smothered chicken and corn bread, and I'm told there is something really good for dessert."

Trey smiled. "Can we keep her?"

Gabriel laughed, tousling his son's hair. "I'm going to try, kiddo. I am really going to try."

Chapter 15

Gabriel lay between Malisa's legs, the woman wrapped around his waist as he rested his head against her torso. The oversized sofa supported them as they reclined in front of the big-screen television, catching up on the nightly news.

As the local weather announcer forecasted another bout of light snow and colder temperatures, Gabriel massaged her feet, gently kneading every ounce of stress from her limbs.

After dinner, the family had spent the rest of the evening simply enjoying each other's company. Malisa had challenged Trey to a game on his Xbox 360, and even though he was on punishment, his father had permitted him a few minutes to show the woman what he could do. After beating her three games to two, he'd excused himself and had gone back to his room, accepting the balance of his punishment without complaint.

Naomi had made date plans with an old flame from high school and had disappeared out the front door shortly after. After stacking the dirty dishes into the dishwasher and packing up the leftover food, the couple had retired to Gabriel's library and the sofa in front of the big-screen television set. It had been an hour and they were still there, still comfortable, still in awe of the depth of feeling that they were having for each other.

Malisa traced her hand across his forehead as she leaned to kiss him. She shifted ever so slightly beneath him.

"I'm not too heavy on you, am I?" Gabriel asked, concern rising in his tone.

"No. Not at all. Are you comfortable?"

"Extremely."

Malisa draped her arms around his shoulders and hugged him close. "How's your bedroom? Do you need any help getting it clean?"

He shook his head. "No, it's done. It looked worse than it was."

"I am so sorry."

"You have nothing to be sorry about."

"I feel responsible. None of this would have happened if you and I . . ." She paused.

Gabriel clasped her hand beneath his and kissed the palm of it. "If you and I hadn't met, I wouldn't know how incredibly blessed I am. What Delores did is more about her own unhappiness than anything else. Do not let that spoil what we have between us, please."

She smiled sweetly, meeting his stare as he looked up at her. "I won't. I promise," she responded. "Right now, though," she said, gently pushing him from her, "I need to head home. I have a very long day tomorrow."

"You can always stay. I do have a spare bedroom that you can have all to yourself."

Malisa laughed. "And how long would that last?"

He shrugged. "You'd start off there, I'm sure, and then I would probably get lonely and have a bad dream in the middle of the night and you'd have to come comfort me."

"And then neither of us would get any rest and all of my holiday orders would be a bust."

"That might happen too."

She shook her head as she leaned to kiss his mouth. Her lips brushed his, just barely touching, and Gabriel purred, a barely audible "mmmm" spilling out of his mouth. Their lips came together again, gently at first and then with increasing passion, their tongues taking turns probing and receiving.

Malisa pulled away just as she was wanting him to touch her, knowing that it would take very little to have her buck naked and in heat across the cushioned sofa.

Racing from the room, she grabbed her coat and hat out of the hall closet and exited the home. As she pulled her car out of the driveway, Gabriel stood in the entranceway, his hand lost down the front of his slacks, wishing her to come back to him.

Miss Etta entered her daughter's room with a large basket of freshly washed clothes. Baylor was lost in front of the computer screen atop her desk, barely acknowledging her mother as she twittered back and forth with some stranger the young girl called her friend.

The matriarch shook her head. "Baylor, did you

finish filling out that application you need for the summer dance program?"

Baylor shrugged. "Not yet, Mama. I'll get it done."

"If you really want to go, you will," her mother said as she carefully placed each stack of clothing into the appropriate drawer. "I am not doing it for you, Baylor. I told you that, so don't miss that deadline."

"I won't!" Baylor whined, annoyance tinting her words.

Miss Etta raised her eyebrows, a reprimand perched precariously on the tip of her tongue. She bit back the words, opting to save that battle for another day.

She stood watching as Baylor clicked the mouse and navigated from one Web page to another. She had no understanding of the obsession young people had with computers and smartphones. As far as Miss Etta was concerned, the devices had stifled their social skills and made most of them as brain-dead as dry toast. Few knew how to carry on a successful conversation that wasn't peppered with "you know what I'm saying" or "ya know" or "do you hear me?" Only a select few would ever be able to successfully build careers around the darn things, and yet far too many of them felt like it was the end of the world if they couldn't twitter or Facebook with thousands of folks they knew absolutely nothing about.

She'd been threatening to take Baylor's laptop from her for months now, and she knew that if the first report card that came after the holidays did not show a marked improvement in the girl's grades, Baylor Ivey might not ever see another computer again until she was grown and gone from the Ivey homestead.

As she headed toward the door, Baylor called out to her. "Mama, is Malisa here?"

"No. Not yet. I think she had a date with that nice Mr. Whitman."

Baylor cut an eye at her mother, noting the woman's wide smile at the prospect of her sister being with a man the matriarch wholeheartedly approved of.

Miss Etta winked at her youngest daughter. "If I see her before you head to bed, I'll tell her that you're looking for her."

"Thank you!" Baylor chimed as she went back to her Internet search.

Shaking her head, Miss Etta exited the room and headed down the hallway to her own bedroom, bemused by the antics of all her children.

Baylor was anxious to see Malisa before she took off for the bakery. The young girl had set her alarm to go off at the crack of dawn, knowing that if she timed it right, Malisa would be downstairs in the kitchen consuming her first cup of morning coffee. Racing into the room, her arrival was a surprise to all the members of the family, each of them knowing that Baylor slept in late whenever possible. Since there was no school and no reason for her to be wide-eyed and awake, they knew something was seriously amiss.

Miss Etta pressed a palm to her daughter's forehead. "Baylor, baby, are you all right?"

Baylor shook her mother off. "Yes, ma'am. I needed to catch Malisa," she said as she dropped her laptop onto the kitchen counter.

Malisa had just taken her second sip of morning

brew, the hot cup of coffee warming that early morning chill away. She eyed her baby sister with surprise.
"What's up? And before you ask, no, you cannot
borrow my clothes."

Baylor shook her head. "I don't want your old
clothes. This is serious," she said, lifting the top to
her computer and powering the device on.

Gattis and Etta stared curiously. Anitra and Malisa
both moved to stand behind Baylor.

"What is it?" Anitra asked.

Baylor said nothing, pausing as her computer
flicked on. The girl typed quickly and waited as a Web
site loaded on the screen. "This," she said, turning the
device so both of her sisters could read the screen.

Anitra gasped first, a hand flying up to her mouth in
shock. Malisa's eyes widened as she read and reread
the words across the page. She reached over her sister
and scrolled down the page.

Seeing her daughters' distress, Miss Etta moved to
where they stood, leaning to read whatever was causing them all such angst. As she read what they were
reading, she could feel the protective mother in her
surging to the surface.

"Who would write such a vile thing?" the older
woman questioned. "And put it on the Internet?"

"How did you find this?" Malisa asked, turning her
gaze to Baylor.

"My friend Sam sent me the link. His dad found it.
Apparently, they Googled you when he found out you
were my sister. But it gets worse, Malisa," Baylor
said, typing a second time.

Malisa watched as her sister pulled up the Goggle

search engine and typed in her name. Scanning the headings on the list of articles about her, it appeared that almost overnight, the Internet, which had been one of her best marketing tools, was no longer her friend.

Malisa was shaking as she dialed the New York telephone number of her publicist, Charles Dwayne. She knew it was early, but she had no fear of waking him up. She knew the man had been up even earlier than she had. He answered on the first ring.

"Malisa, do not panic, baby!"

"Charles, have you seen it?"

"It came across my desk late last night. Do you have any idea who would have written it?"

Malisa heaved a deep sigh, meeting her mother's gaze as her whole family stood staring at her. "Yes," she said, the response a loud whisper. "I can't be positive, but I have an idea."

The man on the other end shook his head. "Now listen to me carefully. I am going to make this go away as quickly as I can. So I don't want you to panic. If anyone in the media calls for an interview, refer them to me. Don't even bother to say you have no comment—just hang up. Is that clear?"

"Yes. Has the network seen it yet?"

"Probably, but don't you worry about them either. I have a call in to your attorney, so he's already in the loop. I assure you that this will just feel bad for a moment; then it will go away as if it never happened. There is far more good publicity out there about you than there is bad."

Although Charles Dwayne was trying to be comforting, Malisa wasn't finding an ounce of assurance in his words. As she disconnected the call, her mother wrapped her arms tightly around her shoulders, whispering into her daughter's ear as she hugged her tightly.

"We're all right here for you, baby. Everything is going to be just fine."

Gabriel turned on his computer before he headed into the bathroom for his morning shower. He had a long list of things he needed to accomplish before the day was done, and first on the agenda was going through his e-mails. He hadn't looked at an e-mail since Christmas Eve, and he could only begin to imagine the number of responses that needed to be made.

As his computer booted up, he scrolled through his iPhone. There were almost fifty-four text messages that beckoned for his attention. At least forty of them had come from Delores. Gabriel deleted each one, in no mood for his ex-wife's antics.

Signing into his mailbox, an even lengthier list of messages awaited his consideration. One hundred eighty-seven of them, to be exact. His attention was drawn to the fact that each one listed Malisa's name in the subject line. The sender's name for every one read *Anonymous*. He clicked the first message, and the message linked him to a Web site, also titled with Malisa's name. He clicked the link, then settled back in his seat and waited for the page to load.

The Web site was titled THE REAL MALISA IVEY. A dozen or more promotional photos of Malisa graced the page. They made Gabriel smile as he thought about the woman who had come to mean so much to him. And then his smile faded as he began to read the text. His phone rang as he was rereading the hateful words for the third time. Delores's number was reflected on the caller ID.

He answered on the first ring. "Hello?"

"Are you ready to talk to me yet?"

"Why did you do this, Delores?"

"Do what?"

"You know what. Why would you smear Malisa's name like that?"

"I don't know what you're talking about, but if I did do something to that woman, she deserved it. I don't take kindly to anyone messing with my son or my family. You know how protective I am of Trey, and Malisa Ivey is not a good influence on my child. I don't lay down for her kind of foolish mess."

"Well, I can assure you, Delores, that Trey isn't going to take kindly to your foolish mess either. He likes Malisa. I'm not sure your son likes you. You may very well have damaged your relationship with Trey beyond any kind of repair."

There was silence on the other end. Gabriel could hear her breathing heavily.

"Well, like I said, I didn't do anything."

Gabriel shook his head. "Delores, this has your fingerprints all over it. And I hate that you would stoop so low."

"I think we should take Trey to dinner for some quality family time," she said, moving to change the subject.

Gabriel sighed. "I'm sure you do, Delores, but please know, it will be a cold day in hell before you and I share anything else ever again. Call your son if you want. If he answers and wants to speak with you, then that's between the two of you. He's old enough to make his own decisions about the relationship you two share. I'm not going to encourage him or push him to spend time with you, to speak with you, nothing. If it works out between the two of you, it will do so because you and Trey put forth the effort. I have had enough."

"I don't see why you—" Delores started before Gabriel disconnected the call.

Powering off his computer, he rushed into the bathroom, needing to take a quick shower. He needed to get to Malisa.

Chapter 16

Malisa hadn't realized how angry she was until the third customer asked her about all the hate sites that had sprung up with her name on them. A pot of confection had begun to burn on the stovetop as Malisa stood staring off into the distance. She was reflecting on the sheer magnitude of what had been done to her.

It had taken some serious maneuvering for Delores to initiate the dozen or more Web sites all purporting to reveal details about Malisa and her personal life. The writings had been ridiculous ramblings about her sexual predilections, assumptions about her previous relationships, and horrific reviews about her skills as a bakery chef.

One site implied that she had interfered in other people's marriages and had engaged in questionable activity with teen boys, and that her educational and cooking degrees were fraudulent. Her image had been Photoshopped onto other people's bodies, some of the images sexually graphic and deeply disturbing.

Under normal circumstances, Malisa might have

been able to ignore the loathsome rantings, but somehow Delores had managed to ensure every search engine imaginable found those sites about her before all others. To add insult to injury, the creator of each site had registered them in her name, making it look as if Malisa had done this to herself.

She fought back tears, her head waving from side to side. This was not supposed to be her life, she thought, wrapping her arms tightly around her torso. She had worked much too hard for her success to have her reputation trashed so callously.

Gabriel calling her name tore her from her reflections. She shook the unhappy cloud from her head, rushing to the stove and the sugar paste that had begun to char in the bottom of the pot.

Grabbing the pot with a dishrag, she tossed it and its contents into the sink, then ran cold water over it. Staring at yet another mess had her on the brink of breaking down completely.

Sensing her distress, Gabriel stepped into the room, moving to where she stood. Stepping behind her, he wrapped his arms around her torso and hugged her tightly.

Leaning her back against his chest, Malisa allowed herself to fall into his strength, grateful for the support that she hadn't even known she needed until he'd reached out to hold her up. She started to cry, her tears coming despite her efforts to stall them. Gabriel allowed her to cry until she was all cried out, holding tight to her.

Minutes later, she sniffed back the last tear, gasping for breath. Gabriel kissed the top of her head, rubbing her shoulders.

"I'm a mess," Malisa said, swiping at her eyes with the back of her hand. "And I have three cakes to finish by tomorrow." She turned to face him.

"You'll get them done."

He cupped her chin and lifted her gaze to his. He gently kissed her mouth, savoring the sweetness.

"I keep asking myself why?" Malisa said, pulling away from him. "Why me? Why would she do this to me?"

Gabriel took a deep breath. "I am so sorry," he said, apologizing for the umpteenth time since he'd called her that morning, discovering that she'd gotten wind of the news well before he had.

Malisa looked up at him. "I don't deserve this, Gabriel. I do not deserve this."

He nodded his agreement. She didn't deserve the mistreatment that had befallen her, and he felt responsible in a way that he would never be able to explain to her. He slid his hand against the back of her head, his fingers tangling in her hair as he pulled her to him. He kissed her again, wishing that he could turn back the clock to a point where all of it could have been prevented. But he couldn't. What he could do was make sure nothing like this ever happened to Malisa again.

"Your mother gave me the contact information for your publicist, and I put him in touch with my legal staff. Every one of those sites should have been inactivated by now. My team is also researching what legal recourse you may have against Delores, and I will ensure that every avenue is pursued. She won't get away with this."

Malisa leaned her forehead into his chest. She took a big inhale of air before lifting her eyes back to his.

"Just help me get them down and then let it go. Please."

"But we can—"

She shook her head, stalling his words. "No. If we don't try to put an end to it, then it may never stop. I can't let Trey go through that. It's his mother and their relationship is challenged enough without him being torn between his mom and his dad's new girlfriend. And I don't want the relationship between him and I to get started with his mother and me in litigation over foolishness."

Gabriel stood staring at her, reflecting on her words. Malisa showed more concern for his son than did the woman who'd given birth to the child.

After a few minutes of thoughtful reflection, he clasped both of her hands between his own. "I love you," he said, staring deep into her eyes, every ounce of emotion spilling out of the dark orbs. "I love you, Malisa Ivey. I love you like I have never loved anyone else in my life."

Malisa took a deep breath, Gabriel's words dropping like a blanket of comfort around her shoulders. She stepped back into his arms and nestled close against him. The hurt that had been in her heart was suddenly feeling less painful.

"I really have to get some baking done," Malisa said after standing in his arms for a few minutes. "And I can't get a thing done with you distracting me."

Gabriel laughed, the warmth of it making Malisa smile. He nodded, leaning to kiss her cheek. He winked in her direction as he headed for the door.

Malisa called out after him. "Gabriel?"

"Yeah?" He turned back to stare at her.

"I love you too."

Miss Etta poked her head into the kitchen, calling for her daughter's attention.

"Malisa, do you have a minute?" she questioned, gesturing in Malisa's direction.

Malisa nodded, her gaze locked on the cake that she had just draped with fondant icing, the sweet confection lying perfectly in place. She looked up and smiled at her mother. "For you, I have two minutes." She moved to where her mother was waiting patiently.

Miss Etta pointed to a table in the front of the restaurant and the woman who was sitting alone, pretending to be interested in a menu. "Do you know that woman sitting there?"

Malisa stared momentarily. "Yes. I do," she said. She took a deep breath and then a second.

Miss Etta noted her rising anxiety. "Is that Gabriel's ex-wife?"

Malisa nodded.

Her mother dropped both hands to her hips, huffing harshly. "Well, she's got some nerve. I have a few words for that heifer!" Miss Etta proclaimed.

Malisa dropped a hand on her mother's arm. "Watch the bakery counter, please. I'll take care of this," she said as she brushed her palms down the front of her apron. She untied the garment and tossed it over a hook on the wall. With another deep breath, Malisa moved through the swinging doors and headed to where Delores Winn sat in wait.

Sliding onto the cushioned seat opposite the woman, Malisa greeted her sweetly, her sugary tone belying the thoughts running through her head.

"Delores, good morning!"

Delores was momentarily stunned. "Malisa."

"How are you this morning?"

She smiled. "I'm sure I'm doing better than you are."

Malisa smiled back. "Actually, I'm doing very well. You just missed Gabriel," she said smugly.

Delores pursed her lips as if she'd bitten down against something sour. Her eyes narrowed, her expression hostile. "You know this thing with Gabriel isn't going to last, don't you?"

Malisa shrugged, her smug smile starting to rattle Delores's last nerve. "I'm actually thinking that it will probably last a lifetime."

Delores snorted, her eyes rolling skyward. "Not if I have anything to do with it. I'm not done. I will make your life miserable."

"No, you really won't," Malisa said, her head waving from side to side. "You might try, but you'll never succeed."

Malisa leaned forward, her elbows on the table, her hands clasped together as if in prayer. "See, what you don't seem to understand is that you are only helping Gabriel and me discover that we can get through anything as long as we support and love each other. And we *love* each other. I'm not going anywhere. You don't scare me. I have no intention of running and hiding from your foolishness. I can give as good as I get. So if you want to play games, bring 'em. I'll play and I won't lose."

Delores rolled her eyes skyward. "You talk a lot of trash."

Malisa smiled. "Not really. I just know that all of this is sheer madness. It is anger and frustration coming from this deep, dark, ugly place of total unhappiness. It is jealous rage masked behind righteous indignation. You're determined to prove a point where none exists. It is bad behavior at its worst, and although you want to pretend that you're doing all of this to protect your family, it is your family that you are hurting most. Not me.

"I don't harbor any ill will toward you, Delores. My heart actually breaks with sadness because your bad behavior will inevitably leave you all alone and much unloved, while on the other side of town, I will have Gabriel. Gabriel loving me and me loving him back.

"So, can I get you a piece of cake?"

Chapter 17

Malisa stood in front of the full-length mirror, staring at her reflection. The perfect little black dress she wore fit each and every one of her curves like a glove. The Manolo Blahnik pumps had been a gift from Gabriel, the high-heeled adornment complementing her toned calves and thighs.

The week had been a whirlwind, nothing at all happening the way one would have expected. And it had all begun with the massive cake sitting on the stage in the grand ballroom of the Biltmore House. Malisa chuckled at the memory as she ensured her makeup and hair were perfection.

Gabriel and Trey were waiting patiently in the other room of the massive suite. Malisa knew that it was taking her twice as long to get ready, but she wanted to ensure that when Baby New Year kicked Father Time to the curb, gleaning the possibilities the next three hundred and sixty-five days had to offer, everything went off without a single hitch.

She took a deep breath, finally satisfied with the

woman staring back at her. Crossing the room, she threw open the door. Gabriel and Trey stood at the windows, looking out over the snow-covered gardens below. Father and son turned around at the same time.

"Wow!" Trey exclaimed. "You look hot!"

Malisa laughed. "Thank you!"

Gabriel nodded his agreement. He strode to Malisa's side and kissed her cheek. "Trey's right. You look incredible!"

Malisa grinned, her smile stretching from ear to ear. "I like you boys." She gave them each a thumbs-up. "And we need to hurry," she said, grabbing her beaded purse from the end table. "We need to make sure the cake is ready for your presentation." She gestured for Gabriel and Trey to hurry behind her.

Minutes later, the trio stood stage center in the meticulously decorated ballroom. The room was aglow with sparkling white lights, crystal tableware, and massive floral arrangements.

The cake was a spectacular work of art. The massive structure was comprised of three separate units, only two of which were edible. The center structure was the housing unit that Gabriel was supposed to jump out of. Each compartment was an elaborate design of white icing swirls, silver candy dots, and hundreds of sparklers. Just before midnight, Malisa's staff would light the sparklers, open the plush velvet curtains to showcase the structure, and Gabriel would make his appearance.

Gabriel nodded his approval. "Nice job. It's gorgeous!"

"It also tastes good," Malisa said. "One of my best. This side is a raspberry cake with a chocolate ganache filling, and the other side is lemon cake with a mixed berry filling, all of it encased in sweet buttercream icing."

"I want a piece," Trey exclaimed excitedly.

"You can have two pieces." Malisa smiled.

"So what time does this party start?" the boy asked anxiously.

Gabriel shook his head. "In a few minutes. Malisa just wanted to make sure everything was working properly."

"That's right," Malisa said, moving to the back of her design. "Gabriel, I need you to get inside to make sure everything is working okay."

Gabriel cut his eye toward Trey, who was grinning broadly. "Now you're sure it's going to work this time, right?" he asked, his expression teasing.

Malisa tossed him a look of annoyance. "I'm a professional, Mr. Whitman. I take my business seriously."

Gabriel and Trey both laughed.

"Go ahead, Dad! Get inside! I'm sure if Malisa says it's safe, then it's safe."

Following Malisa's directions, Gabriel stepped carefully into the box, kneeling down until he found a comfortable position.

"How long do I have to be in here?" he asked, popping back up to see Malisa's face.

She chuckled softly. "Just a few minutes. Stop being a baby! Get in, let me get the top closed, and then you need to make sure it opens easily. Okay?"

Gabriel nodded. Dropping back down, he positioned himself accordingly as Malisa secured the top.

"Okay!" she said, indicating that he should open the top and pop from the inside.

As instructed, Gabriel pushed at the latch, the top popped open with ease, and he stood tall. He nodded with satisfaction.

"Good job!"

"It's a great job," Malisa said, smiling. "I need you to do that one more time, please. I just need to make sure we won't lose the trim around the edge here."

"Okay," Gabriel said, dropping back down again. "But make it quick. I'm ready for a glass of champagne."

Malisa looked down into the unit and grinned. "I love you, baby," she said sweetly.

Gabriel smiled back, his gaze meeting hers. "I love you too."

Winking, Malisa closed the top one last time. When it was secure, she pressed her index finger to her lips, gesturing for Trey to shush. She grinned widely as she secured the box from the outside. Trey pulled his fist into his mouth, fighting not to laugh out loud. Slipping her arm through the teenager's, Malisa and Trey tiptoed across the stage and down the stairs.

Minutes later, Gabriel called out to them. "Malisa? Trey? Hey, where are you two?"

He listened intently, silence the only response. "Malisa? Hey! Someone? Anyone?" And then Gabriel laughed, understanding that he was the punch line to one of his family's jokes. He laughed, realizing that his holiday gifts couldn't have been any better and the New Year was starting off with one heck of a bang.

Don't miss Regina Hart's
Fast Break

On sale now from Dafina Books

Prologue

"Clock's ticking, Guinn."

DeMarcus Guinn, shooting guard for the National Basketball Association's Miami Waves, looked at his head coach, then at the game clock. Thirteen seconds remained in game seven of the NBA finals. The Waves and Sacramento Kings were tied at 101. His coach had just called a time-out. DeMarcus stood on the sidelines surrounded by his teammates. He wiped the sweat from his forehead and drained his sports drink. It didn't help.

He looked into the stands and found his father standing in the bleachers. He saw the empty seat beside him. His mother's seat. DeMarcus rubbed his chest above his heart.

"Guinn! You need to step it up out there." His coach's tone was urgent.

Why? What did it matter now?

His coach grabbed his arm. "Do you have this, Guinn?"

The buzzer sounded to end the twenty-second time-out.

DeMarcus pulled his arm free of his coach's grasp. "I've got this."

He joined his teammates on the court, walking through a wall of tension thick enough to hammer. Waves fans had been cheering, stomping and chanting nonstop throughout the fourth quarter. DeMarcus looked up again at the crowd and the empty seat.

"Are you with us, Marc?" Marlon Burress, his teammate for the past thirteen years, looked at him with concern.

"I'm good." *Was he?*

DeMarcus saw the intensity of the four other Waves on the court. He looked at his teammates and coaches on the sideline. He saw his father in the stands. He had to find a way to play past the pain, if not for his team or his father, then for his mother's memory.

DeMarcus took his position near midcourt. The Waves' Walter Millbank stood ready to inbound the ball. Marlon shifted closer to the basket.

The referee tossed Walter the ball. The Kings' Carl Landry defended him, waving his arms and leaping to distract him from the play. Marlon balanced on his toes and extended his arms for the ball. Thirteen seconds on the game clock. The referee blew his whistle to signal the play.

Ignoring the Kings' defender, Walter hurled the ball to Marlon. With the ball an arm's length from Marlon's fingers, the Kings' Samuel Dalembert leaped into the lane. Turnover. The crowd screamed its disappointment.

Eleven seconds on the game clock.

Dalembert spun and charged downcourt. Marlon and Walter gave chase.

Ten seconds on the game clock.

DeMarcus saw Dalembert racing toward him. The action on the court slowed to a ballroom dance. The crowd's chants of "Defense!" faded into the background.

DeMarcus's vision narrowed to Dalembert, the ball and the game clock. From midcourt, he stepped into Dalembert's path. His concentration remained on the ball. He smacked it from Dalembert, reclaiming possession. Waves fans roared to the rafters. The arena shook.

Seven seconds on the game clock.

DeMarcus's vision widened to include his teammates and the Kings' defenders. With Marlon, Walter and the other Waves guarding the King, DeMarcus charged back upcourt. His goal—the net, two points and the win. He felt Dalembert closing in on him from behind.

Five seconds. Four seconds. Three seconds.

DeMarcus leaped for the basket, extending his body and his arm, stretching for the rim.

One second.

Slam!

Miami Waves, 103. Sacramento Kings, 101.

The crowd roared. Balloons and confetti rained from the rafters. The Waves' bench cleared. The team had survived the last-minute challenge from the Kings to claim the win and the NBA championship title.

DeMarcus looked into the stands and found his father. He was cheering and waving his fists with the other Waves fans. Beside him, the seat remained empty. His mother would never cheer from the stands again.

Less than an hour later, showered and changed from

his Waves uniform into a black, Italian-cut suit, De-Marcus entered the team's media room. Reporters waited for the post-finals press conference. They lobbed questions at him before he'd taken his seat.

"What does this championship mean to you?"

"Why did you seem dazed during the fourth quarter?"

"You made the winning basket. What are you going to do now?"

He latched on to the last question. "I'm retiring from the NBA."

DeMarcus stood and left the room.

Chapter 1

Two years later

"Cut the crap, Guinn."

DeMarcus Guinn felt the sting of the honey-and-whiskey voice. It slapped him from the doorway of his newly acquired office in the Empire Arena. He looked up from his National Basketball Association paperwork and across the room's silver-carpeted expanse.

Standing in the polished oak threshold, Jaclyn Jones radiated anger. It vibrated along every curve of her well-toned figure. Contempt hardened her long cinnamon eyes. The media had nicknamed the former Women's National Basketball Association shooting guard the Lady Assassin. Her moniker was a tribute to her holding the fewest number of fouls yet one of the highest scoring records in the league.

As of today, DeMarcus called her boss.

DeMarcus pushed his heavy, black executive chair back from his massive oak desk and stood. He didn't understand Jaclyn's accusatory tone or her hostility, but confusion didn't justify poor manners. "Excuse me?"

"You took the Monarchs' head coach position." She threw the words at him.

DeMarcus's confusion multiplied. "Why wouldn't I? You offered it."

Jaclyn strode into his office. Her bloodred skirt suit cut a wave of heat across the silver carpet, white walls and black furniture. Her fitted jacket highlighted the rose undertone of her golden brown skin. Slender hips swayed under the narrow, mid-calf skirt. Three-inch red stilettos boosted her six-foot-plus height.

She stopped behind one of the three black-cushioned guest chairs facing his desk and dropped her large gray purse onto its seat. Her red-tipped nails dug into the fat chair cushion. "That was my partners' decision. Gerry and Bert extended the offer. *I* was against it."

Her admission surprised him. DeMarcus shoved his hands into the soft pockets of his brown khaki pants. Why was she telling him this? Whatever the reason, it couldn't be good. "I didn't ask to interview for the Brooklyn Monarchs' head coach job. *You* came to *me*."

Jaclyn shook her head. Her curly, dark brown hair swung around her shoulders. It drew his attention to the silver and black Brooklyn Monarchs lapel pin fastened to her collar. "Not me. Gerry and Bert." Her enunciation was crisp and clear.

So was her meaning. *You don't have what it takes. Stop wasting our time.*

Confusion made a blind pass to bitterness. De-

Marcus swallowed it back. "Why don't you want me as your coach?"

"The Monarchs need a winning season. We need *this* season. You don't have the experience to make that happen."

"I don't have coaching experience, but I've been in the league for fifteen years—"

Jaclyn raised her right hand, palm out, cutting him off. "And in that time, you won two NBA Championship rings, three MVP titles and an Olympic gold medal. I saw the games and read the sports reports."

"Then you know I know how to win."

She quirked a sleek, arched brow. "You can *play* to win, but can you *coach?*"

"Winning is important to me."

"It's important to me, too. That's why I want an *experienced* head coach."

DeMarcus clenched his teeth. Jaclyn Jones was a pleasure to look at and her voice turned him on. But it had been a long, draining day, and he didn't have time for this shit.

He circled his desk and took a position an arm's length from her. "If you didn't want to hire me, why am I here?"

She moved in closer to him. "Majority rule. Gerry and Bert wanted you. I'd hoped, after the interview, you'd realize you were out of your element."

DeMarcus's right temple throbbed each time he remembered the way she'd interrogated him a month ago. He should have realized she'd been driven by more than thoroughness. Gerald Bimm and Albert

Tipton had tried to run interference, but the Lady Assassin had blocked their efforts.

DeMarcus shook his head. "I'm not out of my element. I know the game. I know the league, and I know what it takes to win."

Jaclyn scowled up at him. A soft floral fragrance—lilac?—floated toward him. He could see the darker flecks in her cinnamon eyes. His gaze dipped to her full red lips.

"But you don't know how to coach." Her expression dared him to disagree. "When you were with the Miami Waves, you led by example, picking up the pace when your teammates weren't producing. You were amazing. But I don't need another player. I need a coach."

DeMarcus crossed his arms. "We went over this during my interview. I wouldn't have taken this job if I couldn't perform."

Jaclyn blinked. Her gaze swept his white shirt, green tie and brown pants before she pivoted to pace his cavernous office. "We're talking about coaching."

"I know." DeMarcus tracked her movements from the black lacquered coffee service set against his far left wall and back to his desk. Her red outfit complemented the office's silver and black décor, the Monarchs' team colors.

The only things filling the void of his office were furniture—his oak desk, a conversation table, several chairs and a bookcase. The tall, showy plant in the corner was fake.

Jaclyn paced away from him again. Her voice carried over her shoulder. "The Monarchs finished last season with nineteen wins and sixty-three losses."

DeMarcus heard her frustration. "They finished at the bottom of the Eastern Conference."

"We were at the bottom of the *league*." Jaclyn turned to approach him. Her eyes were tired, her expression strained. "What are you going to do to turn the team around?"

He shrugged. "Win."

She was close enough to smell the soft lilac fragrance on her skin, feel the warmth of her body and hear the grinding of her teeth. "You sound so confident, so self-assured. It will take more than the strength of the Mighty Guinn's personality to pull the team out of its tailspin."

"I'm aware of that." He hated the nickname the media had given him.

"Then how are you planning to win? What's your strategy?"

As majority owner of the Brooklyn Monarchs, Jaclyn was his boss. DeMarcus had to remember that, even as her antagonism pressed him to respond in kind.

He took a deep breath, calling on the same techniques he'd used to center himself before making his free throws. "I'm going to work on increasing their speed and improving their defense. Your players can earn style points, but they do everything in slow motion." Jaclyn stared at him as though expecting something more. "I can give you more details after I've studied their game film."

He glanced at the tower of digital video discs waiting for him to carry them home. It was late September. Training camp had started under the interim head coach, and preseason was two weeks away. He didn't have a lot of time to turn the team around.

Jaclyn settled her long, slender hands on her slim hips and cocked her right knee. The angle of her stance signaled her intent to amp up their confrontation. DeMarcus narrowed his eyes, trying to read her next move.

"Maybe I should have been more specific." Her voice had cooled. "The players no longer think they're capable of winning. How are you going to change their attitudes?"

"By giving them the skills they need to win."

"These aren't a bunch of high school kids. They're NBA players. They already have the skills to win."

"Then why aren't they winning?"

Jaclyn dragged her hand through her thick, curly hair. "Winning builds confidence. Losing breeds doubt. I'm certain you've heard that before."

"Yes." But why was she bringing it up now?

"Even with the skills, they won't win unless they believe they *can* win. How do you plan to make them believe?"

DeMarcus snorted. "You don't want a coach. You want Dr. Phil."

Jaclyn sighed. "And you're neither. I'd like your resignation, please."

DeMarcus stared. He couldn't have heard her correctly. "What?"

"It would save both of us a great deal of embarrassment and disappointment."

His mind went blank. His skin grew cold. Jaclyn had landed a sucker punch without laying a finger on him. "You want my resignation? I've only been here one day."

"Think of your reputation. Everyone remembers

you as a winner. You're jeopardizing your legacy by taking a position you're not qualified for."

Blood flooded his veins again, making his skin burn. "I disagree. I have what it takes to lead this team."

Jaclyn didn't appear to be listening. She dropped her hands from her hips and paced his spacious office. "You can keep the signing bonus."

"It's not about the money." The vein above his right temple had started to throb. He heard the anger in his voice but didn't care. He was through playing nice with his new boss. She was threatening his goal and maligning his character.

Jaclyn frowned at him. "Then what *is* it about?"

DeMarcus doubted she was interested in his motives for wanting to be the head coach of the Brooklyn Monarchs. "I'm not a quitter."

"You're not a coach."

DeMarcus studied the elegant features of her golden brown face—her high cheekbones, pointed chin and long-lidded eyes—searching for a clue to her thoughts. What was her game? "Do you have someone else in mind for my job?"

Her full, moist lips tightened. "We interviewed several candidates I consider much more qualified to lead this team."

"Gerry and Bert hired me. Your partners don't respect your opinion."

Jaclyn made an irritated sound. "I've realized my business partners don't have the team's best interests at heart."

"Careful, or you'll hurt my feelings."

Jaclyn's eyes narrowed. "Are you helping them destroy the team?"

"What are you talking about" Was Jaclyn Jones unbalanced?

"Why would you stay where you're not wanted?"

He gave her a wry smile. "But I *am* wanted. I have the letter offering me this job to prove it."

"I didn't sign that letter."

DeMarcus turned to reclaim his seat behind his desk. "Two out of three isn't bad."

Jaclyn followed him, stopping on the other side of his desk. "You should be more careful of the company you keep. Gerry and Bert don't care about the team. They don't care about you, either."

"I don't need your help picking my friends." DeMarcus pulled his seat back under his desk before giving Jaclyn a cool stare. "Now, you'll have to excuse me. I have work to do."

Jaclyn straightened. "I want your resignation. Now."

DeMarcus dropped his mask and let her see all the anger he'd been hiding. "No."

"Then you're not getting my support."

"Lady, you don't scare me." He leaned back in his seat. "You're convinced I don't have what it takes to coach your team, but you haven't given me one damn reason why you've made that call."

"I've given you several."

DeMarcus held up one finger. "You want someone who'll get in touch with your players' emotions. Look, if they don't want to win, they don't belong on your team."

"You don't have the authority to fire players." There was apprehension in her eyes.

He raised a second finger. "You think your partners

aren't looking out for the team. That's only because you didn't get your way."

"That's not true."

He lifted a third finger. "You don't think I can coach." DeMarcus stood. "How do you know that? Have you seen me coach?"

"Have *you* seen you coach?" Jaclyn clamped her hands onto her hips.

DeMarcus jerked his chin, indicating his office. "This is what I want, an opportunity to lead the Brooklyn Monarchs to a winning season. And, in a few years, bring home the championship. We have to be realistic. That won't happen this season. But it will happen. That's my goal. And I'll be damned if I'm going to let anyone deny me."

Jaclyn's gaze wavered. But then she raised her chin and squared her shoulders. "That's a very moving speech, Guinn. Can you back it up?"

"Watch me." DeMarcus settled back into his seat and nodded toward his doorway. "But do it from the other side of the door."

The heat of her anger battered his cold control. DeMarcus held her gaze and his silence. Finally, Jaclyn inclined her head. She grabbed her purse from the guest chair and left.

DeMarcus scrubbed his face with both hands, hoping to ease his temper. The Lady Assassin had charged him like a lead-footed defender at the post.

Why?

They shared the same goal—a winning season for the Monarchs. Then why was she determined to get rid of him?